Joan,

Thanks so much for the fine interview on WBUX,

Warm Regards,

Jonathan Newman

(Philip Kimpers)

Simon & Schuster
Simon & Schuster Building
Rockefeller Center
1230 Avenue of the Americas
New York, New York 10020

Designed by Deirdre C. Amthor

Manufactured in the United States of America

1   3   5   7   9   10   8   6   4   2

Library of Congress Cataloging-in-Publication Data

Harper, Philip.
Payback / Philip Harper.
p.   cm.
I. Title.
PS3558.A62484P3   1991
813'.54—dc20   91-7857
                                                          CIP

ISBN 0-671-72328-6

PAYBACK

Philip Harper

SIMON & SCHUSTER

New York   London   Toronto   Sydney   Tokyo   Singapore

1

HE PICKED HER OUT at a red light. Before it turned green he knew he'd be late to work that morning. She was blond, and singing along with the car radio. When she slowed her red Camaro at the next light, Reidus pulled up in his dark green Jaguar and offered a smile.

Reidus preferred to pick victims at random. That was his pleasure—teaching that the unexpected could happen to anyone any time. Stepping out of the office for a quick errand, throwing a load in the washer, driving to the bank. Those were the good times to pluck people out of their routines. And the unexpected life was the only life worth living, he thought, because people get trapped in ordinary living. He couldn't understand why people seemed to enjoy following the same patterns day after day. He liked changing all that, showing people they were free to act differently.

Reidus was wearing a light wool suit. He was tall—just over six feet—and fit snugly in the Jaguar's leather seat. His face was strong, well-defined, charcoal gray eyes under dark curly hair. His smile brought on thin creases in the skin around his eyes, the narrowing made them shine, almost glare. The woman in the Camaro didn't see the glare, just the smile, and she returned it, then drove off. This was a good person, as of course most people are, Reidus thought. He followed her onto the highway.

When he was a grade school kid in a small town near Pittsburgh, he went to the library and looked through dozens of phone books. He knew he was different, despite what his parents and teachers said, but it wasn't easy to show it. Eight Reiduses in Cleveland, four in Baltimore,

5

five in Philadelphia, thirteen in Manhattan. And more Williams on any page than he cared to count. Nothing distinctive there. On the very day you're born, he used to think, there are hundreds of thousands of old people who've been around for seventy or eighty years before you arrived, and had already done in their lives almost anything you could think of doing, which itself must have been done a million times before.

He remembered standing in a row with the other kids in school, the teacher gazing at them with a look that said to Reidus: There have been dozens of other classrooms of kids precisely like you kids, and there is nothing different about you, about the routine, about anything.

He came from a family that for generations had made trouble. In many instances they simply took things they wanted, but more often they settled their disputes with violence. Nature had given them the basic tools to survive. They were big and smart. The Reidus boys who worked at it were especially strong, but even the ones who didn't had a bred-in savage bent. Most of them eventually landed in jail, and despite their natural talents, most of the family died by forty, often in prison.

But Reidus's father was different. He thought of himself as the first to break the pattern, holding down a "real job" running a hardware store. His son was handsome, and the father thought, decent. As Reidus grew, he kept his great looks. But he was a natural scion of his family, the long line of it.

By ninth grade, when he was fourteen, he'd started to think about what he could do to show he was different. His father died of a stroke that year and Reidus made plans. He left school, already tall for his age, and strong, and with a talent for the impassive face that made one seem older. He went to the Caribbean islands and worked on fishing boats. He knew that many people went to sea to be free. But was he?

The problem, he discovered, was that he was one of only a few white men down there working. All the rest were black men from the islands. Therefore he was noticed a lot. People assumed he was down there to escape his routine, or to escape something, or for the freedom there, and all of that was so. And because they all knew that, he didn't feel free. To be free, he thought, meant being uncategorizable, unpredictable in some important way, meant not meeting the countless expectations other people had for you.

PAYBACK

He began to think about that. What exactly is it, he wondered, that other people count on in their own lives, and expect of you? By the time he was sixteen, he had figured out that one of the basic assumptions people make is that others will not hurt them. So he began to play with pain. He began to hurt people, and took it to the point that several people died.

One afternoon he broke the neck of a man waiting for his wife in a double-parked car on a busy street in Pittsburgh. He did this without noise or notice, and it took only seconds. He wasn't interested in the man's dying, paying little attention to his struggles and small sounds, just before he snapped the large bone. He had only a short time before the wife returned, and he thought of it as creative inspiration to rest the body's head on its arms as if asleep. When the wife got back she spoke to her hunched-over husband for a moment, then, looking uncertain, she reached down to stir him awake. When she raised his head and saw the lifeless white of his rolled-up eyes, she screamed.

That was a satisfying response, Reidus thought, but he wished he could know exactly what expectations of hers he had shattered, and how, exactly, he had changed her path. He wondered whether killing people was best, or whether there was more unpredictability and surprise to be gained from just hurting them. He eventually decided he would hurt people, and save killing for when it was unavoidable, for instance, to keep from being caught.

But he realized that getting caught was unlikely. His reasons for hurting people didn't fit any of the assumptions the police made when they looked for criminals, and that was probably enough to protect him. He also knew that from a certain point of view he was but one of a number of criminals protected from detection by the sheer randomness of his actions and selection of targets. As much as it made him safe, it also bothered him. He didn't like to think of himself as just one of a group.

One day, when he was sixteen, he went to a department store dressed up in a jacket and tie. He walked up to a very well dressed woman who looked about forty and complimented her on her necklace. She thanked him and he reached out slowly as if to touch it, but instead he put his hands under her blouse. With his thumbs he undid her buttons while his long fingers began pinching the nipples on her breasts.

She didn't scream at first. He knew that was because she didn't believe it was happening. People assume that pain is always instant, but they're wrong. Before the pain comes shock and humiliation, then anger. He had studied peoples' reactions to such things. He knew he had time.

The woman looked into his face, his eyes, as if to say, "What are you doing?" She finally grabbed his hands, pulling at the fingers clamped on her breasts. He was squeezing her nipples tight between his thumb and middle finger. He could see the instant she realized the pain was shooting through her body, and finally, after a few seconds—but it seemed so long to Reidus—she began to scream. People are stupid about screaming. He had long ago figured out that screaming had only one predictable consequence: people pay attention. But to what? They don't know what's happening. They need more information. When a baby cries, its mother doesn't always know why. Adults think all they have to do is scream and everyone will understand their situation.

So when she screamed, Reidus was ready. He let go of her and backed away. People nearby came running. He began crying; then he made himself throw up. He could do both whenever he liked. As the crowd gathered, he said with just the proper tone of horror and disgust, "This woman, she . . . she hurt herself, on purpose right in front of me . . . she must be crazy."

The woman stopped screaming. But before her accusations could begin, the crowd was caught up with Reidus's story. They could hardly hear her, this crazy woman, and they felt sorry for Reidus. He leaned onto a sales counter and cried more for them, and inside he was drinking in the way the rhythms of ordinary life had momentarily vanished, and chaos appeared in its place, and it was a wonderful, wonderful feeling.

He attacked people in the open again and again as a teenager, and thought it fascinating that people always took his side because he looked innocent, angelic. He had a full head of curly hair, a square jaw, and an easy smile. As a teenager, he looked, they said, mature for his age; now, at thirty-four, they said he looked youthful.

People will always respond to physical appearance, Reidus knew, which was good because a person can control how he wants to look. Using his looks and his cleverness, he learned how to involve himself in other people's lives. He was interested in the contradictions people lived every day. Most people have only a few close friends because getting to know someone well takes years. But then along come the unexpected exceptions, and one day you find yourself telling the bank teller about some problem with your wife that you've never told anyone else. Or someone new is moving in next door, and as you help him unload some furniture, you tell him a small piece of your life story. Reidus learned to be the stranger people talked to, and a good listener eventually discovers what someone fears: rejection by a loved one, loss of job, loss of money, losing a child, falling from a high place, drowning, being raped. Knowing their fears, he could enter their lives. He himself had no fears.

He once dated a woman a few years older. They spent days discussing the problems men and women had, men trying to be open and women trying to make things happen for themselves without getting too lonely. She liked him, believing, as people did when he wanted them to, that he was older and settled and gentle, and that he understood, or cared. So she told him what she thought women feared, and he knew the fears were hers, because most people really talked only about themselves. Her biggest fear was that her loneliness would make her dependent on a man, and then she'd be hurt by him.

One night they had some beers at an old-fashioned tavern with long, broad, dark wood tables and benches. She was relaxed and talking freely. In the middle of their small talk, he told her he could kill her, and then he showed her how, putting one big hand on the side of her neck. He brought her down into blindness and seconds of sleep, and then let her up into alertness and vision—all this by single thrusts of his thumb against her carotid artery. He kept his hand on her neck so she couldn't scream, and he ordered more beers and a bottle of wine. He made her drink until she wet herself, and all the time he talked to her about trust and honesty between men and women. Then he took her home and left her there, alone. He never saw her again.

He realized early on that to experience his own personal joy—the effect he had on others—he needed other people. But they would never be interested in joining his games; they spent their lives avoiding the chaotic and unpredictable. He had to force them to play. He thought of himself as a monster at the bottom of a deep, placid sea, now and then reaching up through the calm surface to grab an unsuspecting ship or swimmer and bring them down to the deep. He'd read once about a

Greek god named Pan, a god who was ugly and clever. He hid behind trees in the forest, the story said, and waited for travelers. When they passed, he jumped out, trilling high shrieking notes on his flute. He frightened them. Some fled, some died of their fear. His actions made sense to Reidus. Grabbing the weary traveler was the only way to involve him, because no one willingly steps off the path and into the darkness.

In those days, he enjoyed the effects of pain, but now he didn't need to cause physical pain to be satisfied. He had discovered that it was the taking itself that mattered. Not simple things like money or jewelry, or even life. That was meaningless, stupid. There were better ways to get to people. It was surprise that mattered—taking things in a direction not planned, taking the ordinary and making it permanently exceptional. He could frighten people so they could never return to one particular room or one particular street—not for the rest of their lives. That was the thrill. "I'm like art," Reidus once told a woman. "I just happen."

When he was eighteen he took a job at an oil company in New Jersey. He lied on his resumé, saying he had gone to college, when in fact he'd never finished high school. He'd had some experience working at refineries in the islands, and the oil business seemed familiar to him. The company bought and sold oil to numerous firms, never taking physical possession of the oil, making its profit as a middleman. His job was to keep track of the changing prices of oil and of how much the other companies had and needed.

He both liked and hated what he saw of the world of business. The businessmen he met seemed no more interested in following the rules than he was. Their escape was to devise varying ways to steal money from other companies and to embezzle from their colleagues whenever they thought they could get away with it. But they were usually neither smart nor bold. And they were not honest about their corruption. Asked directly if they were thieves and liars and if they were ruthless, they said, "No, we're not bad." Reidus, on the other hand, felt he could tell anyone at any time, "Yes, I am bad, I did that. Yes, I did those things to your child, bound as he was for three days, young as he is. I did it for the way it felt, and because you were sure I wouldn't do it, and because you didn't think it was possible. I did it, yes."

Still, there was more to like than dislike about the world of business, and he took several other business jobs after leaving the oil company.

PAYBACK

For the past four years he'd been working for Jack Carlton, who ran a real estate and land development firm in Chester County, just outside Philadelphia. Reidus fit in well there. He loved to watch Carlton speak at public appearances, and to read about Carlton Associates in the local papers and magazines. Carlton seemed sincere when he was lying. From the start Carlton knew Reidus had thin credentials, but, as Carlton often told him, Reidus had a talent for dealing with people. That's why he'd hired him. His title was "Vice-President for Operations," but in fact he was head of security for the company. Reidus fit in well at Carlton Associates, and he was free to do just what he wanted as long as it made money. Hurting people almost always made money, or easily could.

For the past month, someone had been following him, a red-haired woman who drove a black Nissan Z and carried a .32 pistol. He didn't know what she wanted. Every now and then, someone good enough to pose a threat would come along—either by design or by accident—and get in his way. It was in periods like this that Reidus sometimes felt the coldness replaced by old turbulent feelings, the way he had felt when his parents and teachers praised him, and when the weight of their expectations made him want to do things that were different. He returned to the wilder and more violent disposition of his teens. He found himself going out more frequently to play with people's lives, and in ways totally unrelated to business.

One day he took a baby out of its stroller while a mother daydreamed on the grass nearby. He drove the child across the state line and left it in a dirt lot near a hand-built shack in rural Delaware. He never bothered to find out what became of the baby or its mother.

He was excited, irritated, energized now. Someone else was out there shaking things up. He liked that; he was always looking for people to enhance his feeling of freedom from the expected. The red-haired woman had been moving more aggressively in recent weeks and had been coming closer to making mistakes. At first she'd hidden far in the background. But three days ago, in the middle of the night, there was the shooting incident at Carlton Stables. It was obvious she wasn't trying to kill him. She'd missed completely, intentionally, and hadn't tried again. It could have been more than just that woman. There was a newspaper in West Chester investigating Carlton and the business. There was a reporter, a man named Chris Baines, who had already written some stories. There were always reporters investigating Carlton Associates, but maybe this time the newspaper was working with the red-haired woman. Reporters were usually trivial. Something more serious seemed to be happening now. Carlton liked to handle people by having them followed so that he could develop a dossier on them. So Reidus had ordered some of his men to follow the reporter for the past few weeks—to see who he reported to, and maybe to get something to use on him later, if it came to that. Whatever their motives, people were always zeroing in on Carlton Associates because Carlton was so flamboyant and because he was corrupt: newspapers, TV, the district attorney, spurned customers, business competitors, and sometimes mobsters whom Carlton knew from Detroit. Jack Carlton had lots of enemies. And Reidus was his main protection.

The blonde in the red Camaro pulled off the highway at the Landis Mall exit. Reidus pulled up to the side of the car while the woman was doing about thirty miles an hour. He did not mask his intentions. She glanced at him and saw the message in his face—the dispassionate intensity of his gaze that said he was after her. She pulled away.

Reidus dropped back, cut from the right lane to the far left, and pulled up to the other side of her car. He knew he could cut her off from every entrance to the mall, as the road they were driving was a loop, a three-mile circle that led only into the mall, or out onto three different highways. The traffic was light in mid-morning, and could be of no help to her. As they approached each exit into the mall, she tried slowing down or speeding up to get into the left lane, which Reidus would not allow her to do. Each time he looked into her car, Reidus saw the frustration and fear build in her face. He knew it would be only minutes before she began to feel trapped—trapped by the road, by the speed, by the circularity of it all. The one thing she could not do was stop. She was trapped in motion. He could see panic setting in. They drove nine miles, fully three times around the loop.

The last time, as they approached a mall entrance, she slowed again, then suddenly gunned ahead. She cut sharply to her right, crossed over a small grassy island and raced onto Route 202. She thought she had an escape plan. She was doing ninety-five as Reidus clocked her on his analog speedometer from behind. She was probably good with the car in normal circumstances, Reidus thought, but now she kept crossing onto the left shoulder of the road. Reidus eased the Jag up to her and pressed his front bumper against the rear of the Camaro. He flashed a big smile to her rearview—he knew she was looking—and he slowly mouthed the words "Gooood-Byyyyyy." He dropped back a few feet, pulled to the right of her car, and matched her speed precisely. She couldn't pull ahead of him or drop behind. She had only one choice to get away. He saw her inch her car onto the shoulder, closer and closer to the guardrail. He pulled ahead to watch. He didn't want to be anywhere behind the Camaro. Ordinary drivers going to the mall don't think much about how a ton of red fiberglass and metal reacts to contact with a steel guardrail at 115 miles an hour. What actually happens, Reidus knew, is that the metal of the car compresses and bounces away. The guardrail doesn't give much.

It happened quickly. First came the screeching sparking of metal against metal. Then the Camaro flipped over and slid on its roof across all three lanes and off the road, down an embankment and onto a dry brown field, still doing about fifty. It hit a utility pole and spun around, like a top, turning, turning, and turning, until, at last, it stood up on one side and came to rest. He could see the woman, dazed and bloody, crawl out through a side window.

He was glad she'd survived; he hadn't intended to kill.

He was only building to some higher match-up. He wanted to contend with the red-haired woman who'd been following him. Maybe with the reporter, too, if he was part of it. He hoped there was more to it than just a newspaper story. He hoped the game wouldn't be simple. In all likelihood he would end up winning. But even if he didn't—even if he lost—he might have fun. And, at the very worst, he would die.

2

I RECOGNIZED SIMON GRIFFEY'S QUICK, uneven walk from way up at the top of the hill, a good five minutes before he got down to my house. He had a restless, loping kind of walk and covered a lot of ground fast. He stopped by to see me every now and then, usually to talk over some scheme he'd come up against, or to ask a favor. He'd take a long time getting to the point, but he knew I'd help if I could. Most of the time he'd talk about a woman, or money, or both. I usually told him what he already knew: that he was wasting his time and should drop whatever he was up to. Maybe that was part of the fun—for both of us. What he really wanted was someone to talk to, which was just fine with me. Simon Griffey had his limits as a private detective, but none as a friend.

I'd been out in the garden all morning, even with the rain. I called it a garden. Neighbors thought of it as a small jungle. Maybe that was appropriate when you took a look at my 220-year-old stone-and-brick carriage house. It was a cranky old place with more quirks and sags than I could count, but it fit in just fine on this little street in the rural northwest part of Philadelphia. The old lady who lived here before me had planted quite a prolific and exotic garden, but she forgot to leave instructions when she died. Weeds were fighting with the tomato plants to see which would reach the roof of the porch first. Weeds seemed to have the edge. I only managed to get around to cleaning the place three, maybe four times. I'm usually gone about four months a year working on a case. Most of the rest of the time, I keep myself too busy doing small construction jobs for people in the neighborhood, or going out on the road scouting minor league ballplayers. I like times like these, when I have nothing to do, just hang around, at rest, a bear in the cave.

I thought I'd taken out a big chunk of the garden mess in June when I single-handedly cut down a rotting apple tree and a burly old maple. I took out a nice chunk of skin from my forearm, too, but at least I'd saved the thousand dollars the tree-service people had asked. Trouble was, the vines that used to cling to the trees managed to find new places to crawl, especially when it came to azaleas. And they liked climbing the bricks on my defenseless colonial fortress. The guy at the garden shop said there was a simple solution to that problem. Cut the vines at the bottom of the house and the rest of them would die in a few months. Then you could pull them all off easily. But June and July had passed and the vines were still thriving, almost blacking out a window on the top floor. Hardly mattered, since I couldn't open the ancient thing more than three inches anyway. Of course, I could put in a new modern storm window, but I liked the old one just fine. And I was willing to wait for the vines to die in their own time. You had to have faith.

I let Simon surprise me from behind as I was bagging some weeds.

"Yo, Gray, old buddy. Need a hand with the yard work? I got two green thumbs."

"What if I said yes?"

"Sure. I'd be glad to help. After the rain stops."

I knew that was about as close to Simon's help as I'd get. Actually, if there was real trouble, he could do the job. He was forty-six, ten years older than me. He wasn't too big, about five feet eight, 170 pounds, but he had thick wrists and powerful biceps, and he was quick. Once, when he managed to bring me along on one of his trips to some body-building place up in Montgomery County, he took out two big guys before either one of them could even lift a barbell. The two must have thought Simon brought me along for muscle since I had six inches and thirty pounds on him, so maybe I did serve as a distraction. But I never even took my hands out of my pockets. To this day, I don't remember why we went up there.

"You wouldn't have come by for a reason?" I asked Simon. "Just to help out in the garden, is that it?"

"Thought maybe we'd get something to eat. You and me, we have that in common. We like a big lunch."

"And a big dinner."

"Yeah, but it's only noon. One thing at a time."

I took off the wet garden gloves, stiff and soaked brown, and told Simon to go into the living room and find something to read while I took care of things in the kitchen. I knew he'd do that anyway, he always did. He liked to go through my thick stack of *Baseball America*s piled high on the dark pine floor beside the fireplace. *Baseball America* was the only thing I subscribed to, and I didn't pay a penny for it. I had a free lifetime subscription dating back over a decade. When I was a minor league ballplayer up in Double A at Reading, I wrote a column for them. They liked it and asked me to write something every month or so, and in return I got the free subscription (and twenty-five bucks per column). Probably would have raised my rates if I made it up to the majors, but one day when we were playing the Vermont Reds I made the unwise decision to slide headfirst into home. Their catcher was a solid 240; among other things, I managed to tear up the rotator cuff in my right shoulder. Thus ended what could have been a great baseball career, at the age of twenty-one. I was a pretty decent third baseman, too. Could hit a slider to right as good as anyone in Double A.

Almost every year since then, I spent most of February and March down in Florida, scouting the rookies at spring training. And once or twice in the summer, I travel with a different minor league team or sometimes go out to take notes on a few high school teams. What most people don't know is that the big leagues rely on guys like me to keep an eye out for them, to spot the kids with real talent before they get smart enough to hire an agent. I did some full-time scouting for the Red Sox when I was up in New England about a decade ago, and the last few years I'd been free-lancing part-time for the Phillies.

Simon busied himself with the reading material, and in the big old kitchen I sautéed onions and garlic, then cut up the peppers and tomatoes, fresh off the vine. When the green and red things were simmering in the tall pot, I started to peel the skin and fat off the chicken breasts. I hate fat, and it's worth the time spent cutting away every bit of it before cooking the meat.

As I did the butcher work, I looked across at the coal-burning fireplace. It was about 150 years old and looked like it hadn't been used this century. I'd always meant to try that thing, but never got around to it. The stones on either side of it were cream-colored and soft-looking, like small pillows, and the black iron belly looked like metal made of coal soaked in night. The stove had two high curved handles of the same black metal extending from it, so that one could simply hang a pot and cook away. That's what I'd often wanted to do, but I'd been in the house eight years now and never had, so probably I never would. Heavy cast iron and coal had been replaced forever by Green Giant boiling bags, five-minute rice, microwaves. Our loss, probably, but progress was relative. Simon usually ate out of Styrofoam boxes.

By the time I'd trimmed all the fat from the chicken, the vegetables were ready, and I threw the chicken in the pot, topped with some salt and pepper, spices, and a large dose of paprika. In forty-five minutes: chicken paprikash. A Hungarian dish, passed along from generation to generation. Both of my parents cooked, and they passed the skills along to me when I was a kid. They came naturally.

Simon wandered through the low, arched wooden entranceway that separated living room from kitchen. The smell of food cooking lured him. If he were a taller man he surely would have bumped his head squarely against the wooden arch. I had, a hundred times.

He walked over to the stove and took the cover off the pot, looking in. "Red dye number three?" He looked at me skeptically.

"You say that now, but you'll eat it."

"I don't have to know what it is," he said. "That's the cook's job."

I guess I'd fooled him with the red stuff. Not fair of me, using Hungarian spices.

He opened the refrigerator and took out a bottle of Diet Coke.

"You keep this in stock?" he asked. "Didn't know you liked it."

"It's the same bottle you brought the last time you were here." I didn't bother reminding him that that had been about a month and a half ago.

He held the bottle up to the light, as if it were a fine wine. "Good vintage," he said. The bottle had a cork plugging its neck. "*Marrone*," he said. "No wonder this stuff is always flat."

He drank what was left of it, then got comfortable leaning against a cupboard across from the refrigerator.

"So where's Helen?" he asked.

"We parted ways," I said. The expression sounded odd even as I

17

said it. Helen Frame and I had broken it off four months ago. We'd been getting along well and I had real hopes for us. I always did. But the truth is, I wasn't able to sustain any decent relationship for more than about three months. Eight years since the divorce. About fifteen relationships. Great record for stability.

"You're nuts," Simon told me. "She was great. All the ones you meet are great. I meet them once, twice if I'm lucky. Then I show up a few months later and they're gone. The idea is to hold on to them, not drive them away."

"You know, you're right," I said. "I've never realized that before. I think I'll hold on to the next one, no sweat. It's all so simple."

"It is simple," he said, ignoring my attempt at sarcasm. "Your problem is, you think too much. And they know it. They wonder what you're thinking about. They get nervous about that, and so do you. No wonder you're always ending relationships."

I looked at him and couldn't help being impressed. He wasn't pretty; he was husky but looked fat. I knew that he confined his romancing to secretaries who worked late and ate alone and happened to work in his building; and that he was a nice guy who loved attractive women but couldn't get a single one in the whole grand metropolis of Philadelphia to look past the surface. Their mistake. He was right about me, though. I did think too much. Helen had been fine. So had the others. But I'd always found something wrong—with them, or with me, or with us. I'd drive them crazy or me crazy, and then we'd split up. Then I'd go back into the cave and listen nonstop to baseball on the radio. I'd gotten to be an expert. All it took was a lot of uninterrupted time.

Simon decided to let me alone, laughed to himself a bit, then walked over to the round oak table. He sat down on the far side, closed his eyes and lifted his legs a few inches into the air. It was the dreaded position you take in karate class, the one instructors make you hold for hours to tighten your gut and give you ridges. I'd seen Simon do this before. It wasn't exercise for him. It was more like meditation, his way of telling you he wanted to discuss something serious. I honestly didn't think he did it intentionally, or was even aware of the habit. He may have done it when he was home alone, before talking to himself. I'd never asked.

"You hear about those stories in the West Chester *Tribune* last week, the ones about Carlton Associates?" He asked the question with his eyes still closed.

"I don't read newspapers. You know that. Only the box scores."

"Sure. Anyway, there was some pretty good stuff about corruption at Carlton Associates, how they ripped off a bunch of people who invested in their land developments. I was the one who gave the newspaper that information. Just a small part of the job I'm working."

"So you're thinking of becoming a reporter? If you want my advice, forget it. Won't get you anywhere. Place like Carlton Associates will only clip the stories and laugh about them. Newspapers can't hurt the big guys. They'll flick you away like a dog scratches fleas."

"So you know Carlton Associates?"

"No more than anyone else. One of those commercial developers that's always building suburban malls and garden apartment complexes faster than the population grows. How do they get so many people to buy their properties, anyway? Where do those people come from, and where would they go if the new malls weren't built?"

"How the hell do I know? Anyway, I'm going to Carlton headquarters this afternoon."

"You looking to buy a shop in a mall?"

"Cut it out, Gray. This is serious. I've got an important job, and I'd like your help. To be honest, I think this might be the kind of thing you'd like to get into, long after my little part is over. Bad people, big money. Interested in hearing more?"

I stirred the chicken. Just once, all it needed. "No," I told him.

I had no idea what his job was, but I knew exactly what he meant about me. Since quitting ball, and after trying a couple years at writing articles for a real newspaper (I liked hitting line drives better), I'd more or less settled into my unstructured retirement, taking no more than three cases a year. No, I wasn't a private cop. I was a blackmailer. I kind of just fell into the job in the short time I was a newspaper reporter. I'd dig up dirt on some crooked business, and then, rather than write the story, I'd make a deal: They stop their rip-offs, pay back their victims—and I don't write the story. Oh, and I'd take a cut for myself. Seemed like good business and fair ethics to me, but not exactly kosher in the newspaper business. So I went free-lance. Worked out pretty well. Got dirty at times, got violent, too. But what the hell. The price you pay when dealing with slime. Gave me plenty of free time, and the pay was okay. The thing is, I liked to pick and choose my own cases. No shortage of rip-off artists as far as I could tell. I finished my last one about four months ago—a little scam at a college campus in Virginia—and my take from that one hadn't quite run out yet. I'd probably get along just fine without Simon's gambit.

"My client isn't one of the regular clowns," Simon said. "She's a good person. She's *right*." He grinned at me. "She's also great-looking. Green eyes. Red hair. A good tan."

That was quite an endorsement. Not the looks. When Simon said somebody was *right* he meant he believed in them—an honest person with a good cause. Most of his jobs were for the "clowns." He enjoyed the work, but helping one of them almost always meant hurting someone else who had an equal grievance on the other side. That was never the case when his client was *right*. It was his highest compliment, and he'd been dividing the world up that way for as long as I'd known him. We'd met more than a dozen years ago when I was a reporter and I'd managed to get some confidential information from him. I had learned over the years that while Simon wasn't too clever he was absolutely infallible as a judge of people.

"All I've had to do so far," Simon said, "was deliver some documents to a guy at the newspaper. Today my client wants me to go to Carlton headquarters and steal something."

When he decided someone was *right*, he was quite willing to work that way.

"Carlton has all sorts of art in his building," he said. "There's a collection of hand-carved ebony horses he says he brought back from Asia himself. My client says he never left town to get the horses. She says he stole the stuff."

"How does she know?"

"It was her father who collected the ebony horses. He spent twenty years of his life putting the collection together. It's not really worth very much, if anything, in the art market. But for him, it was a lifelong passion. It meant everything to him."

"He's dead?"

"Yeah. Died a few months ago. Guess that's what sparked my client's sudden interest in getting the horses back. You see, her father worked with Carlton years ago, when the company was still pretty small. At some point my client's father and Carlton had a real bad falling-out— I don't know all the details, but I think they were even physically fighting with each other. Anyway, they stopped working together. Split up all their business interests. But apparently that didn't satisfy Carlton. He sent out some thug to take the collection of horses. He not only got the collection, he also somehow managed to stop my client's father from fighting back. Don't know exactly how he did that. Like I say, those horses aren't worth much in money, but they represented a whole lifetime to my client's father. Carlton did it just for spite, just to hurt the guy. Gray, there's something really wrong with this man. He really is a rotten person. See what I mean?"

I was putting on a pot of hot water to boil the noodles. The paprikash would be ready in a couple of minutes. When my grandmother made the dish, she'd make noodles from scratch—actually her noodles were more like dumplings. Called the stuff *nockerle*. Mueller's would have to do now. I didn't have much interest in Simon's story, but if it was true, Carlton did sound like a complex individual. And he definitely had a lot of money. The type I'd usually choose to take on.

But it was an in-between time for me, and I liked it that way. I wanted to stay in my cave a little longer. I had no local construction jobs lined up, and the minor league season was already winding down. There was plenty of work to be done in the garden and around the carriage house. The world was in its place, and I was in no hurry. Spend a couple of hours a day running, half an hour with the weights, and maybe two hours a day cooking and eating. Every Friday, the all-night poker game at the Quill & Ink Club. Although, I have to admit, I'd been feeling kind of itchy for a while, bored, a little empty. The last time I'd spoken to my ex-wife—maybe two months ago—I was left with that usual stale feeling, still angry that she'd remarried and I hadn't. After all, she was the one who had wanted the divorce—her career came first. And it always bothered me that her career didn't really take off until after we split up. When we were married she was a perennial graduate student, always in the lab at the university, doing her cell-biology research. Then, two years after the divorce, she finished her Ph.D., moved to the West Coast, got a great job at a lab in Portland, and married the vice-president of the firm.

I threw the noodles in the pot, a little harder than I should have.

"Your client asked you to plant those stories with the newspaper?" I asked.

"Yeah, she really hates Carlton. Wants to get back at him in the worst way."

"How do you know she's telling the truth?"

"She's got pictures of the horses. A whole lot of pictures, with her father standing there, holding each piece. And others with the pieces displayed in his den. Gray, if you saw those pictures, you'd know the horses belonged to my client."

"So maybe everything she says is true. Except, maybe, there could be something she doesn't know. Like when her father split up with Carlton, maybe part of the deal could have been that the horse collection stays with Carlton. That could have been written into the settlement."

"You think so?"

"No, not from what you've said. But it's possible."

"Anything's possible. Maybe Carlton's really Santa Claus. But for my money, I'm convinced he's a thief and a turd, and I'm stealing that ebony horse for my client."

"Just one piece? Or the whole collection?"

"For now, just one. She's got a plan to go after him one step at a time, one piece at a time. That's the way she wants it. And she's paying the ticket."

The food was ready. I put out plates and silverware and dumped good-sized portions of the stuff for both of us. I sat down across from Simon.

"So what do you need me for?" I asked.

"Delivering documents to a newspaper I can do," he said. "Keeping the name of my client quiet, I can do. Stealing something—you know I can do. But I think she wants a lot more than that. Too much hate for all the little horses to heal it. She wants to bring down their whole business. The crazy thing is, this woman is more like me than like you. She doesn't come across like a lawyer or a banker, or even just the bereaved daughter. She likes to fight. I can tell." I'd never heard him say that about a woman. Not the way he meant it. "And she's alone," he said.

He genuinely cared about her.

"These are the kind of people you can't take down just by fighting," he said. "They don't stand up straight, they go sideways. They won't go down doing it my way. Or hers. You . . ." He jabbed a finger at me. "You could handle them. It's your kind of thing. The big lie. The big money. I don't know who else they hurt, but you know what I mean."

What surprised me was that a part of me wanted to do it. And I hadn't even seen this beautiful woman yet. Though, I have to admit, it was Carlton who interested me more than the woman. At least at the moment.

"You don't need me," I said. "If the collection is that casually displayed, you can steal the whole thing on your own. If it has no cash value, they probably won't have high security on it."

"Okay, then, solo it will be. Just thought you might want to tag along."

I started eating. He didn't seem quite ready. "How about we get together tonight for dinner," he said. "Say, seven o'clock, at my office. I'll show you the horse, tell you all about it. What do you say?"

I'd said no to everything else he'd asked. What could I lose? I was curious.

"You're buying?"

"Hey, I'm getting a thousand dollars for one afternoon's work. Anything you want."

"All right, I'll be there at seven." We dived into the paprikash, stuffing it in like madmen for the next fifteen minutes, too busy to talk. After lunch he headed out toward Carlton Associates. I watched him walk his funny walk all the way up the hill. He was in very good spirits. He'd told me that his client had green eyes and a very dark tan and sexy red hair. But he never did tell me his client's name. The man had ethics.

3

I GOT TO SIMON'S OFFICE EARLY, and while I was waiting I decided to take a walk around Market Street. The crowds and noise reminded me for the thousandth time why I hated living in a city and why I'd never sell that old carriage house near the woods. In the space of less than a block I saw a pinball arcade, two cheap jewelry stores, two subway entrances, a McDonald's, a step-downstairs porno shop ("Live Girls for Only One Dollar"), a step-in peep show (video for twenty-five cents), a pizza parlor, a stereo-electronics shop—and each of them, it seemed, was blasting out its own version of the same rock music. All this was happening on the ground level of a thirty-story office building, right there on Market Street between Thirteenth and Juniper, directly across from City Hall and the Mayor's office. This same building housed, on its more respectable floors, many of the offices for the judges of the Court of Common Pleas and Superior Court, various other city officials and bureaucrats, a large number of criminal defense lawyers, and, in the back, a handful of private detectives, including Simon.

I stood there in front of the pinball arcade, staring at my reflection in the window. Was I getting old? Or did I always look this way? The first impression people usually had of me was tall and thin. But then they get to the shoulders, which are wide, wrong for the body. It isn't muscularity, just wide—the hands, the arms, the bones, wide. A woman once told me I reminded her of a reed tree with an armor top. I liked the sound of that, but I didn't know what to make of it. I'd never seen a reed tree. My face goes with thin: bony jaw, hazel eyes, almost green,

24

and lots of wavy light brown hair. Nose and cheeks and chin all angles. My ex-wife said I looked old-fashioned in some way, patrician, she called it. Maybe I just looked old. Didn't feel old. If it weren't for the injury, I'd bet I'd still be playing ball, probably in the bigs. Could go another four years, figure, till I'm forty. Hell, Pete Rose played till he was forty-five. But then, he used hair coloring.

By seven o'clock, most of the rush-hour business people were gone and only the more serious downtown evening folks stayed behind. The two jewelry stores had pulled down their locked metal armor for the night, but all the other establishments were still going strong. I decided to stroll around the corner to Commerce Street, the back of the office building, where Simon usually made his entrance. There was a little coffee shop on the corner of Commerce and Juniper. Simon was late. I might as well get comfortable.

From the table by the window I could see the entire back of Simon's building, including the fourth-floor window of his office. If I looked across the street, I was staring up at the pigeon-stained tower of Billy Penn atop the City Hall building.

Commerce Street was neither alley nor sidewalk nor gutter. It was a filthy mess. You walked along it in a series of steps, up a little on a few feet of brick shelf, down a little over some slabs of broken slate. Halfway down the street was a pile of garbage that was hard to figure. There were wires and liquor bottles in it, but the glass and metal looked like they might have come from another planet. Every few feet was another pile of garbage.

The street was shaped by the back wall of the office building, which had so much dirt on it, the lines where the bricks met were no longer visible. I was always mildly surprised to see windows. One expected bare holes, like the entrances to caves, in no particular order, all the way up. Near a garbage dumpster, a black iron ladder curved out from the building and headed up. Wherever it was going, it never arrived, the end rung broken off and leaning out over the alley.

On the wall were signs of various kinds and graffiti, some of the latter scrawled in chalk, yet looking very old and very permanent. Morgan's Outlet, one of the signs read, and written over it in several places was the word Fayva. There were several doors leading into the back of the building, including one that Simon used to get to his office. Next to the doors were small windows with black bars spaced so tightly together it wasn't possible to see more than an inch of glass at a time.

It was ten after eight and starting to get dark. Simon was not usually late. Looking up at his office, I saw no light and no other signs of life. For the first time, I began to worry. What if the woman was lying to Simon? What if the ebony horse hadn't been just a personal passion of her father's, but actually something of real value? What if the security was a lot tighter than Simon had expected? What if Carlton did more than build malls and apartments, did things he didn't want people snooping around?

Commerce Street was beginning to show forms of its own nightlife. A woman wearing layers of filthy clothing and clutching a dark brown basket was lying on the sidewalk, alongside the dumpster, drinking from a long dark bottle. A man came along and sat down near her. Two men staggered toward the door of Buddy's Bar, but didn't quite make it in. They were kind of moving in slow circles. Apparently they weren't yet ready for their bed in the gutter.

Across the street a couple of long black limousines were pulling up to the sidewalk at the Mayor's entrance to City Hall. A small group of men dressed in black tie and a few women in long gowns came out of City Hall, along with four uniformed policemen. The fancies got into the limos and the cops walked back into the Hall. I didn't recognize any of them.

The coffee shop was closing, and still there was no Simon. I thought about going home. That's what I really felt like doing. I didn't like being near sleaze when I didn't have to be. Simon chose to work here. I didn't. I wasn't supposed to be working at all. I was supposed to be home in my cave. When I came out, it was for business. Being here was too close to business. I wanted out. I should have been back in the casual land of the kitchen, with the radio giving me the play-by-play of the Phillies' loss. The team could have used me at third base. At the very least, they could have used me listening at home. I could be there in twenty minutes, if I forgot about Simon. It could be that easy—just get back in the car and drive home. That would be the wise thing to do. Simon was probably fine, probably eating a classy dinner with his green-eyed client. There was no reason to worry, right?

The dark red door at the back of the building wasn't locked. I used the back stairs. The unlit corridor seemed hotter than the mucky air out in the street. I stepped on surface that was wet, sticky, crunchy, as if someone had lined the path with small bodies. It was too dark to see what was on the floor. I took bigger steps.

The stairway was better. There were sixty-watt light bulbs every other flight and a handrail. The handrail was cold. I took the stairs quickly. The door at the top of the fourth-floor landing was the same dark red as the one at the bottom. It opened a lot less easily. I couldn't see why Simon used it so much for entry and exit if it took such muscle just to open. On top of that, it was noisy. A piece of metal was jammed into the hinges. The thing gave out a long scraping shriek as it opened.

Simon's office was toward the rear. I was almost at Simon's door before the stairway door stopped squealing. It was an alarm, in effect, home-made and efficient. I could see his office door. It was open. The light inside was still out, but the hallway lamps did a pretty good job of illuminating the office. Someone was in there with a flashlight.

She was thin and not too tall, and her long, curly red hair almost glistened in the dark room. She was looking through file-cabinet drawers. She had to know someone was coming, even without that metal warning device. She had to have heard the noise. Either she didn't care, which made no sense at all, or she'd already checked me out. The thought was not pleasant.

She was wearing jeans and a dark green T-shirt and sneakers. I stood at the door looking at her profile. This must be Simon's red-haired client; I could see why he had such an interest in her. I still hadn't seen her from the front, but she was impressive enough from behind. She finished with the file cabinet, walked to the desk, and only then did she turn around to face me.

We looked at each other. She had a tough kind of outdoor look. I guessed she was in her twenties, definitely no more, but if I had been free-associating the word "grizzled" would have sprung to mind. She had lines in her face as if she'd been in the sun too much. It didn't take anything away from her. Like a young farm woman in an old photograph. Like she'd been doing a few decades of hard work, but with the health of the sun and fresh air. Her arms were muscular, too, as if she'd done some serious mountain climbing. Neither of us said a word.

Her shirt had patches of sweat, two lines down her back. Her jeans were not tight, but her body was pushing the fabric's limits, all curves, no fat. She wasn't smiling, and her intensity made me think she never did smile.

This might have been nice on another night, but it was feeling increasingly like work. I'd come with a plan: I would wait awhile for Simon, as any friend would, then I'd go home. Now this woman was here. Was I on duty or wasn't I?

I walked in all the way. She ignored me and started to go through papers on Simon's desk. It was a lot of work if one really wanted to find anything there. Simon was forever dumping things on the desk. He was the kind of guy who ran up ten dollars a month calling the information operator because he couldn't find phone numbers. She was about halfway across the desk, going from pile to pile. She in no way acknowledged my presence.

"Simon around?" I asked, talking as if I belonged there.

"You a friend?" It was her first direct sign that she was aware of me. Her tone was serious. No time for nonsense. She had to talk to me, so she was doing it.

"Yes, I'm a friend," I said. Maybe I made an enemy by saying I was his friend. Or maybe I'd put myself on her side. I looked her square in the face. It wasn't a bad side to be on.

I moved toward her slowly. She still seemed to be ignoring me when I put my hand out to stop her from picking up another pile of paper. For my effort, she swiveled hard and pushed my hand away with so much strength I almost lost my balance. I came back toward her, and that's when I noticed she was holding a gun.

I hadn't seen the gun and hadn't seen her take it out, so that was another kind of skill I added to her list. Strong, great at movement, easy with guns. I wondered if it was a short list. I hoped so.

"Go over and sit on the couch," she said, her voice calm, used to giving orders.

I went over and sat on the couch. I didn't say anything and neither did she. Actually, I didn't mind sitting there looking at her. She looked as good from the front as she had from behind, and the side view wasn't bad either. She did a lot for jeans and a T-shirt. After a few minutes she stopped watching me, kept the gun out, but busied herself going through the desk drawers. For some reason I didn't feel especially threatened, and not because I doubted her competence. I wondered how much depth I'd added lately to that particular feeling I had of not caring about things. It was one thing not caring, spending your days at home, the way I'd been doing the past few months. It was something else not caring when someone was holding a gun on you. It seemed like a little too much not caring. I thought I should do something about it.

"Shouldn't you be watching me?" I said. She glanced over at me for only a second, then shook her head and slapped some papers back down on the desk. "I mean, you were worried enough to take out a gun, so shouldn't you be watching me a little more closely? I could run, you know."

She didn't stop searching the desk. "What makes you think I'm not watching you?"

I considered laughing. It was pretty funny. But I didn't think she was trying to be funny. I sat there quietly for a few more minutes, and then I finally decided to take the gun.

Before I made a move, the phone rang. She went on searching. I stood up and started to walk to the phone. Simon's answering machine came on. His taped voice gave a short, to-the-point message, and then there was the beep. A man on the other end spoke loudly: "Hello, hello? Simon, you there? Hello? Listen, this is Greenwell. Simon?"

The woman seemed interested. She looked at the phone and repeated the man's name. "Greenwell . . ." It came out almost as a question. Then he hung up. I chose that moment to close the gap between us. I moved to her left side, and she turned that way, quickly, both with her body and the gun. I kicked at the gun at the same instant she turned, and if she'd fired right then, there was a chance she would have got some part of me, but instead she lifted her arm out of the way, and just as she did I moved in.

She shifted the gun hand back toward me, but by then I was in close enough so that her hand ran out of room between us. I pinned her gun hand against the desk and put my other arm around her. I had one leg and my side against her and positioned myself to throw her down, but it didn't work. She dropped the gun, took hold of my elbow and forearm

29

with both hands, bent down quickly, and pushed me off. I fell headlong. I grabbed one of her wrists as I went down, but she turned the wrist in my hand, and it was like holding a piece of thick rope twisting. My skin felt rubbed raw between my thumb and forefinger. I was down on the ground, and she was already around the desk and against the far wall, by the window.

The door wasn't that far away. The gun was closer. I wasn't sure which she'd go for, but it seemed reasonable one of the two would have some appeal. I went for the gun. Before I reached it, she went out the window. I got there myself seconds later, gun in hand. Simon's window faced out over the alley. The broken metal ladder I'd noticed was over to one side about five feet away. She was halfway down it and I had no idea how she'd gotten there. I had the gun, but I could barely make her out in the dark, and I had no intention of shooting. I was pretty sure that if I called out to her she wouldn't come back.

4

JACK CARLTON TURNED THE KEY to the warehouse door and opened it quietly. He walked through a long corridor and stopped at a large room with no door. He looked to his left, and there he could see the back of a man tied and bound to a chair. He knew it was Simon Griffey.

Carlton imagined what it must feel like to be wrapped so tightly in rope. Particularly if the man who had beaten and gagged you was Willie Reidus. Whenever Carlton saw someone in pain, he liked to think through what it would feel like, and how he would deal with it if it were he. It was something he was good at, and an old game of his, imagining himself having someone else's problem.

It must feel as if you're encased in something, he thought while studying Simon; as if your body had another part, a new hard skin that was, and wasn't, yours. There was this shell outside you, and it was stiff, ungiving. Inside it was soft. At first, maybe, you'd strain to free yourself. But you could not. You'd feel your feet pressed together, the bones meeting.

As Carlton stood there, he saw Simon's head moving. It went up and down, left to right, up and down. Then it just fell, as if to rest again. He probably felt nothing, Carlton decided. He'd been hit hard. He probably couldn't even remember who'd hit him.

He could see Simon begin to take in deep breaths. Maybe he was coming to, regaining his senses.

His head was free. But he hadn't yet glanced around. The room was very large, but confined as he was to the two-foot-square of space of the chair, he might as well have been in a closet. Carlton could see

31

him now gaining control of his breathing, calming his body, maybe thinking about how he had gotten here, and coming up empty for any answers. The pain would be the problem, not the numbness. His legs no doubt were raw and bruised where the rope was tied. He tried to flex his legs, and Carlton heard him gasp in pain. A pain like that, Carlton knew, moves through you like a wall of water hitting a hill of sand.

Carlton imagined what it must be like to look out from Simon's eyes right now. His vision would be more inside his head than out of it, he'd probably see the room in front of him as a blurred display of moving walls and black dots in empty space.

If he were very strong, and he looked like he was, he would try to focus himself. He'd have a thought like this: Hold on, hold on. He'd try telling himself, very firmly, to be quiet and look around and remember all he saw. At that moment, he'd promise himself he'd get out of this.

Carlton saw him straining against the ropes. There wasn't any give. Simon slumped for a minute, just gathering himself. If I were him, I'd be making plans, Carlton thought. First get untied, but then what? He's a private eye on a case, so he'd call his client. To report in about the ebony horse. To say yes, he stole it, but then they took it away. Where? Don't remember. A bar. A motel and bar near Carlton Associates. Maybe he would remember. He drove away with the piece, went to the bar, and then they came at him, blind-sided him.

If Simon was just a private eye on a case, there'd be no problem. But he was also feeding information to a newspaper. Reidus's men had found that out while following the reporter, Baines. Why Simon was a source for the newspaper wasn't yet clear, but that didn't really matter. He was a source. That could be a problem. Reidus had made a mistake, no doubt about it. He'd taken things too far, as he often did. He shouldn't have kidnapped the man. Now Carlton was here to fix things.

Carlton walked farther into the room, and even before Simon could react to the sound of footsteps, Carlton said, "Don't worry. There's been a mistake. I'm here to take care of it. You'll be okay. I promise."

Simon swung his head back toward Carlton as he approached. He was gagged so he couldn't speak. But his face didn't seem to be frantic, didn't show a sense of panic. Carlton liked that, even respected it. More than anything, Simon looked curious. If he'd been kidnapped, fine. If he was to be killed, then, well, he needed to know. Tell me. He made his expression ask the question.

"No, no," Carlton said, his voice soothing, even as he knelt down and reached around Simon to feel for the knots of the ropes. As he worked, Carlton could see Simon had large bruises on his face and arms, and a cut had opened below his right eye, bleeding into his mouth, the trail of blood crusted. Reidus had caught him full in the face. The punch had done damage, all right. It looked like he'd broken Simon's nose. Carlton wondered, as he looked at him, if Simon knew how close he'd come. Perhaps he should find a way to tell him, Carlton thought. It might make him grateful both to be alive and to have Carlton's help and comfort now. He decided not to tell him yet.

Carlton finished untying Simon, and he was free to rise, but Simon didn't move at all. He seemed pasted to the chair, part of it. He looked dazed and incapable of motion on his own.

"I'll get you out of this," Carlton said. He put an arm under Simon's elbow and helped him stand, half carrying him toward the door. He wanted to begin talking to Simon, but knew he had to wait for him to recover, at least a bit. He walked him down the long corridor and took him outside. Simon's hands were still tied tightly behind his back.

It was dark out.

"It's only been a few hours," Carlton said. "You really haven't lost anything. Just a few hours. We'll get you back on your feet like nothing ever happened."

They walked a small circle on the dirt, Carlton guiding him, saying nothing, until finally Simon managed to walk on his own. Carlton led him to the Cadillac.

If he could convince Simon of his sincerity, Carlton thought, then the incident had been worthwhile. Having people's trust was the thing most worth having. Get that from people and you can do anything. They'd help you, even help you take their possessions. With anyone, including this private eye, that was worth pursuing. It was his talent, as Carlton thought of it. Even someone like this, even in the state he was in now, even thinking, as perhaps he did, that Carlton was responsible for what had happened, he could even bring someone like that around to his point of view. That was worth more than the crude power of a punch.

"I'll take care of everything," Carlton said after they were in the car. "Just try to relax. I'll explain to you as we drive. It was all a mistake and as soon as I found out, I came to get you."

When Reidus told him he'd snatched the private eye, Carlton had been upset, but he kept it to himself because he knew Reidus had good intentions. He was just narrow; the only thing he knew was violence. Oh, he was good at that. But it was all he knew. Carlton, on the other hand, was, as he saw it, anything but narrow. Yes, he was comfortable with violence. He'd come up that way. He'd never have made it past the guy who killed his cousin when Carlton was sixteen if he hadn't been comfortable with killing. At a certain point in a man's life, there was no other way. But he had grown. Because he had so much more to work with than the narrow, single-minded Reidus. He inspired people, won their belief in him and his endeavors. Stealing was one thing. But to actually get them, as he did, to voluntarily put their own hands in their pockets and offer you their possessions, that was a kind of worship. He had never had that thought before, and it stunned him. He felt energized by it.

Carlton pictured for a moment all of his holdings. The land he personally owned, the greater amount he leveraged—the houses in Hatley (albeit that was at Reidus's urging), the office buildings, the stables. He saw himself in his domain, a god walking. He felt swelled. He glanced at Simon. He was coming around. It was time to explain, to convince, to inspire. There was no need for Reidus's violence, for an approach based on threats. Carlton had words.

"In our world, there are constant attacks," he began. His voice reached out for Simon's attention—Simon was staring out the windshield, but there was nothing to look at out there, so Carlton knew he was listening. "The public hears about industrial espionage, corporate competition, but what it really amounts to is that everything we've earned by our hard work, people try to take away. Other companies. The government. Individuals. All with plans of their own."

Although Simon was still gagged, he turned Carlton's way. This was all the reaction Carlton needed, just his attention. He could do the rest. "So we defend ourselves. We protect our property. We keep what we have by being alert."

Carlton pulled over to the side of the road, removed the gag from

Simon's mouth and untied the private eye's hands. When Simon's mouth was free, he took in a long deep breath, then flexed his jaw, maybe just to see if anything was broken. He rubbed his hands, but he didn't say anything.

"It was our security people who followed you after you took the ebony statue from my collection," Carlton said. "That was a mistake on your part. You shouldn't have done that. But then our people made a mistake also. Two wrongs don't settle anything. All I want you to tell me is why you stole the horse."

Simon didn't say anything.

"Did you think it was valuable?" Carlton asked. "If so, you were wrong. It's not an expensive piece. It's worth twenty-five bucks, fifty, tops."

Simon didn't respond, and Carlton wondered if perhaps the private eye knew something that Carlton didn't. Could there be some value to the horse that Carlton didn't know of? Or was Simon really after something else, and perhaps was scared off before he got to it?

"I know you're doing work for the newspaper," Carlton said. "My people have no intention of interfering with that work. We happen to believe in the First Amendment and we support it strongly. I want you to understand that one of my men overreacted, did an impulsive thing. He was angry, but that was all."

Simon still said nothing. He stared, expressionless, at Carlton.

"I'll see that everyone involved in what happened to you will be disciplined severely," Carlton said.

It took a great salesman to say things like this and make it believable.

"I'll take you home now, and then I'll arrange for a doctor to see you. Where do you live?"

"No," Simon muttered. "Not home. To the office."

Why would he want to go to the office this late at night? It was past 10:30.

"Come on," Carlton said. "Let's get you home."

Simon sank into the soft leather comfort of the car seat and stared out the windshield at the onrushing road, which was essentially darkness broken by the rhythmic flaring of other car lights and the orange tubes of the roadside markers. In the silence, Carlton thought again about what must be going through the private eye's mind. The newspaper,

35

that must be it. Simon was planning to go to the reporter. That's why he was so silent. He had an urgent idea, like a solid thing inside him, something that had kept him going. He was so calm because he had this picture in his mind, this vision he had focused on: seeing himself walking the flight of steps to that newsroom in West Chester, walking up to the reporter, Chris Baines, the guy Reidus's men had been following. And then Simon would fill him in on every detail of the kidnapping. That must be his plan.

Carlton noticed that every minute or so Simon's eyes started to close. He'd taken a really bad beating. He shook himself awake. His head came up too fast, but it seemed important to him to make sure he kept his eyes open.

Once, when his eyes closed again, Carlton tapped Simon's shoulder, and Simon snapped his body, pushing Carlton away.

"Hey," Carlton yelled. The car swerved sharply. "Listen," Carlton said, regaining his hold. "You've been through something rough. Let me take you home, we'll have my doctor check you out—he'll come right away."

"No," Simon said, not sounding quite as shaky. "Not home. To my office."

"You can't consider going there now," Carlton said. "Not in your condition."

For all his impulsiveness and preference for the dramatic, Carlton thought, Reidus had good instincts. His feeling had been that this man was capable of taking his investigation to a level that was more than just helping a newspaper with a story, and that it was possible he had enough strength and will to have actually either mounted an operation against the business or at least to have played a role in someone else's operation. It was certainly possible he was being paid by someone outside the newspaper. If so, it was probably good money. He'd survived an encounter with Reidus, which was as good as you could get. He could easily have been killed.

"Would capturing somebody be a standard security procedure?" Simon asked calmly.

Carlton didn't answer. It was the kind of question that had no legitimate reply. It implied that Carlton was the head of the team that had snatched Simon. That was the conclusion Simon had reached, and no doubt the one he planned to tell the newspaper.

Well, he'd given the private eye the opportunity to save himself, Carlton thought, and he'd turned it down. Whatever happened to Simon next would therefore be his own doing, not Carlton's. The thing about Reidus was that he was completely unworried about the consequences of his actions. He would automatically do whatever was necessary to protect whatever he'd done first. He'd kill three people if necessary to protect himself from the consequences of having killed one. There was no limit to it. It was narrow and one-dimensional, but also very effective. At this point, Reidus would probably kill Simon. After all, what was the problem with that? Done Reidus's way, by the time a couple of days had passed, he'd have located the people who'd paid the private eye and planned the operation, and either handled them permanently, or made a deal with them to call off the hostilities.

Carlton saw that Simon's expression was no longer dazed. The private eye was alert and concerned.

"All right," Simon said. "Take me home. I live near the Art Museum."

He imagined Simon was trying to size up the change in Carlton's mood, to figure out why Carlton had suddenly grown quiet. Simon was trying to read Carlton's feelings. He had none.

He took the interstate turn toward Carlton Stables, where he could find Reidus. Simon tried asking more questions and Carlton told him to be quiet.

5

REIDUS WAS AT the small dining area in the guest house at the stables. On the table was a spread that included a large sliced turkey, bowls of vegetables, and a basket of bread. He ate with no relish; it was a necessity of life to feed himself, nothing more. But as he ate, he thought, as he often did, of his background, and how well his family had prepared him for the man he was today.

As a child, Reidus had heard the stories about the many generations of violence in his family. His grandfather and two of his grandfather's brothers had each ended up in jail for a series of rapes and killings. His grandfather died there at the age of forty-two, killing a guard, then being killed while trying to escape. Reidus's Uncle Joe had made more of an effort to stay out of jail. He was once acquitted of a murder. He liked telling the eight-year-old Reidus how he beat the rap by crying in front of the jury, looking as innocent as he could, and swearing that he would never hurt another human being. He knew well how the courts worked—that despite the fact that he committed the murder, the evidence was not strong and the jury could not be told a word about his family background. "People will believe anything," he told Reidus.

Reidus's father somehow managed to avoid any trouble during childhood, and he decided to live an ordinary life. He worked at the store twelve hours a day and spent most of his free time with a religious group in town. He married a woman he met there.

Reidus, an only child, avoided the church and spent much of his time instead with his uncle. He believed, as did his uncle, that his father's allegiance to the church was fake. He imagined it was part of

38

some scheme, though he had no idea what that might be, but Reidus was convinced his father's devotion to his mother was part of it. He couldn't believe his father loved a bland, empty, opinionless woman with no spark.

One Sunday, when he was eleven, Reidus was supposed to meet his parents at church. Instead he went out with his uncle for the day. They spotted a teenage boy and his girlfriend parked in a red Corvette convertible. Joe walked up to the car and started saying things to the boy, speaking calmly, but making little sense. Then he reached in to grab the boy, who protested but was immediately silenced by one hard punch to the face. Joe pulled the boy out of the car, threw him on the ground, then motioned Reidus into the passenger seat, next to the girl.

Joe drove fast and they were quickly out of town. He looked at Reidus. "Having fun?"

Joe stopped the car on a rural road and led the girl and Reidus into the woods. "Did your father get you laid yet?" he asked Reidus.

When Reidus said no, Joe spoke quietly to the girl. After he did, she had sex with Reidus as the uncle watched. When they got home, Joe told Reidus's father what they had done. He seemed to be taunting his brother with it. Reidus's father ordered his brother out of the house.

That night Reidus's father talked to him for a long time in his bed, warning him, for the hundredth time, about the family and its troubles. And as Reidus listened, he thought that for no good reason his father refused to use his strength, denied he had any. His father's whole life, not just church, was a lie, a voluntary lockup, a way of throwing aside the power passed on to him.

When his father died of a stroke three years later, Reidus remembered seeing the body lying dead on the floor, the medics failing to revive him. He was a very big man, even in death—dwarfing the people around him who were feeling for pulses and tending their machines. There are natural kings in the world, Reidus thought, and the great and only sin was to live tied down.

He worked hard to get stronger. For years after his father died, he spent hours every day working out, by himself. He wanted no involvement with other people's regimens. His own rule was that if everyone was doing it, it wasn't good enough.

When he was nineteen, he developed what he thought of as a training program that suited him. Every other night he selected a spot on a map—a place within five or ten miles of where he was living. He'd run at a fast pace to the location, dressed in jogging clothes, pick out a house or a shop, break in, assault anyone inside, and take something—usually just an object, a few times a pet, and once a child. He'd run back home, and drop whatever he'd taken along the way. He'd sprint the last few miles.

On the nights he didn't run, he'd do two hours of repetitions with free weights. He'd bench-press 350 pounds. He'd read once that the strongest football players could press 350, so he was satisfied. If he'd wanted to do more, he believed he could.

He'd stopped the rigorous workouts four years ago when he'd taken the job with Carlton. He realized that the daily challenges of the job and his occasional violent assaults were enough exercise. More than that, he knew his strength was largely a gift in the blood from the generations of Reiduses who'd made their own rules.

He heard the sound of the approaching Cadillac and walked casually to the front window. He watched the big car come to a full stop, and then smiled as he saw Carlton help the private detective out of the front seat. Carlton was much bigger, and Reidus had the image of a father leading a sleepy child to his bed. Let's get physical, Reidus thought, imagining Carlton's reaction when he'd seen the bound man in the warehouse. With Carlton, everything had to be indirect and subtle, people had to be talked to and understood and guided. Carlton's pride in convincing people to go along sometimes evoked Reidus's admiration for the skill he had at getting his way, and, just as often, Reidus's contempt, because Carlton cared so much what others thought. He talks to him, thought Reidus, then he brings him to me for the kill.

Reidus stopped smiling, but had a general feeling of content and pleased anticipation as he opened the door and stepped out onto the dirt.

Carlton brought the private eye up to the front of the guest house. Reidus gazed first at Griffey, then at Carlton. "I'm glad you got to see him," Reidus said to Carlton. "Now let me help."

Carlton stood in front of Simon. "I've always said that knowing other people's strengths is my key to doing business," Carlton told Reidus. "Knowing their weaknesses is yours."

They were talking as if Simon didn't exist. As if he were already dead. Suddenly, Simon tried to run. But Reidus grabbed him and pulled him in, his back to Simon's side, his arm crossing Simon's body from his shoulder down to his leg. He pressed Simon's ribs inward and a gasp of air pushed past the private eye's lips and exploded.

Simon inhaled as much air as he could and made an effort to wrench free. He didn't get anywhere. The fact that Reidus was tall made it hard, because he had leverage. Reidus was stronger as well. Simon couldn't move.

Reidus stretched out his other hand and gently squeezed Carlton's shoulder. "It's no problem. I'll take care of this."

Reidus wondered if the private eye, in his present condition, was physically capable of putting up a fight. Show me something, Reidus thought, letting him go. As he did, Simon bunched a fist and swung it up into Carlton's neck, just behind his ear. Carlton went down. Simon turned around to face Reidus.

"Did he tell you who he works for?" Reidus asked Carlton as he got to his feet.

"No."

"Then tell me," he said to Simon. "Who are you working for?"

Simon didn't answer.

"Okay," Reidus said. "We'll have some fun getting the answers." He took a step toward Simon.

"No," Carlton said. "I don't care. Just get rid of him."

"Sure thing," Reidus said. "But I am interested in the redhead. If it's okay with you, I'll just get her name."

Reidus took Simon's face between his hands, and blocked all of the smaller man's attempts to get free. He put his mouth against the detective's ear and Carlton could hear him whispering but couldn't make out the words. A steadily louder moaning rose out of the smaller man, a painful keening. Reidus was doing something to his face, but Carlton couldn't see what. He stepped closer to hear the detective utter two single, well-formed words: "Fuck you."

Reidus released him only slightly, but Simon stepped into him, going

41

low, digging both hands in and trying to punch with one hand and grab with the other. He committed himself to the blow, wanting the man lower to the ground, where Simon could deal with him. But Reidus avoided the brunt of Simon's blows and didn't go down. Instead, he took Simon's head in both hands, his elbows locked below so that Simon couldn't get in another punch. Simon's head started to move up and back, the pressure in his ears and the force on his neck increasing.

Carlton started for the car. He heard a snap—a thin, small sound. He got into the car, closed the door, and drove off.

Reidus dragged the body to the storm-cellar stairs, opened the wide wood doors and dropped it in. He'd decide how to dispose of it later. He went back to finish his dinner.

6

I'D BEEN SITTING THERE in the dark office for over an hour, turning her small gun over in my hands again and again, staring out into the alley, waiting to hear the sound of the screeching door, anything, just some sign of Simon. I was tired of talking to the answering machine at his home phone. I knew I wasn't going home till I found him. I finally decided to walk the five blocks up Broad to the *Inquirer* building on Callowhill. I figured I'd be able to get some information there; staying in Simon's office wasn't doing either of us any good.

No one was in the newsroom when I got out of the elevator on the fifth floor, a few minutes before midnight. It looked like a still picture on a TV screen, no sound. All the cogs and wheels were in place—telephones, computer screens, swivel chairs, stacks of books—but nothing stirred. Newsrooms were like this everywhere. The hours aren't nine to five, more like ten to ten. But after that, at night, the place goes to sleep. Maybe news never stops, but newsrooms do. Oh, there'd still be a few people on duty now—a reporter over at police headquarters, a night rewrite guy, probably in the bathroom or library, a copy boy (these days they're called "editorial assistants"), probably in the cafeteria. But no one gives a second thought to leaving the newsroom unattended at night. Newspaper people are probably the least security-conscious professionals in the world. Very few reporters put their notebooks away when they leave the office, and even fewer lock their desk drawers. And the newsroom itself is never locked. Most newsrooms don't even have doors, just elevator exits and stairs. At night, the places are left alone, with the lights on, and the security guards making their usual rounds. I think it has something to do with reporters not feeling they're worth very much, so how could their working tools be of any value? Go ahead, steal my notebook. It won't do you any good.

I'd left the news business more than ten years ago, but I still felt at home here. I remembered the feeling of always having the newsroom available, open twenty-four hours every day. I'd come in at any time, sometimes instead of going home after a date or party, just because settling in at the desk was easier than going home alone. Even when no one else is here, you don't feel alone.

The basics of being a reporter never change. And feeling unimportant was one of those basics—having the notion that nothing you do, no bits of writing, big or small, made a lasting difference in the way the world worked. But there was another side to it, and I remembered it strongly, felt stirrings of it in me now, as I looked around. It was the sense of knowing that on any day you might hit on a small story, usually by accident, that could mean something special to one person. That felt good.

I hadn't been looking for anything special when I started out reporting. Just washed out of the minors with my bum shoulder, the muscle healed well enough for anything except to swing a stick and send a hardball flying over a fence. Since I'd found it easy to write the columns for *Baseball America*, I figured why not try to get a job as a sportswriter? I talked to a few sportswriters I knew, and one guy at a small paper in Delaware County introduced me to the news editor, Mike Shannon.

For no money, Shannon told me I was free to go out and write some features about anything local. He'd be glad to read my stories and let me know what he thought.

I liked Shannon. He was straightforward and simple, and he made no promises. Managers and agents in the minors had made me a lot of promises, telling me all about the great things that would happen. They talked about my "potential" and how far I could go, and how I'd probably have a multi-year contract for several million by the time I was twenty-five. They lost interest when my shoulder went out. Shannon said he'd love a twelve-inch feature story about a sixty-seven-year-old woman who drove a taxi. If I could give him that, he'd pay me. Fifteen bucks. Now that was a man I could trust.

I wrote the story, and a dozen more like it, and in two months Shannon hired me as a reporter. He said I had an "eye," which wasn't something I knew then as part of journalism, but which I certainly understood from baseball. I guess it helps to have an "eye," no matter what field you're in.

At the city desk, a list of city and suburban police telephone numbers was taped to the side of a computer terminal. Standard procedure for city desks. Call the numbers every couple of hours, see if anything's happening. I took the list to a Xerox machine, made a copy, then retaped it. I found a bank of telephone books just to the side of a glass-windowed office. Harrisburg, Wilmington, Trenton, Philadelphia, and all the suburbs.

Greenwell. That's all the guy said to Simon's answering machine. I didn't have a first name. The red-haired woman wasn't polite enough to give me that. Or an address. Not even a town. I flipped through the Gs in the Philadelphia white pages. Eight Greenwells. I checked the suburbs. Only three more. I wrote down all the numbers and addresses. It struck me that in one way I was lucky it was late at night. It was about as likely a time as any for most people to be home, so at least I could go through the list right away and eliminate the wrong Greenwells. I'd probably wake up most of them, but I'd say it was urgent, that I had a message from Simon. The right Greenwell would show interest. There'd be no reason for him to deny knowing Simon. Anyone else would tell me to shove it.

As I walked to a desk, a chubby man, mid-twenties, came into the newsroom from a corridor. He was wearing blue jeans and a dirty white polo shirt. My first guess had him as the copy boy on his way back from the cafeteria. He could have been the rewrite guy, but he looked too young. He was the first person I'd seen in the newsroom and I said hi. He ignored me and walked out toward the city desk. Okay. So maybe the Pinkertons would be a little tougher. But you can't blame this guy. Newspaper people always let other reporters use their newsrooms. They don't even think about it. If I were him I'd probably do the same thing. In fact, when I was a reporter, I had done the same thing. A hundred times.

The first Greenwell to answer the phone was a woman. She had been asleep. I asked to speak to Mr. Greenwell and she said there was no

Mr. Greenwell. The next woman I reached said her husband was out of town on business for the weekend. The third put her husband on the phone, and he assured me I had the wrong number and he didn't seem very happy about it. Of the remaining five Greenwells in Philadelphia, three told me, with differing degrees of emphasis, that I had the wrong number, one line was busy, and one didn't answer.

In the suburbs, two were wrong numbers, and the third didn't answer.

I tried calling Simon again, and again got the machine.

I went up to the library and pulled the clips on Carlton Associates. Not too many. I photocopied what there was and quickly read through them. Then I went back down to the newsroom.

I took out the Xeroxed list of police phone numbers and called the Philadelphia police. I said I was calling from the *Inquirer,* which, after all, I was, and asked if there was anything to report. All's quiet, they said. I asked if any dead bodies had come in. No, nothing going on, they told me.

It felt strange remembering that when I had the night shift as a reporter, I'd made that same phone call about ninety times each night to each of about thirty different local police and fire stations, night after night. That was the routine covering night police. You go right down the list, cop shop after cop shop, and ask the same tired questions again and again. Maybe a little variety: Any banks get robbed? Valuable gem collections stolen? Celebrities bound and gagged? Dead bodies come in? No, the cops almost always said. Everything's quiet. Okay, thanks, 'bye. And the thing is, when you make all those calls, you never expect to hear anything, and if you do, after all, so what? You take down the information—maybe a body found stabbed—and you tell the night city editor. A short story. A metro brief. Most papers didn't even report all the murders, let alone other crimes that came in each night.

You'd make the calls and you'd do it all in an even tone, over and over, and sometimes, pleasantly, someone would be in a good mood and joke around, and you'd respond to that, and there'd be some laughter. Or you'd be covering for someone else and the cop would first think it was the usual guy, but you'd say, "No, I have the night," and there'd be silence on the other end. And the tone would change as the night went on. By 4 A.M., talking to the same guy for the fourth time, you'd hardly have anything to say, it was all mechanical, hard black plastic at ear till you wore out any feelings about deaths and fires and body counts.

I went down the list for suburban Philadelphia, including Chester County, where Carlton Associates is headquartered. They all said the same thing. Nothing. A good sign? Maybe. Maybe not. Simon could be dead and buried for two years before anyone even reported him missing. I called back the Greenwell number that had been busy. This time it rang. Turned out to be another wrong number. I tried the two that hadn't answered. Still no answer. I went to the crisscross phone directories, the ones that listed street addresses first, then names and phone numbers. I took down the names and numbers of neighbors of both Greenwells, then called them, saying it was an emergency. A neighbor of the Philadelphia Greenwells said the family had been on vacation for the week. A neighbor of the suburban Greenwell, out near West Brandywine, said he had no idea where Dave was.

It was a long shot, but it was the best I could think of at the moment. I decided to drive out to Dave Greenwell's house.

7

THE LAST TWENTY MINUTES of the hour-long drive to Greenwell's house was on a winding two-lane road in the dark meadows and woods of the Brandywine horse country. I'd taken the expressway from Center City almost all the way out to Valley Forge, then picked up 202 to go south into the Chester County farmland. My old Civic did well enough on the narrow Doe Run Road, but it wanted the expressway, the turnpike, the big routes, the ones with lots of lanes and fewer bends. I liked the car, had had one just like it before. I'd run that one up to 150,000 miles, and missed it like a friend when it died. As I took the curves, weaving from side to side, I thought this was the kind of road that frustrates city people, makes them dizzy and scared. The never-ending curves, the lack of shoulders, and the way cars coming the other way blind you with their headlights popping out of nowhere. Leaves you feeling stunned, like some animal with big eyes, frozen immobile by the presence of bigger things owning the night.

I turned off Doe Run onto Stottsville Drive. The land was no longer for horses or cows. There were houses in a new suburb, land and trees and properties wide apart. You could hardly see one place from the other. Nicely developed.

It was past midnight by the time I found Greenwell's house on a newly paved road without street signs. There was no car in the driveway. But parked across the street was a black Nissan Z, and the woman sitting behind the wheel had lots of red hair that almost glistened in the dark. I parked behind her, got out and walked up to her window.

"My name's Gray," I said, resting my hands over the open window

48

of the driver's side door. "I'd give you back your gun but I don't have it with me. I left it in Simon's office. Sorry."

"You didn't follow me, I know that for sure. How the hell did you find me out here?"

"I wasn't looking for you. I was looking for Greenwell. Remember? The voice on the answering machine. Actually, I don't care about Greenwell, either. I'm interested in Simon. I don't know where he is, and at this hour Greenwell seems like the best place to start. What brought you out here?"

She didn't answer.

"You think Greenwell has your ebony horse?"

She grabbed one of my wrists, hard, as if she were planning to pull me into the car. "Who are you?" She kept her voice low.

"Ouch," I said, meaning it. I was a lot bigger than she was, and I pulled my wrist free but with more effort than I thought it would take. "I told you, I'm Simon's friend. Who are you?"

She unlocked the passenger door. "Get in," she said. "I'll tell you."

I walked around, and as I got in, I couldn't help noticing that the back was stuffed with several bags and small suitcases. "You live in here? Or just always on the move?"

"Yes to both," she said, then laughed. "You know, that pretty much sums it up." And she laughed again. I didn't get it. "My name is Sara. Sara Mitchell."

"Nice to meet you." I paused. "How come you're not holding me at gunpoint this time?"

"I know you're not one of them. I believe you are who you say you are—Simon's friend."

"You're right, I'm not one of them. By the way, who are they?"

"Carlton's people. Like Reidus and Greenwell. You're not one of them."

"How can you tell?"

"Well, for one thing, they would have used my gun. Probably would have shot at me from the window. Would have missed, but would have shot anyway. And they wouldn't have said they were Simon's friend if they weren't. Makes no sense. And most of all, they wouldn't have said ouch when I grabbed them."

49

"Oh." Simon was right. Even in the dark I could see she had beautiful eyes. "So why are you interested in Greenwell?"

She started her answer by telling me about Greenwell's boss, a guy named Reidus. For about a month now, she said, she'd been following him. She'd watched him hurt people, hurt them in sick ways, like pulling them out of their house in the middle of the night and making them stand almost naked outdoors. Or taking people from their cars and throwing their keys in the sewer. Or shutting down small shops just by putting "out of business" signs on windows and telling customers to go away.

"I've seen him do things you wouldn't believe," she said. "He fucks around with people, hurts them, the way you or I might go for a walk or eat lunch. A few weeks ago, I saw him drive a woman off a road, just for kicks. Almost killed her. He does something like that almost every day."

"Okay," I said. "The guy sounds like a nut. But why are you following him?"

"Reidus works for Jack Carlton," she said. "You ever hear of him? Reidus is Carlton's right-hand man. Anything Reidus does, he does with Carlton's approval."

"And you hate Carlton because of what he did to your father?"

She almost jumped out of her seat. "How do you know that?"

"I really don't know anything. Just the little bit that Simon told me this afternoon. That's how I know about the ebony horse. He told me he was going in to steal it. We arranged to meet for dinner when he was done. I got worried when he didn't show up so I'm looking for him. I read a few clips about Carlton in the newspaper library tonight. Not much there. But they did write about the breakup of the company, when your father left four years ago."

She sat back in her seat. She stared through the windshield at the little wooded area in the undeveloped lot just in front of the car. Then she turned to me.

"I don't want to talk about Carlton or about my father. But let me tell you about Reidus and Greenwell. Let me tell you why I'm waiting for Greenwell right now."

She rested her hand lightly on top of the steering wheel and leaned with her side against the driver's door.

"The first time I saw Greenwell," she said, "was on a day I'd been trailing Reidus, about three weeks ago. It was maybe a half hour from here, almost in Delaware, near a small town called Hatley. Reidus and Greenwell were driving in separate cars. They finally parked just off a dirt road and I found a spot for myself up a hill. A couple of minutes later, a big pickup came along, carrying four workmen. Greenwell pulled a rifle from his car and shot out one of the tires. When the truck stopped, Reidus herded the men out, and Greenwell covered them with the rifle. Reidus spoke to the men too quietly for me to hear. The funny thing was, Greenwell stood near them and kind of put on a show by emptying the rifle's bullets into the ground. Then he tossed the gun away and kicked dirt over the bullets. He smiled at the men. I thought it was an invitation to fight, but that's not what happened."

She was thoroughly involved in her story. I could see her anger. More than that, hatred. This was a woman who had already crossed the line. But where she was headed, I didn't know. Maybe she didn't, either.

"How do you even know their names?" I asked. "Reidus and Greenwell. Who told you their names?"

"Oh, come on," she said. "They're in the personnel directory at Carlton Associates. I've seen their files. I have connections; some of my father's friends are still there."

I believed her, but I didn't understand her.

"Reidus talked to the men a while longer," she continued. "Then he signaled to Greenwell and they both got in their cars and drove away. But before the workmen repaired the tire, Greenwell came back, this time alone, in his red Corvette. One of the guys ran to the van and took out a crowbar, but another guy, an older one, stopped him, then went to Greenwell."

" 'What do you want?' I heard him asking. Greenwell stepped up as if to answer, but instead he dropped his shoulders and brought one arm up, using his elbow to lead. I saw it coming but the workman didn't. He took the elbow in the throat, then he dropped to the ground. The three other guys ran in, led by the one with the crowbar. I was watching from above and I could easily see their approach was wrong. They moved in one at a time. They should have taken him from three sides, or jumped him all at the same time. They had no chance one on one."

"You talk about fighting as if you're an expert," I remarked.

51

"I've become one." There was no hesitation in her response. "But that doesn't matter. Just listen to what happened."

"The guy with the crowbar swung down and across Greenwell's body," she went on. "It wasn't a bad move, but Greenwell handled it easily. At the time, I thought his response was also a show, like his throwing the bullets at the dirt. He was all bravado, lots of flash and guts. He didn't turn away or back up to avoid the crowbar. Instead, he dropped to his knees and raised his hands over his head. The timing was perfect. He caught the blow with his palms and just turned it around, sending the blow back up through the crowbar. You know what it looked like? It was like the workman hit rubber and metal with the crowbar. He sort of just bounced off Greenwell's hands.

"Greenwell was definitely exhibiting himself. I even had this feeling— although I knew it couldn't be—that maybe Reidus, with his incredible talent for combat, had somehow divined I was there, and he'd sent Greenwell back to show me this, to show me, I don't know, that this is how good even his assistant is, so that I could imagine what it would be like to face Reidus himself, directly."

If she was a cop or someone like that, then why had she hired Simon? I wondered. Simon was good physically, but this woman was twenty years younger and, having seen her in action for just a few minutes, I couldn't believe she'd have trouble handling any man.

"I watched as Greenwell bent forward," she went on. "He grabbed the ankles of the man with the crowbar, and yanked his legs up, so the guy fell hard on his back. Then he hit the guy in the groin. While that guy was rolling in pain, Greenwell spun and moved toward the other men. Again, it was a show by Greenwell—for Reidus, I realized, even though he'd left. What must it be like, I thought, to be Greenwell, and work for someone like Reidus, going with him on his rounds? You'd feel pale, thin, like a piece of tin next to a bar of gold. Always second place. Reidus's business with these men had been over when he'd driven away. But Greenwell felt he had to come back.

"I could see by then that the two other guys didn't want any part of Greenwell. They'd backed away. But Greenwell came at both of them, side-kicking the older man, knocking him down, then swinging a ridged hand into the face of the younger man, breaking his nose. The younger guy fell, holding his face, rocking on his knees. Greenwell turned and whipped a roundhouse kick into him. As he turned for another kick, I noticed again his broad smile. He was beaming. He swung his hips smoothly and landed with all his weight on the workman's face. A line of blood slowly covered the workman's forehead. After a while, he sat up, barely able to move.

"Greenwell turned and headed for his car. I could see him clearly. You watch someone do what he did, it's like being connected. The part I hated most was the way he kept smiling."

She seemed to remember every detail, as if she'd studied a videotape.

"Why didn't you do anything to stop him?" I asked. "You're an expert at fighting, you claim. Why did you let those guys get hurt?"

"Simple. Reidus. He might have still been around." She put her hands through her hair like she was trying to pull some out. Then she hit the steering wheel with a fist. "You don't know a thing about this— you ask me questions like that!" She grabbed my arm and pulled me toward her so our faces almost touched. "I've gotten very good at watching things and doing nothing. Things that are hard for a person to watch. Do you think I like it?"

I twisted my arm to break her grip. "Hey, easy. I'm not one of your targets. I need to know more about what you're doing. Tell me about Simon."

"Maybe Greenwell can tell you," she said, opening her door.

"Wait a minute." I put a hand on her arm. "Stop it. Stop fighting me. I might be able to help you. But first you have to convince me you're not crazy. Okay?"

She leaned back. She spoke more softly, and slower. "My guess is that Carlton would have had Reidus get the horse back from Simon. And a job like that is so simple, it's possible Reidus had Greenwell do the dirty work. I don't know why Greenwell called Simon's office, but I assume it means he was involved."

"Maybe," I said. "But you're not really interested in Simon, are you? You want Greenwell because of what you saw him do. You're taking him on instead of Reidus, right?"

"Yes," she said. "But it's also a way of letting Reidus know I'm around. I want Carlton and Reidus to know that I'm the one who's after them, not Simon, and not the newspaper. I'm sorry about Simon. Really. I shouldn't have involved someone else. It's my fight. I shouldn't have asked him to steal the horse. That was too dangerous. I was just trying to up my odds—not do everything myself."

I'd met a lot of screwed-up people over the years. The ones that were actually crazy never apologized for what they did. They never admitted they made mistakes. So this one probably wasn't crazy.

But what of it? My only goal was to find Simon. And here I stumble into this woman, pursuing the source of some pain. Should I help her? I'd stopped letting other people pick my battles a long time ago. It didn't feel right then, it wouldn't feel right now. If Simon shows up, okay, I'm out of it. This woman may need help because of high stakes and heavy weapons on the other side. So what? Most of the world needs that kind of help.

We sat there in the damp night air waiting for Greenwell to pull into his quiet suburban driveway. We both knew we'd wait all night if we had to.

"Look," I finally said, "I don't really care what you do with Greenwell. But when he gets here, I want to know whether he can lead me to Simon. Fair enough?"

"Okay. But I handle Greenwell. Alone. I'll find out if he has Simon. You wait outside."

I agreed.

About ten minutes later we heard the smooth hum of an engine before it turned the curve and pulled up to the driveway. It was just before 1 A.M. It was raining lightly, but Greenwell strode unhurried from the Corvette. He looked drunk. I could see a small green frog hop onto the blacktop in front of Greenwell. The motion stopped him. He bent over a bit to see it, then straightened and stepped over it. When he was inside, Sara and I took a walk around his house, checking the yard, the windows, the land. The nearest neighbor was a quarter block down and across the road, too far to hear whatever might happen. She went to the front door. I stayed by an opened side window to watch and listen.

8

THERE WAS A BLACK KNOCKER shaped like an eagle's wings on Green-well's front door. Sara hit it hard. Greenwell was closing his windows because of the rain when he heard the knock. He had a beer in his hand as he opened the door, and he smiled broadly when he saw Sara. She smiled back. She started to tell a tale about her car breaking down, but he held up his hand to stop her.

"I don't care why you're here," he said. "You look great. That's all that matters. A gift, to me. From God." He paused. She said nothing. He trailed the hand with the beer across his chest, pushing open his shirt as he did, matting the hair on his chest with the wet roll of the can. He rested the gold bottom of the can on the similarly colored belt buckle, pushing his fingers below the belt.

He started to take off his shirt. "Let me show you," he said. She half turned away from him. "Yeah, babe," he said. "Show me your ass. But don't go anywhere. Nearest house can't even hear us."

As he grabbed her, she pushed down on her left foot, turned into him and drove her right foot up. Even drunk, his reactions were good. She drove the kick through his block and caught him just above the groin. The pain bent him quickly and stiffly. Before he could regain his wits, she jammed her knee fast and hard to his head three times. He fell to the floor, out cold. She bent down and ripped his shirt the rest of the way off and tied his hands tight behind him. She did it all with swiftness and ease.

It was stunning. She kicked the shit out of this guy as well as I've

55

ever seen it done. And he was big. She'd taken him down like a dummy on a football-practice field.

I went in through the opened front door.

"I thought we had a deal," I told her. "You do what you want, but first we find out about Simon. It looks to me like you're planning to kill this guy."

She didn't say anything. Instead, she went off to the kitchen, looked through it in a hurry, and came back with tape and cord. She bent down and tied his hands tighter with the cord, and also tied the cord around his arms, chest, and back. She stood up and looked at me.

"I haven't forgotten Simon," she said. "Be patient."

In a few minutes, Greenwell regained consciousness, but he was too dazed to stand.

"Simon," she said. He looked up through groggy eyes and said nothing. He didn't even see me. She slapped his face with the back and front of her hand four times, very hard. Each slap had the sound of a dead branch snapping in the woods.

"Tell me where you have Simon. What did you do to him?"

"You're crazy," he said. His voice was dull. "I don't have Simon. I'm looking for him. We have business to do. You're crazy, lady. Nuts. You'll die for this." He probably meant to sound tough, but his voice came out sleepy and not very threatening.

Sara sealed his mouth securely, wrapping the tape around his head several times. Then she lifted him; I tried to help, but she got him all the way up on her own in a fireman's carry. She threw a jacket over his back to cover the tape and cord and walked him out of the house and to the Corvette. I followed. She opened the passenger door and let him fall into the leather bucket, then strapped him in with the shoulder belt, which, in his condition, was as good as an iron chain.

"Keys," she said to him, softly.

The noise that came from beneath the tape was muffled, but it sounded like laughter. Sara reached for the holster under her shirt, on her right side just above the waist of her jeans. She took out a .32 and showed it to him. I was surprised to see she was carrying the gun. I wondered how many more she had stashed on her body or in her car.

Greenwell didn't make a move, and she used the butt of the gun to strike him across the forehead. A line of blood welled. Greenwell either nodded to his left or just dropped his head that way. Sara reached into his left pants pocket, and the key was there. She got in the driver's seat and backed the Corvette out of the driveway. I got in my car and followed.

After half an hour, she pulled off into what looked like a large private estate. A small tile sign on a stone wall said "Carlton Stables."

Low, dim lights at ground level were surrounded by flowering shrubs and bushes. Stone walls set off a series of about a dozen quaint small guest houses, each one a slightly different pastel shade. Bermuda style. Quiet elegance. Acres of meticulously gardened landscape, the kind that needed tending every day by a crowd. It was just past 1:30 in the morning and the place looked deserted. Sara drove about a half mile beyond the guest houses, past a stand of pines, and stopped near a small house that was ringed three-quarters around by a pen with a high outer wire-mesh fence.

The house looked out of place because it wasn't elegant at all. There was no sign of activity inside. Even before Sara stopped the car, two dogs came charging out of the house into the yard, as if bursting through paper walls, barking, wailing, slamming their claws up on the wire-mesh fence. German shepherds. I was fifteen yards away and on the other side of the fence, but I drew back anyway. If they could eat metal, they'd already have been through the fence and half the engine of the Corvette.

Sara just sat in the car, with the dogs clamoring on the other side of the fence. Finally I got out and walked over to her.

"How about a clue?" I had to yell over the dogs' barking. She didn't answer. Instead, she leaned across the seat and put her mouth next to Greenwell's ear.

"You know what they can do," she said loudly and slowly. She ripped the tape off his mouth.

"I'll ask you for the last time. Where is Simon?"

He was afraid of the dogs and breathing hard. He was also shaking.

"I told you the truth," he finally said. "I don't know where the man is. You're making a big mistake. Your only chance is if you let me out of here right now."

She gagged him again.

"This is Reidus's place," she told me. "And these are his dogs. I've seen him with them. Purebred. Very loyal. Once they get going they're hard to stop."

I knew she was right. A cop friend had once told me that police preferred Dobermans because shepherds sometimes got crazy and you couldn't call them back.

"I'll leave Greenwell here," she went on. "He'll be really shook by the time Reidus finds him. He won't suffer any serious harm, but he'll do well as a messenger. Let Reidus know someone can get to his place, to him. That's what I want."

I still wanted to ask Greenwell my own questions, but I realized I could do better by returning to his house and searching it while he wasn't there.

She took out the extra cord she'd brought from the house and tied him tightly to the back of the seat.

"I'm leaving you here," she told him. "Be good and the dogs won't bother you."

She got out of the Corvette and walked with me to my car. She got in on the passenger side.

"Drive away," she said, "but not fast. When we're around a few curves, we won't be visible from the house." I drove slowly.

"Pull off here," she said, after a minute.

We got out and walked a circular route back toward the house, taking ten minutes to get there.

"The dogs aren't barking anymore," she said. "I guess because we left."

We stopped behind a low stone wall about thirty, forty yards from the house. From our view we could see nothing moving. No dogs, no Greenwell, no Reidus.

"I want to wait here until Reidus arrives," Sara said. "It may be a long time. You don't have to hang around if you don't want."

"I'll stay for a while," I said. "If nothing happens, I'll go back to Greenwell's house to check it out. I can pick you up later."

Almost a half hour passed and we saw and heard nothing.

"Something's wrong," I said. "There's no movement in the car. I don't see how Greenwell could have gotten out. Still, we should have seen some movement. And what happened to the dogs?"

"Let's go and check," Sara said.

We came up slowly from behind the wall and walked toward the car. As we approached, we could see that the side of the Corvette was wet. Blood was dripping to the ground from the bottom of the passenger door. And the fences were opened. Someone had unlatched the gate, but the dogs were nowhere to be seen. Sara took out her .32.

I walked to the car, Sara staying a few feet behind me with the gun. I looked in. The top of the passenger seat was soaked in blood. Greenwell was no longer sitting where she'd left him. Sara came up next to me so she could see inside the Corvette.

The two great animals sat in the well behind the seats. They were breathing slowly. The two sets of canine eyes stared at Sara's gun. Their paws and necks and faces were covered with blood. Greenwell's body was torn open. His head was by the stick shift, split and crushed by the dogs' jaws. His eyes stared up. The taped mouth had stifled the screams. The twine around him had been bitten to shreds, as was the seat belt. He must have died within minutes of our driving away. Whatever sequence of noises and motions he'd tried to make, they were over long before we returned.

Still pointing the gun at the dogs, Sara stepped back and glanced at the small house behind the fences. I knew what she had to be thinking. I had already come to the same conclusion. Reidus had been inside the house the whole time. He'd seen everything she'd done. He'd raised the gates and let the dogs have the tall man. Their gift for the night. Then he'd left the animals in the car, stilled by whatever command it was that held them motionless in our presence. And now he was gone again. Before we even knew he'd been there. It was his territory and his timing. If he wanted Sara, he'd have had her already. I think she realized that at the same moment I did; she shuddered as she lowered the gun. She'd left a message. She'd gotten one.

9

WE DIDN'T SPEAK to each other as we walked back to my car, and we held the silence for five more minutes driving the winding roadway out onto County 842. I'd seen violent death up close maybe a dozen times in my life, and the thing I remembered about it most was how long it took to get it out of my mind. I'd find that two, three weeks after the death I'd go to bed and instead of falling asleep, I'd focus on this clear image of the body. The image would come and go all night, until the sun rose, and then the body would fade, and I'd finally fall asleep.

I really didn't want to talk to a woman who was an expert at fighting, who was always ready for conflict. I could have used someone softer than that now. But there was the matter of going to the police. So I turned to her.

"We might as well drive to the state trooper barracks," I said. "I'm not sure, but I'd guess it's in Wakefield."

"No," she said quietly. "It's in Avondale." Her voice was different, and I looked over at her. She was trembling.

"This particular one get to you?" I asked. "I had the impression you deal with this kind of thing a lot."

She took a breath and let it out. "If you think I don't have feelings about death, you're wrong," she said. "Feelings are what this thing is all about. But we can't go to the police. I'll tell you why."

We were driving by a large old farm that was mostly pastureland and a few ponds. I pulled off the road and parked on the grass by a long wooden fence. There were a couple of signs on either side of an open gate that said "Free Nolly Farm." The fence rambled both ways as far as I could see. At the base of the near pasture, just beyond a pond, there was a small stone house, two stories, and behind that, several acres of cornfield.

I got out of the car and she followed. We walked alongside the fence. The dark wood was old but well tended. It was a good ten minutes before she spoke.

"My father died six months ago," she finally said. "He killed himself. But the truth is, he'd been dead for the past four years. That's how I see it, anyway. Four years ago, he and Carlton had the falling out. As far as I'm concerned, Carlton killed him. Carlton and Reidus."

A small animal stirred up some leaves nearby, and she tensed till it settled. She was wired.

"When my father died, I made a vow to myself that I'd get revenge. I've spent the past months getting ready, training."

She had stopped walking and was leaning on the fence, holding the wood in both hands, not looking at me.

"I had to convince myself that I could do it, that I had it in me to kill them."

"You must have done some things like this before," I said. "My first impression was that you were a cop."

"No," she said. "Not a cop. I was a gymnast in high school and college. I graduated five years ago and since then I've stayed in shape. I've spent a lot of time mountain climbing and skiing in the Rockies. I taught climbing in Colorado for a year."

"You mean you left your father after Carlton got rid of him?"

"It was pretty depressing at home," she said. "My father kept telling me I had to get on with my own life and not worry about him. My mother died when I was a kid and I don't have any brothers or sisters. So I left, but I still worried about him a lot. I called and visited regularly. But it never seemed to make any difference."

She let go of the wooden fence and we walked some more.

"I got the call from my uncle the night they found my father," she said. " 'Your father's out of his misery,' he told me. As if that would make me feel better."

"My uncle *is* a cop. I told him I was going after Carlton and asked him to help. He gave me bullshit about how it wasn't Carlton's fault, that my father drank himself to death, and there wasn't any point in trying to blame someone else. Maybe my uncle was worn down himself. So I gave up on him and went back to Colorado, where they have some of the best sports-training facilities in the world. I have a friend there— a black belt in martial arts—who trains women in self-defense, runs the rape-prevention program and all that. We're close. She agreed to have someone cover everything else for her and just train me. And for five months, that's all we did. There isn't anything in the world you can't learn in five months if that's all you do, and if you want it badly enough. Cops go to police academies, the FBI does it the same way, and they learn to shoot in even less time. I was already in shape. I needed to know the things cops know.

"I practiced shooting every day. Guns and rifles. I also practiced following people, and driving fast, and every damn thing I thought I'd need in taking Carlton and Reidus down. Getting out of the window at Simon's office tonight was something any rock climber could do. But having a rope ready to escape that way—that's the sort of thing you prepare for in combat training. That's the type of thing I've been thinking about when I haven't been thinking about Carlton."

A breeze came up from a grove of maples and oaks. The grass was still wet from rain, but the sky was clear.

"Thinking what, exactly, about Carlton?" I asked.

"My father and Carlton were partners in starting up what's now called Carlton Associates. Carlton probably needed a legitimate businessman to get the company off the ground. My father was an important reason the company got so successful. He was good at everything he did. I know he was a good father. He always took good care of me.

"When the company was established and doing well, Carlton decided to take my father out of the picture. My father wouldn't leave. That's where Reidus came in. They did just about everything short of killing my father on the spot. It might have been better for all of us if they had."

"What do you mean?" I asked.

"A woman schoolteacher in Wakefield was raped and my father was accused. Lots of people believed he did it, and they hated him for it. He was never arrested because the woman was afraid to talk to the D.A. My father didn't rape her. He was set up. He thought eventually he'd clear his name. Never happened. Everyone just treated him like shit, like he really was a rapist."

Her face got tight again, her eyes burning with intensity. "That man was a straight arrow. Everyone knew that before the rape thing. But afterward, Carlton used the rape charge to get rid of my father. He forced him out. Gave him a little bit of money to live on, but nowhere near his share of the company. My father had no choice. I was twenty-two then. I didn't know what was going on. The only thing I knew was that my father was innocent."

Her tone was flat now, as if without feeling. But there was strength in her way of describing a painful story directly, and I knew then that she'd been telling the truth, had told Simon a version of the truth from the start, and that these were things that were absolutely new for her to say out loud. She seemed very alone as she told her story.

"The one thing my father still cared about, other than me, was his collection of ebony horses. He'd used all his spare time for years, before this thing happened, to go halfway across the world to Ceylon—Sri Lanka now. He'd visit small mountain villages and buy the little statues. The collection made him feel good. I don't really know why. Maybe just because it was his, and no one else had it. Carlton knew that. As if taking his job and his reputation weren't enough, he didn't want to leave him any damn thing. So he took the horses, too. He stole them from our house—and my father did nothing to stop him. I never really understood how Carlton could do that. Not until I saw how Reidus operates. Now I understand."

"What do you mean?" I asked. "What does Reidus do?"

She stopped, swallowed hard, glanced at me briefly before looking away again.

"I was following Reidus one day in Chestnut Hill," she said. "It's very nice there, cobblestone streets, families walking around in the afternoon. He was on Germantown Avenue pretending to be window shopping. I was across the street. There was a young mother with a baby in a stroller. Reidus began talking to the mother, smiling, laughing, having a good time. Instinctively, I sensed that whatever his plan was, it was too much, had to be too much, with a baby involved. So I crossed the street, heading for them. He turned his head, just a little, like a bird, and he saw me. He gave me a wink. Actually winked at me! Then, the next second, he stepped hard on the left rear wheel of the carriage— real fast, so the mother didn't even notice what he'd done. The carriage tipped over and the baby came flying out. The mother screamed, and everyone on the block suddenly stopped. But before the child hit the ground, *Reidus caught the baby*. Smooth as silk. Everyone came over and patted him on the back and said he was a hero. He looked at me, and winked again, then disappeared into the crowd."

"What happened to your father after they stole the horses?" I asked.

"Things got worse. He was too scared to go to the police. Eventually, my father gave up. He drank. He fell apart. All I could do was watch as it happened. Then, six months ago, he shot himself. When I found out, I decided I had to learn what really happened between my father and Carlton four years ago. I knew that's what really killed him. So I went to the schoolteacher who was raped. I talked to her. Believe it or not, she said she was glad I had come."

Sara leaned toward me. "My father didn't rape her!" she shouted. "The man who raped her did it in her house in the dark and she never saw his face. But he made sure she saw a photo ID—my father's—then he took it with him. No evidence, just my father's name and face left in her mind.

"A few weeks after she went to the police, the guy who raped her came back. He barged into her house. He beat her, hurt her badly but left no marks—she described to me how careful he was when he hurt her. The guy sat her down, took a chair and sat right opposite her— their knees touched, she told me, and he held her hands in his lap. He looked right into her face and told her his name." Sara picked up a leaf off the ground and crushed it in her hand. "Reidus."

I put a hand on her shoulder. I thought she might pull away or brush the hand off. She did neither.

She told me earlier that she'd become an expert at watching. It wasn't just watching Reidus and his men, I realized. It must have been agony watching her father lose everything, like a surgery on his life taking him apart piece by piece, so that what was left was intact but empty. He faded before he died. There are lots of ways to lose someone you care about in the world. The worst is to watch them hurt for a long time and not be able to do anything about it.

"For so long now," she said, "every time someone's touched me it's been the opening move in a fight. And for the last month the only men I've been near were hurting people."

She took my hand off her shoulder and put both her hands around mine and squeezed, as if we'd reached some agreement. She looked down at the wet grass, let go of my hands, and took a few steps away. She continued her story.

"Reidus told her to withdraw her complaint about my father because—after all—it wasn't my father. She was terrified. He told her if she didn't do as he said, he'd come back and hurt her the exact same way—rape her again. Can you imagine?

"She's lived with this for four years. She never saw Reidus again. She did just what he said. She withdrew the complaint, said she couldn't bring herself to testify. That's how scared she was.

"But the crazy way these things work, her dropping the charges was what really convinced everyone my father had done it. People figured my father had scared her somehow. What a plan! And that plan was the key to my realizing it couldn't have been Reidus alone who did this to my father. It had to be Carlton. Carlton was smart enough to figure out that if the case went to trial my father could probably prove his innocence and maybe even get to the truth of it. But with no trial, with no charge at all—everyone assumed my father was guilty."

I could see her regaining her balance as she talked. Some of her hard attitude was returning.

"I've tracked Reidus," she said. "Followed him like an animal in a hunt. He knows I'm following him now. I don't hide it anymore. I know he's crazy, but it's like he wants me to fight with him or something." Suddenly she smiled, a big satisfied smile with no warmth in it. "I'm going to take Reidus up close, tell him who I am. Then I'm going to kill him. With him gone, Carlton will be easy."

"Don't you think murder is going a little too far?" I asked. "If Reidus is responsible for that many things, and you're a witness, why not go to the police and have him arrested?"

"No, not the police. They wouldn't stop him. You don't know Reidus. I mean, look at Greenwell, tonight. How can anyone prove Reidus did it? If anything, I'm the one who's in trouble. I took the man to the dogs. Reidus can say he knew nothing about it, wasn't even home."

65

She was headed for a cliff and didn't care. I knew something about vengeance, or what they called payback on the street. I'd never been anywhere there wasn't some form of it driving people up glory roads or off cliffs. But so far, my own family hadn't been touched. Maybe it wasn't real until it was that close. They got her father. Her plan was to get them back. But when it was done, I bet she'd still feel empty. She needed help, in more ways than one. I could provide it.

I dropped her off at her car and she left. I had to go into Greenwell's house. Simon was still missing.

10

THE LIVING ROOM of Greenwell's house smelled of stale beer. An open aluminum can was on the floor beside the couch, most of it spilled out on the carpet. I looked through the other rooms. Nothing out of place, nothing that might lead to Simon.

The large bedroom closet was stocked with finely tailored suits and shirts, as well as a collection of knives, guns, and ammunition. They were all neatly arranged, undisturbed. I needed more information on Greenwell, needed to learn about his dealings with Simon. In the den, I looked through desk drawers. I found stationery with the letterheads of Carlton Associates and Carlton Stables. Blank white sheets. There were some letters and notes and bills, but nothing that seemed tied to Simon's case in any way. In the middle right-hand drawer I saw a file filled thick with photographs, the glossy edges of prints extending from the sides of the folder.

I spilled the sheets of photographs out onto the floor. It was a dossier on a man and a woman, in some cases just the woman. What the black-and-white grain of the photos, as well as a few typed sheets, had captured was a portrait of the things people sometimes did when they were alone, and free not just of clothing but also of fears and rules. You could see clearly in the pictures that the man was wearing a wedding ring, the woman was not. As in a children's game of one step, two step, the more their targets lost themselves in the pleasures of the moment, the closer the photographers crept, and the more detailed the photos, a running description of sin. But the couple seemed to have run out of deviations

67

fairly quickly. There wasn't anything here blackmailers could use if these people stood up to them.

Modern corporate security. They send out spies to collect all the dirt they can on anyone who might be or become an enemy. Then they have leverage, when and if they need it. The first time I'd seen this sort of thing was when I was a reporter, writing about police corruption. The police had followed me and I didn't even know it at the time. They had been following me for weeks, trying to get anything they could. They wanted dirt—drugs, prostitutes, the usual.

I had found out by accident. A couple of years after it was over, when I wasn't a reporter anymore, I was talking with a cop who'd quit and opened a bar. Turned out he was once a spy himself, and he knew the guy who'd been following me. Never led anywhere. They didn't find anything bad enough on me. I was too dull. They should have waited a few years.

I could see that Greenwell and Simon had some things in common. Like Greenwell, Simon enjoyed solving problems with a gun or a fight. So when he found a job that was right, right for the gun, right in that it was something you had to be tough for, he liked that. Clarifying, he called it. He told me once that if someone threatened him, taking care of it always felt good. Get back to basics. He enjoyed the way he had directed his life—"mud with momentum," he called it—and made it provide him with some pleasure.

I got out of Greenwell's place, not sure where to go. I decided on Simon's apartment. The people in Greenwell's portfolio meant nothing to me, but I decided to take the photos anyway. Simon might know them, or Sara might.

I let myself into Simon's apartment with the spare key I knew he kept under his neighbor's doormat.

The front door opened into a large living room that was messier than his office. The couch was dark green and old, with four wooden legs carved into animal shapes. The rest of the furniture was new and metal, a display table with a glass plate balanced on four thin, shiny tubes; a long, high bookshelf with a brass frame and clear plastic panels; a sleek silver-plated console holding stereo, television, and VCR. There were some small framed pictures over the couch: a faded watercolor of pastel houses, thatched roofs, deep red and green foliage, masts of sailboats in the distance, high white clouds. Everything looked as if it hadn't been dusted for a year.

I walked through the room, glanced into the empty kitchen, then made the turn through the short corridor to the bedroom. The bed was unmade and there was a small pile of laundry on the floor next to the dresser. The closet doors were open. I looked in, saw nothing unusual, then checked the bathroom. Nothing. There was one other room, more of a small storage space than a room, and it contained cardboard boxes, a worn sleep sofa, and a few folded beach chairs.

I went back to the kitchen and took from my pocket the Xeroxed list of police phone numbers. Might as well go through the routine again. I checked the time: 3:15. I called the Philadelphia police. Nothing to report. I called West Chester police. Again, nothing. Tried the Wakefield police. Nothing. I went to the living room, dropped to the couch and dozed off. I woke up in about an hour, took out the list and went to the phone. Philly police: nothing. West Chester: nothing. Wakefield: no answer. I tried the state police barracks in Avondale.

"I'm calling from the *Inquirer,* anything happening?"

"Yeah, we might have something for you." The voice on the other end was enthusiastic. I'd heard that tone before, the odd swell of excitement, the ordinary dullness of night awakened by violence, and now a chance to tell the world. An explosion, a train crash, a triple murder. "Big mess at Carlton Stables," the cop said. "Attack dogs somehow got loose. Two people killed. Wakefield police are up there now. We sent assist. Call back in about a half hour, I should have more by then."

Two people killed?

11

CARLTON STABLES was as long a drive from Philadelphia as Greenwell's house, just over an hour. By the time I got there, the sky was still dark, but there was a tint of the sun rising. As I drove the winding entrance road, I could see the flashing red and blue car-top lights in the distance. There were four police cars, two vans, and a truck called a Mobile Crime Unit parked around the red Corvette. The dirt around the car was stained with blood and bloodied pieces of torn clothing that weren't there when I'd left a few hours ago. The man in charge was Captain Brock from Wakefield.

I wasn't the only civilian around. There weren't any reporters yet, but several curious neighbors were standing behind a barricade the police had already put up, the thick yellow tape blocking off the patch of land. The bystanders were talking about dead bodies, but they didn't know any more than that. No names, no details. They didn't even know if they were male, female, or both. I forced myself to wait until the captain finished talking with the assorted people roaming the scene on the police side of the line, then I called out to him. Brock walked over with one of his men.

"I'm looking for a Simon Griffey," I said. "He's a private investigator. About five eight, one-sixty, stocky, short dark hair. Forty-six years old. He's a good friend."

They immediately took me off to the side, and we stood by the hood of one of their cars.

"I'm truly sorry to give you bad news," Brock said. "Your friend's dead. Killed by dogs. It's a gruesome sight. I don't want you even looking. He carried ID. We'll confirm his dentals this morning. Horrible thing. How did you know to come here?"

"Simon was working on a case involving Carlton Associates," I said. "We were supposed to meet earlier tonight. When he didn't show, I started calling the police. About an hour ago they told me you had two bodies here at the stables."

Brock had a pleasant face. He looked me over, but the feeling he put out was sympathy, not suspicion. That's a real talent; most cops can't do it.

"Yeah," he said, "the other one's named Greenwell. You know him?"

"No," I lied. It had to be that way. Sara was right. If I told the police what I knew, I'd implicate her—and myself. And what I knew wouldn't help them in finding the killer, since I hadn't seen what happened.

I didn't like it, lying to the police, but I'd come to accept that, being a blackmailer. If I always told the cops what I knew, I'd be out of work. It's not that I wanted to make it harder for police, but there are things I can do as a blackmailer that they can never do. They can make an arrest, that's it. I can make a deal, keeping a guy like Carlton out of jail to ensure that his business no longer breaks the law. Cops can't do that. Once they make an arrest, there's nothing to stop someone else from coming along and continuing the dirty business the first guy started. And that's what usually happens.

"Do you know what happened?" I asked.

"They were both drunk," Brock said. "The way it looks now—and this is sketchy, from body positions, that kind of thing—we figure Greenwell killed Simon, then planned to leave him to the dogs, to use that as a cover. But the dogs got him before he could get away."

Sounded like a good story. I had to find a way to steer them in a different direction, without telling them what I knew.

"There could be more to it than that," I said. "Simon's client was an enemy of Carlton Associates. It's possible someone from the company would have had a reason to go after him."

"Who was the client?" Brock asked.

"I don't know. He didn't tell me. I might have found out if we'd gotten together last night. I think he wanted to talk to me about the case. We've done that before. I help him out sometimes."

71

I guess I've gotten pretty good at lying while also telling the truth. It's not something I'm proud of.

"We've had a rough string around here the past few months, and we're a bit stretched," Brock said. "What happened to your friend is— what can I say? I'm very sorry." It was plain he was trying to mix two impulses: one to console me, the other to remind me whose opinions counted the most at the scene of a crime. He talked to me in the particular cadence of police to civilian, or maybe to reporter, someone who could understand his world if he wanted to, but might not try.

"A few of our men knew Greenwell," Brock said. "He drank a lot. And he fought over women a lot. A drunk man doesn't always stop to clean up his mess or look behind. Maybe there was some business involving Carlton's company, and maybe Greenwell was part of it. But it ended up something other than business. Greenwell assaulted your friend, then he meant him to tangle with the dogs, but got them loose too soon and died from it. Nobody sober would have tried to open the gates, not with animals like that. That's what we've got."

He was right, that's what they had, but it wasn't the truth. As we were about to part, one man who'd been talking to some other cops walked over.

"This is Will Reidus," Brock told me, "an executive with Carlton Associates."

He wasn't what I'd expected. From Sara's descriptions of his actions, I hadn't expected this relaxed, well-dressed man with a certain innocence about him. He didn't look like a killer. But then, he didn't look very shaken up by the double murder, either.

Brock introduced us. "Gray was concerned about Simon Griffey. Came down here from the city when he heard someone was killed at the stables."

Reidus smiled and shook my hand, and I thought he was about to say something, but he didn't. There was an odd calmness about the man, unsettling under the circumstances.

"Guess you're on your way back to the city now, huh?" he asked me. The tone was as if the man were a ticket clerk at an airline, checking his schedule. There was no evidence to indicate the recent and brutal death of someone you knew and perhaps valued, and therefore all of your next journeys are going to be different in some important way. The man showed none of that. I wondered what kind of answer Reidus wanted to hear, and when I had decided what might please him—that I was leaving now—I said instead, "I'll probably stay around here for a while, maybe check into a hotel."

Brock immediately said, "That's fine. We can help you with that, if you want."

Reidus nodded but didn't say anything. I thanked the men and asked if I could look around. They let me walk beyond the police lines to the Corvette, where workers were still cleaning up. Greenwell had been removed from the car and put in a body bag, which was in one of the vans. Simon had been found a few feet away from the car, according to the workers. They said he'd been mauled even more severely than Greenwell. His body had also been bagged and moved.

I studied the ground, walking slowly, and then realized someone was standing next to me. It was Reidus.

"So you stayed up all night, calling police again and again, because you were worried about your friend? Must be a close friend."

"Actually," I said, "we were supposed to meet for dinner. I don't like being stood up."

"But you thought he was in some kind of trouble down here?"

"Well, he was working on a case around here."

"So you came down," Reidus said. "That's going above and beyond, I'd say." Now he appeared concerned. "Look, I'm sorry about what happened. If there's anything I can do, give me a call."

"That's nice of you," I said. "Tell me something. Are attack dogs always kept here?"

Reidus sighed. "It's the times we live in." He motioned with a sweep of his arm to the land on both sides. "We don't want to put up fences, keep people from seeing the grounds, close things up the way it is in the cities. But you have to keep the property safe. Lots of different kinds drive by, get curious when they see a nice estate. Dogs help keep the fences down, keep things open."

"Are you a trainer?"

"Not really. I have some knowledge of guard dogs only because I'm in charge of security operations for Carlton Associates."

As we walked, Reidus occasionally bent down to pick up a stick or a stone from the ground, then tossed it away. As we reached a small

73

slope, he casually picked up a small dark object. At first I thought it was a piece of metal, and I strained to see it. Then I realized it was actually a piece of clothing soaked and now stiffening with drying blood. Reidus tossed it from hand to hand.

"That thing you're holding," I said, not masking my disgust. "It must be a piece of clothing from one of the dead men. Must be the dogs somehow carried it all the way over here."

"Yes," Reidus said. "They run in circles for a while after a kill."

I was looking at the cloth and picturing the dogs roaming in a circle around the red car, each carrying a piece of their target's clothing, like a piece of death they had captured for display.

"I'd better take this over to the chief," Reidus said. "Too bad about what happened."

Reidus was walking slightly uphill and into the glare of the police lights. The bloodstained cloth that was a part of what remained of a man trailed from his hand. He was holding it so that the end of it plowed through the taller bushes. As it passed each strand of dark growth, it brushed them a bit with its weight, pressing down the tips of the leaves so that a line of blood was drawn across the foliage. This man was numb. Sometimes people got that way when they'd seen a lot of killing. Or done a lot of it.

Someone had primed an animal to be a weapon and unleashed it last night. I thought about exactly what was needed to get an animal to obey a command to kill, not in a single decisive act of conquest, the ripping out of a throat, but to rend and tear in a frenzied dissolution of flesh. People judged deaths according to the mess they made. Being ripped up was somewhere in the deep hole of the imagination, as final moments went. Most people had the one single nightmare they wanted most to avoid, and felt they could tolerate most else. I wondered whether Simon's personal list of fates to avoid had included being torn to shreds by dogs.

I got back in my car, and as I drove off, it hit me hard and at once. I was angry. Simon had been murdered. I wanted information about that, wanted to start knowing. I had questions for Sara—about the object Simon went to steal, about why she wanted the newspapers to write stories on Carlton, about Carlton and Reidus and the kind of people who talked casually in the face of death and didn't mind blood.

I was compiling a long list of questions. I felt myself getting to that place where, when I worked, the questions started lining themselves up in the most efficient way, and the thought process started categorizing and focusing on information or lack of it. It was an unexplainable process, and an unplanned one, the stages of gathering and sorting moving inexorably into place. It was the thing I knew best how to do, guided by reason and not emotion.

I felt clearheaded for the first time in the long night. It had been Sara's battle until now, a blood feud for her, and one that couldn't end peacefully. Up ahead was a run of violence bigger than anything I'd handled in years. But it wasn't someone else's pain anymore. It was mine, too.

12

REIDUS DROVE DOWN to Hatley in his Jaguar. He took a long route, circling through Carlton Stables first, cutting off Route 30 three times and looping through the business districts in Downington and Wakefield. He'd been followed often lately, and he hoped he was being followed now—by the red-haired woman. He drove slowly. He knew his pursuer was good but he didn't want to take the chance of losing her, if she was there. It was time they met.

He felt fine as he drove through the semi-deserted streets of Hatley. Two years ago this town had been strong, with a sense of community. Now it was falling apart. That gave him a measure of consolation for the bad experience he'd once had here.

He drove slowly down Meadows Street, pulling up to the curb and parking across from the house where Laura Thompson used to live. The house was vacant and the front door was securely shut. Like nothing had happened. Just his little secret. And hers.

Reidus had seen Laura Thompson for the first time two years ago, the day before Memorial Day, and not in Hatley. He'd been cruising the small convenience mall in Avondale, not more than thirty minutes from the stables. There was a store, Comics Crack, whose front window was filled with posters of comic-book superheros. There was a huge mural on one outside wall, with various heros either poised aggressively to defend against some unseen major threat, or standing with their mouths open and eyes wide, surprised.

Reidus had stopped to look at the mural, with one eye on the customers entering the store, most of whom were teenage boys. The first adult he

76

saw caught his interest. It was a woman in her late twenties, tall, brunette, attractive. She looked happy, bright, as if she'd thought about it and knew a good weekend was ahead. He had followed her in. She announced her business openly as some people do, talking casually with the salespeople. Her husband and little boy were in New York and wouldn't be back until the picnic tomorrow afternoon. She was buying comics as a special present for the boy, who loved the "X-Men." She said she and her brother had read "Archie" and "Superman" when they were kids, but stopped when they were about ten years old. Her opinion was that comics today weren't simple enough. She didn't like the complicated plots; the events in the latest "X-Men" were too fantastic.

Reidus went out to his car which he'd parked in an empty row in the large lot, and pulled up outside the store, waiting for the woman to leave. He hadn't yet decided what to do. He was enticed by her implicit belief in the straightforwardness and plausibility of everyday life. No doubt she'd been lovingly sheltered, as many people were. There was no gap in her misplaced loyalty to simple realities. She was confident, comfortable, pragmatic, nice.

Reidus described reality this way: that tables are hard and solid, and roads do not dissolve away while cars are on them because there's always a large number of people in the world at any given moment who agree strongly on what reality is. Their belief makes the things real. This was one of the believers, Reidus thought. She helps keep things the way they are. Could her faith be shaken? And if it were, would things change?

He followed her home. It was already suppertime when they pulled onto the highway, and though she didn't go far, it was close to twilight when he drove past her driveway, watching the garage door close to lock her in. It was too close to nighttime. He didn't want that. Nighttime was when such things might happen, however unlikely, and he preferred a less predictable hour. It would have to be morning, in fact, first thing— 7 A.M. He drove back home to Carlton Stables, slept, and rose at 5:30. He didn't take the Jaguar, but the white van, the one that looked like a workman's truck.

He pulled the van up in front of her house. At first, all was quiet on the street. Slowly, some neighbors woke, a few front doors opened for papers, and there were the sounds of breakfast dishes lightly clanging in the kitchens. The woman who bought comic books as gifts was not

77

yet up. No lights were on inside. The only noise was the hum of the cylindrical central air unit on the side of the house. The windows were all closed. Windows are weak, Reidus thought. So much of a house is no more than thin panes of glass. Even locked shut they're little more protection than clothing. It's all a matter of image, one of those common agreements about reality, a general consensus in a community that windows can keep people out of your house. Yet a child can break a pane of glass with ease. So it's not a real wall, but a mutually accepted buffer zone. Don't look in, keep out.

Reidus didn't have to be an unexpected presence in this house. The woman had several opportunities to see him in the shopping center yesterday, when he'd been following her openly, and then slowed in front of her house. Trusting as she was, she'd never bothered to notice. Now there was surely nothing but the walls to keep him out. Unlikely she had an animal or a gun to get in his way. People like her had faith in their homes and in the basic goodness of others. For the most part that faith was justified. He decided to take the front door off.

He put on a dirty light blue work suit and took out a toolbox and a ladder. Down the street two blocks away he saw an old woman walking a dog. He hoped there was a good range of people of various professions and inclinations in the surrounding houses. He enjoyed knowing some variety of reaction was at least possible, though there was usually only one reaction: No one did anything to help.

He'd read a lot about the Kitty Genovese case—the prototypical one in New York City where a woman had been stabbed, her screams heard, and the crime witnessed by scores of neighbors from their apartment windows, and no one had called the police. A psychologist named Milgram had explained in one article he'd read that the city, with its strangers and crowds and anonymity, had accounted for why the neighbors had done nothing to help.

Milgram thought people would be different in rural areas. Reidus disagreed. With rare exceptions, he'd found that, given a chance, people stood idly by and did nothing. And it wasn't because they didn't care or didn't feel responsible. They knew exactly what was at stake in getting involved—and knew that on that one decision to act, their whole lives might change for the worse or at least become uncertain. People said they wanted excitement, but when it was available, he had found that most people turned away.

Reidus was at the front door, a tall rectangle set between the front two windows of the A-frame. He opened the stepladder, reached up with the largest of the straight-edge screwdrivers, and, using his hand heel as a hammer, pushed the metal tool under the top hinge to pop it slightly out. There was a series of bracing screws to undo. It took only minutes. The engineering was simple enough to do the work quietly, but Reidus deliberately made noise. The woman inside remained asleep.

He continued on to the other hinge and soon had both of them off. There was nothing holding the door except the fit of its swelled wood in the frame and the hardware of locks, possibly a chain on the inside. Once freed of the frame, the door could be swung out at its unlocked end. He stepped down from the ladder, spread his long arms out over the wood and began to pry the door slowly out of its fit. This made more noise.

It was 7:30. A few houses away he noticed a man looking out the window toward him. He noted the man's appearance and expression, especially the gaze, which was open, direct, and lingered on him and the van. The absense of wasted motion registered on Reidus; there was no gratuitous closing of the drapes. The man wasn't embarrassed to be looking, for instance. That meant he was capable of intervening. But he wouldn't, Reidus thought, because there were kids' bicycles left out on his front lawn. People with kids didn't get involved in other people's dangers.

Once, making a similar frontal assault, Reidus had delighted in the fact that the victim's next-door neighbor was a retired cop who hadn't interfered because he was too frightened. The old man came out and identified himself and made a mild threat against Reidus, telling him to leave. At that point Reidus smiled and walked up to the man. "So, you were a policeman?" Reidus asked. "Did they train you to deal with men like me? I hope so. Because if they didn't, I will." He wrapped a hand gently around the old man's wrist. He squeezed hard and twisted the man's wrist—just for a second—then let go. He saw the fear in the man's eyes. "Go back inside," Reidus told him, "and do whatever you want. Feel free to call the police. But if you do, you'll answer to me

79

on my time, and the police won't be there to help you." The old man went back in his house and did nothing, as Reidus went into his neighbor's house and assaulted a woman. Reidus later sent the ex-cop an anonymous note reminding him of it. His fantasy was one day to gather in an auditorium all those who had witnessed his various exploits, including the victims, and talk with them. He wanted to hear them comfort and torment each other with their laments and explanations.

He practically had the door off now. There were several strollers and dog walkers out, and activity was visible through the windows in several houses. Yet even in so small a town as this, thought Reidus, with both disappointment and satisfaction, no one had so much as approached him with a question. Just a workman doing a job for their neighbor, early though it might be.

He heard his target in the house; she was awake now. He greeted her with noise, letting one of the screwdrivers scrape wood scraps off the door edge. He heard her coming down the stairs.

He left the door momentarily in place. He didn't want her to see anything so unusual it would decide her action for her. She was at the door. "Who is it?" he heard her say.

"Repairman, about the door," he answered gruffly, too low for her to make out the words. She tried to open the door. "Wait," he said, "it'll be finished in a minute." He was still talking too low for her to understand but he knew the sounds of a sentence in familiar rhythms are soothing. He waited to see what she'd do. Show me something, he thought.

She tried the door but couldn't budge it from his grip. She didn't seem scared, not yet, at least. He wasn't expecting that. He liked it.

She came to the window on the left, to look out at him. He raised his head briefly and smiled at her, then turned aside. She was still for a moment, looking at him. What would she decide? Was he a threat? On a sunny weekend morning in the center of her town, with all her world right here? Could a man pull up to her house, take her door off, assault her, hurt her, and make her do unspeakable things? Is that the way the world works?

Reidus was delighted. He felt dizzy, powerful, short of breath with excitement. The muscles in his shoulders tensed, as if moving on their own, already in motion. He pictured himself striking the woman down, her shocked look as he picked her up in one swift motion. She knows

80

the danger, he thought, knows it but is denying it. She only has to admit it's real, here in broad daylight at her door. Someone isn't following the rules and is very dangerous. She can leave by the back door, go across yards from one neighbor's house to another, run away.

But she stood there. He looked up at her through the window, smiled again, and braced to wrench, with one exultant motion, the door of her house off its hinges. Suddenly he was aware of noises behind him. He relaxed the door down and turned around. A group of people stood together.

The man Reidus had seen earlier at the neighboring window was at the front of the group. Two other men were at the white van, looking it over. Several other neighbors were there with their dogs. A small group of women walked straight past Reidus and into the house. When they came back out, they were escorting the woman.

Reidus sized up the man in front of him. He was big and muscular, about Reidus's height. He was evidently some kind of group leader. He seemed calmer to Reidus than he should be, confronting a stranger, despite the crowd support. Reidus thought he might have to eliminate him before he could deal with the others, and began to think of ways to do it.

First he needed to split up the sympathetic crowd. He began to cry out, pleading, "Where are my kids?" His demand was aimed at the woman from the house. She stared at him and said nothing.

The group leader moved closer. "What's the problem, friend?" he asked gently.

"This woman," Reidus answered, making his voice break, not looking directly at her. "We have children, we were married ten years ago. She took the kids. I haven't seen them since the oldest was six. I've got a picture."

He'd done versions of this before. It had always worked. No one knew anyone else's life so long or so well these days to say what could not have been a part of that life. And no one was willing to arbitrate two peoples' conflicting and passionate claims. Reidus had long experience in planting seeds of doubt in people's minds.

"Don't go on," the big man said. "We don't know what you're doing here. I'm not sure what kind of problem you have, or whether we should call the police. You haven't done much yet except fool with a door. We

81

can fix that. You don't know this woman. You don't seem drunk, yet you talk this nonsense. You can drive. Go on now. Leave. Don't come back."

Reidus looked over the crowd. Normally, there'd be divisions all over, people disagreeing about what to do or who to believe. But this group was united; this man was acting for all of them. No one was complaining or uninvolved. No one had gotten scared and left. There was no one here for him to shake up, he realized. They had decided, all of them and at once, that Reidus was crazy in some way. They didn't want to understand it. They'd get rid of him and go on to enjoy their Memorial Day picnic. The actions he'd taken had no impact here. He looked at the woman he'd been threatening. She was used to the comfort of neighbors. He thought of fighting them all, but instead walked back to the van, trying to let it go, not wanting to. He was uncertain as he hadn't been in a long time. Yet he'd been challenged by these people. That was good, he needed new challenges. He got in the van, put it in gear, and drove away. He glanced back. They were talking to one another. No one was looking after him.

When he got to the edge of town, he suddenly stopped the van and got out. He stepped near a tree and threw up, uncontrollably. He'd been thwarted so easily; ignored, really.

It had never been like this before, not even close, Reidus thought, struggling to understand. As much as he strived for the unpredictable, when it came to violence he had rarely been surprised. He held onto that thought and searched for memories to help bring him back.

In Philadelphia, he recalled, he'd once read a newspaper article about a newly married couple who opened a little shop specializing in 1960s records and memorabilia. He went to the shop one evening, and after it closed he made the newly married wife dance for him—entirely to Rolling Stones albums, every one in the shop—until she fainted. Her new husband had watched for several hours and had done nothing. He wasn't physically bound, but he was clearly terrorized, in what looked to Reidus like a catatonic state. Finally Reidus roused the husband from his stupor and sexually assaulted him in front of the wife. *She* attacked Reidus, tired as she was, pounding him harmlessly with her weak fists. He decided not to kill them because he knew his assault had changed their lives forever.

PAYBACK

The private security guard who had taken an interest in Reidus had been a similar delight, some years ago. There, it was the unexpected intelligence of the man that was worth remembering. He had been able to see, soon after Reidus began torturing him, that he would die. Despite his pain, he had deliberately become quite playful. Reidus had enjoyed seeing an astonishing display of laughter and casual acceptance of his fate, until he broke down and sobbed in prayerful surrender. It was a creative bid for survival, but it didn't work. Reidus killed him because he knew this man might go to the police if he were left alive.

By recalling these experiences, Reidus began to feel better. If the town of Hatley had things to show him, things he should see, that was fine. The more bound they seemed to each other, the more protective of their land and themselves, the more it would demand from him to undo them, to see what part of them was real, and what was just a pose. An entire town, a specific people and place, had offered him a challenge. He only needed a plan.

It was dark now. Reidus got out of the Jag and walked slowly to the empty Thompson house. The door was locked. He poked out three front windows and climbed in. He stared out and waited. Finally, after fifteen minutes, a car pulled up and stopped behind his. It was a black Nissan Z. A woman got out, red hair tied back, dark slacks, a dark blue long-sleeved shirt. She peered into the Jag, then looked at the Thompson house.

Reidus put a foot on the sill and smiled at her. He felt good. He waved. She turned and headed to her car. That she turned her back on him took Reidus's breath away. She's into danger, he thought, exuberant with the realization.

She got in her car. Between them was only the modest breadth of the front lawn and the wide sidewalk.

She leaned across to open the passenger window. She wants to talk, Reidus thought. He saw her bend slightly to lean on the window with both arms, then noticed the slim tube edge and tiny black hole. He stayed centered in the window frame.

As the rifle barrel poked out a little more from the window, he called out, "Get a good bead, honey." He'd identified the weapon. It was a sharpshooter's .32. To stop him, she'd have to be very accurate. The bullets were light. She raised the weapon slightly cradled on her arms. She was smiling. It must mean a lot to her to have me under the gun, he thought. She's been following me for weeks, but lying in the grass. Would she go for the kill tonight? He decided not to wait to find out.

He pushed off the wall with one thrust. She could manage two or three shots, but she'd almost surely miss. He was surprised by her reaction. She realized right away that she'd lost the shot, so she dropped the rifle on the seat and started the car. So she didn't want him now, Reidus thought. But he wanted her.

He hit the ground six feet from the window and rolled in one motion to the sidewalk. He jumped up like a gymnast coming off the mat and was on the roof of the Z before she had it in gear, one of his arms already reaching in the driver's side window.

He slid from the roof, crouching outside the car, and grabbed her upper arm. He expected no resistance at that point but she brought her right fist around with great force and smashed the middle knuckles into the softer tissue of his wrist just below the bone. The pain was intense. Reidus yelled and immediately opened up the fingers holding her arm. With both hands now free, she caught his right wrist, pulling up on his arm, while aiming one hand under his chin to the soft front of his throat.

She hadn't shot him, but she was apparently willing to kill him by hand. He admired the quickness and strength of her moves, while he automatically countered them. He blocked her slash at his throat, turned his wrist in her other hand so she let go, then grabbed the front of her shirt in the same motion, pulling her upper body toward the window between his arms. He was leaning well into the car now and was choking her. In a moment he'd have her subdued, and he could think slowly about what to do with her.

She rammed her head at his chest, then whipped it up at his chin. His arms flew open and she was free of his grip. She dropped back into the bucket seat and used her elbow to bring up the electric window. Reidus retreated quickly. Another moment and she'd have locked his head in the window.

Reidus stood there, staggered, as the car disappeared. He pictured his decapitated body lying in the brush a hundred yards away, his pursuer driving off with his head in her car. She's good, he thought, so good. He was thrilled.

13

I TOLD THE SECURITY GUARD at the West Chester *Tribune* that I had a noon appointment to see Steve Foley, a police reporter. The guard gave me the official look first, noted no obvious dangers, then took her time. My posture is too relaxed for my size. I slump, don't take up much space, and people who have to deal with me usually conclude I'm the kind of big guy who isn't intimidating. The guard asked me to wait in the lobby until she could get Foley on the phone. I walked to the base of a tall and wide sheet of glass and looked in at the huge, stilled presses.

Among my friends, being a reporter was an absolute good. People I knew who did anything else—doctors, lawyers, even construction workers—envied what they saw as a reporter's freedom to "uncover wrong and do something about it." It was hard to explain, to convince them if I'd have tried, how useless the whole process was most of the time— the uncovering, and confirming, and checking with the lawyers, and satisfying the editors, and after ten other totally unrelated things had been done, finally printing the story. How often it turned out that nothing important happened as a result of the story, and nothing really changed. Oh, there were times, maybe once or twice a year, when a story made a real difference. And for those times alone, the job was worth doing. More often, though, there would be a flurry of controversy and noise, and soon after, business would return to normal. It was easier, and I used to find myself doing this all the time, to just accept the unspoken praises. "Gray the heroic." The cachet: Investigative Reporter.

At parties, I'd sometimes get cornered by acquaintances telling me their great wish—if they could just take off for a month or so, and "find out what was really going on" in whatever place it was they spent their days, but wished they didn't. Then—the great wish culminated—they'd put the story in the newspaper. That was the wonderful, magical thing. The sword of the righteous. The wizard's potion. Like a kid's dream power, the threat eight-year-olds always used: "I'll tell everybody everything."

I myself had believed the Myth of the Reporter, sort of, for several years at least. And the truth is, many reporters *are* white knights, putting everything they have into their work, and getting little in return. But what I had concluded—and this was the part that was so hard to explain to friends—was that reporters can't really accomplish much *because* they're honest. They even have a written code of ethics. Looks great on paper, but crooks don't give a damn about ethics. It's like trying to catch trout without bait. Even harder. Like hanging out a line with no hook at all. Crooks have dirty hands. Even the shiniest, best-manicured bastard in a boardroom on Wall Street has dirty hands, if he's a dishonest bastard. The only way to stop him is to crawl down to his level, into the mud and the scum, and look him right in the eye. He'll listen only if you threaten him with what he cares about—his money or his power, or the loss of same. You can't do that if you're a reporter, following a code of ethics. If you're serious about getting it done, you're going to get dirty. And that's the part of blackmailing I didn't like to talk about, and what made it so different from being a reporter.

Ten minutes later I was in the newsroom. At midday, it was crowded, busy, and the volume was on high. Desks faced in every direction, people trying to eke out privacy and territory, with no chance of finding either. The newsroom arrangement assumes reporting is a communal task and requires neither quiet nor calm. Phone lines, computer cables, and extension cords were tangled in masses under desks. The reporters' desks were too close together to distinguish one conversation from another. I could hear only fragments. "I'm trying to reach Mrs. Hamner . . ." "Well, what if the sewage plant isn't completed by then . . .?" "No, the *Tribune*, it's a newspaper in West Chester, Pennsylvania . . ." "How do you spell that . . .?" "Is the councilman ever in . . .?"

Foley was in his mid-fifties, tall, balding, overweight and sloppy. His corduroy jacket was wrinkled, and his shirt hung out the front of his pants, the cuffs of which were frayed. He looked like someone who'd stopped caring about his appearance years ago.

"I appreciate your giving me the time," I told him. "Is there a lot of talk about the double murder?"

"It's a good story," he said. "About five reporters are on it."

"Do you know anything more than the police version?"

"No, that's all I've heard. Most people believe the police account—that it was a drunk, crazy guy, not a plot by Carlton, if that's what you mean. In fact, some people are afraid Carlton may pull his advertising if things get too controversial. So we're kind of staying clear of the guy."

"I understand one of your reporters has done some stories about Carlton in the last few weeks. Is he in?"

"No. That's Chris Baines. He's out sick. He did some pieces about a real estate scam by Carlton, something like that. You can look up the clips. I helped him out on a few things, here and there. He needed to check a couple of police records and I'm the only one here with good access to that sort of thing."

I noticed the newsroom was filled with people mostly under forty. By that age reporters usually get out of the business, go into public relations or publishing or politics. Some become editors but don't like the job, restless not writing their own stories. Older reporters watch the younger ones grab all the big stories because good reporting often means running around looking at things and badgering people and staying out until all hours. The older ones get bitter. Foley was by far the oldest in the room.

"What's the Wakefield P.D. like?"

"The chief, Reynolds, has a great reputation. But he's semi-retired. The guy in charge is Stanley Brock, a captain. He's another story. He's been here about four years, up from Wilmington, where he left in a hurry. A few years ago there was a scandal over evidence room thefts in Wilmington, and Brock was in the middle of that. He got out, somehow."

"Would Brock take orders from Carlton if he wanted things covered up?"

"My guess? He'd cover for anyone, if the price was right."

"The police seem satisfied with their conclusions—that Greenwell

87

was drunk, fought with Simon over a woman, killed him, then got killed himself accidentally by the dogs. I get the feeling nothing would change their minds. Does that surprise you?"

"If Reynolds was still there, I'd say yes. He didn't get bought off by anybody. But Brock and his crew are pretty much out for themselves. I don't think you can count on them for anything serious. Know what I mean?"

I asked Foley if he knew which editors were involved with the Carlton story, and how much they knew.

"Well, you know how it works," Foley said. "The story was never assigned. Chris just got some leads and pursued them on his own, the way most investigative stories start. He told his editor what he was doing, and that was about the extent of it. The editor's too busy moving daily copy to think seriously about a long project. He certainly doesn't see himself as the kind of person who'd kill an investigative story. So he just hopes Chris comes back with a story that makes him look good, or at least doesn't get him in trouble."

"Sounds like you love the business," I said.

"You ought to know. You say you were a reporter once?"

I nodded.

"Why'd you get out of the business?"

I didn't answer.

"Well, I can't say I blame you, one way or the other. Most papers these days are like the *Tribune*, soft and safe. The Chicago papers, the *Inquirer, The Washington Post*, some small independents still expect reporters to hunt down tough stories. But they're exceptions."

A young woman walked by to ask Foley when he'd have a story on police contract negotiations. He told her, she left, and I said, "Is there any chance I could look through Chris's desk? His notes could help me out a lot."

"You know I can't let you do that. Why do you need them, anyway?"

"I think Chris might have known Simon. I think Simon was a source." Foley seemed mildly surprised, but it was obvious he really didn't care. "Forget I asked about the notes," I said. "Just point me to his desk. You can do that much, all right?"

Foley shook his head and laughed under his breath. He took me to Baines's desk. Then he left, saying he had to make a few phone calls on a story. He was the kind of guy you could buy off with the right expression or tone of voice.

I needed to see if Baines had any notes about Carlton. If Baines was in town, I could look him up later. If his notes were here, there was no assurance they'd remain here for long. They killed Simon; they could go after Baines, or his information.

I found a dozen notebooks in the bottom right-hand drawer of Baines's desk.

While I looked through them, I heard the quiet voices of the police radio constantly droning on Foley's desk. Sometimes there were sentences with long, long pauses, and the only sounds were the static of the airwaves and occasionally a kind of test noise, like a whistling, whining hum, and the radio got louder. A few times, Foley reached over and turned it up, because the pauses had disappeared and people were hurriedly talking, which meant something might be happening. Usually the voices were a woman and a man, a dispatcher and a cop, and Foley would make a note and then call someone to get more details.

It had been a while since I sat near a police reporter's desk, and what I noticed now was that I was listening to the dull sounds of the radio. For years, when I'd hear it in the background every night, I'd tune it out completely, like the people who live near railroad tracks stop hearing the night sounds of the passing freight.

Baines had very little on Carlton Associates. There were notes about a school board meeting, a highway construction dispute, a change in zoning laws, a move to increase the speed limit, a new mall opening, a city solicitor named, ribbon cutting for a new courthouse, Carlton speaking at a cancer fund-raiser, a thirteen-year-old girl dying in a car crash, a woman celebrating her hundredth birthday. At the end of the notes on a planning-board meeting, I found a Carlton entry:

"G. HOWARD. Maxville General Contracting, Hatley. Carlton." It was dated July 8. Seven weeks ago. There was nothing else on Carlton in that notebook.

I read the calendar on Baines's desk. On Sunday, August 18, was entered, "Meredith. 5:30." On Wednesday, August 14, "Call Meredith." On August 7, it said: "George. 4." All the other notations on the calendar had complete first and last names, most with phone numbers. I wrote down all the names and numbers. It could be that the notations with first names only were related to the Carlton story, and the others were not. A small measure of security by Baines. Everyone had his own code.

Most reporters knew all the routines. I still used most of them. Reporting. Blackmailing. They were professions with a common method. The transition between the two had been easy. The way I looked at it now, reporting was an incomplete, restrained, inadequate version of blackmailing; a self-sabotaging version of the game in which you used talent and energy to get useful information, then scattered the information to the wind. Reporters were eagles who cut their wings, tigers poised for a kill who never leaped from hiding, people who gutted their powers by accepting the view that the highest order of good was informing the public. Reporting was in some ways as arcane as an ancient religious rite. I envisioned a devout religious clan putting in a hard year farming the land, gathering up the food, and then, instead of eating, throwing the pile off the side of a mountain, a token of worship to some god.

There wasn't a piece of information good reporters assembled, as the armies of them roamed the land, that couldn't be put to better use. As blackmail. I sometimes wondered what would happen if all reporters gathered together for warring descent on corrupt neighboring nations. Thus transformed, their normal benign rites of exploration would become something darker and more potent. White ink to black.

I noticed a framed photograph lying face down in the top drawer. I took it out and turned it over, and there, facing the world with a smile and a loving embrace, was the man I'd seen in Greenwell's dossier. But in this picture there was a different woman, and there were three children, and they made a happy family indeed. So that explained why Baines was not in the office. He wasn't sick. He'd been blackmailed. He'd met with Greenwell and seen the dossier. Carlton now had his silence. And possibly more. That also meant they had no need to go after him anymore. They had his silence, which was all they wanted.

I walked over to Foley, thanked him again for his time, and asked if it would be all right if I called him if something came up. He seemed glad to help, even gave me his home number.

I drove down to Hatley to look for G. Howard, the name in Baines's notebook. The rolling pastures of the Brandywine horse country were pretty, with low wooden fences framing green fields, and pine forests off in the distance. Occasionally, alongside the winding road, small metal markers had been implanted, reminding the passerby that this was the site of a certain Revolutionary battle in 1776, that this was where the British attacked an American Wing, or this was where Sullivan's defense line retreated until reinforcements arrived from Chadds Ford.

I drove through the mushroom farms near Kennett Square and Toughkenamon and Wickerton, and in the fields I could see the Mexican workers digging and plowing and planting and hauling, and every now and then there were a few workers lying under trees, hats over their heads, sleeping.

Hatley looked like a lot of the towns in the area, neat, orderly, pretty, small quiet streets with old trees and carefully planted little gardens. The houses were unimpressive by horse-country standards, small, simple, older. There were no big malls, no billboards, no signs of modern development taking over. But as I drove toward the town's center, I saw that a number of the quaint little houses were vacant, some boarded up, all in good condition. Clean, undamaged, and abandoned, as if people had fled from a tornado that never came. Hard to figure. Didn't look like the kind of town people would suddenly leave, more like a place you'd want to move to.

Maxville General Contracting was a small storefront on Main Street. The door was locked. I knocked. I looked through the window.

"Can I help you?" A woman had stepped from a greeting-card shop, just next door. "I own this," she said, pointing to her store, "and couldn't help noticing you."

"I'm looking for Mr. Howard."

"You know him?" the woman asked.

"No. A friend said he could help me out."

"Well, I'm afraid he's in no condition to help anybody," she said. "He's in the hospital."

"What happened?"

"He was beat up. Horrible thing."

She gave me directions to the hospital, about fifteen minutes away. George Howard was asleep. According to a nurse, he had been there for fourteen days with several broken limbs and some internal injuries.

He'd been badly beaten by people who got away. The nurse said he would probably fully recover eventually. I decided not to wait for Howard to wake up. Whoever beat him up clearly could have killed him, but had decided not to. People usually don't change their minds about that kind of thing. I would come back some other time.

On the way back through town, I stopped again at the greeting-card shop to thank the woman who had given me directions and see if there was anything more I could learn from her. She asked me how Howard was.

"Asleep," I said. The woman seemed disappointed. "Do you know what happened?" I asked.

"Before I answer that," she said in a matter-of-fact kind of voice, although she still seemed friendly, "let me tell you that you won't like what I have to say." With that, I knew exactly what she would say, having heard the opening line many times before. Witnesses who had done nothing. A supreme cowardice, no doubt ashamed because she'd done nothing to help George Howard. But it was perfectly reasonable. What should a person do when there was violence around? We'd only spent every second since crawling out of the primal pool leaping, thrusting, lunging, and burrowing our way clear of danger. We managed for days and years and generations to tuck ourselves neatly out of harm's way. So why risk losing our shield by running after the dying, possibly to die ourselves? Made no sense. This woman was normal.

She locked up the shop and invited me to join her as she walked home. It was only a block and a half away. Her house was a simple two-story A-frame with a small, neatly tended front yard. The place was decorated in a way that nowadays would be considered fashionably old, a style for making people feel substantial when they owned only a little. Much of the furniture looked handcrafted, as if someone had tended the joints and welts, nurturing them into things that held and lay and set and stood, taking the test of time by getting better as well as older. We sat opposite each other on the solid pieces of comfortable furniture.

"There isn't much I can tell you," she said. "George made it to the nearest house—Rick Donald's, you might want to talk to him—and we, maybe a hundred of us, went looking for who did it. Some of us walked through the woods out to the roads. Other folks took cars all the way to neighboring towns, just looking. Didn't find a damned thing. No tracks of a vehicle. No sign any groups of men had been in the woods. We ended up making stupid jokes about invisible men. We have nothing but guesses about how many there were. Why was he beaten, and who did it? We know nothing."

She looked at me as if to appeal for my help in making more out of what she knew.

As she spoke, I sat back, humbled. I'd guessed wrong. She was describing a group of people, neighbors, who had jumped out into the flames on only the slim chance they might help. Not even the advantage of the blood ties of family, just neighbors. In the face of danger and the mocking force who'd beaten one of their friends, the neighbors had gone out after their own share of whatever pain was offered. The woman was disappointed, because she couldn't tell me about something she and her neighbors had completed. It had been a process of taking the terrors the night brought and trying to restore the rules these people wanted in their town. This was rare, and made something special of this particular place. It wasn't something I'd seen very often—not in Pennsylvania or anywhere else.

But there was something else about Hatley. I remembered that this was the town Sara had been in when she'd seen Reidus and Greenwell confront the four workers in a truck. Why would Reidus want to intimidate workers from Hatley? And now, as it turned out, George Howard, a contractor, was also beaten without explanation in Hatley. And there were all those shut-down houses I'd passed on the way into town. Based on what this woman was saying, people here were not the kind to leave willingly.

Construction workers beaten. *A housing contractor* beaten. Houses shut down. Carlton Associates *is* a real estate and land development company. There was a connection.

"Did you ever hear of a man named Willie Reidus?" I asked the woman.

"No."

She may never have heard of him, but my guess was she'd seen a piece of his handiwork.

14

EVERYTHING IN WEST MARLBOUGH looked like a landscaped million-aire's ranch. It hardly seemed like the place for a real estate and land development company. Carlton Associates headquarters was surrounded by large, flowing formal gardens and the low-lying buildings were hidden in the trees and shrubs. The lobby of the main building was mostly glass walls looking out onto the gardens. I'd kind of wished they'd put those large pieces of tape up on the windows, like they do at construction sites to prevent people from walking into glass. I kept a hand in front of me as I walked slowly to the reception desk, where a woman directed me to Jack Carlton's office.

What struck me at once, as I walked the spiral stairs and wide corridor, was the apparent lack of security in this building. The recep-tionist didn't even bother to call Carlton's office to ask if I could come up. There were no guards and no video cameras that could be seen. Everything was open, an open invitation to touch. It didn't feel right.

The only person in Carlton's outer office was a very beautiful woman with long black hair. She wore the kind of simple blue-and-white cotton dress that looked like planned enticement, because the clothes were innocent and plain, and the woman who wore them was neither. It was hard to tell her age because she had looks that didn't fade much, a face with strong features, clean lines, a lot of grace. The dress floated up a bit, the hair shook down hard over her shoulders.

She stepped from behind her desk. She was tall and the body also had clean lines, a lot of grace, and a whole lot more. She introduced herself as Meredith McDowell, Carlton's secretary. She welcomed me warmly. I guess maybe she thought I was there to buy some land. Her openness and polish were smooth. She seemed genuine, which was either a matter of her skill or perhaps she was one of those people who felt empathy for everyone. I looked around. The place was set up more like a living space than an office. Lots of couches and low tables with phones that were easy to reach from anywhere. Meredith seated me at a long couch covered with blue silk in a pattern of small rectangles in red and blue that looked like flags.

She asked me what I wanted, which was a good question because I wasn't sure of the answer myself, but I knew I had to meet Carlton. I told her pretty much what I'd told the police at the stables, that I was a friend upset over Simon's death.

"The police believe it was Greenwell who killed Simon. I'm not so sure they're right. I was hoping to talk with Mr. Carlton."

"There isn't anything we could tell you specifically that would help," she said, still warm and smooth. "We agree with the police, and what they've told us is all we know. It's no secret that Dave Greenwell worked for us for several years. We're very open about what we do, and we're very concerned about the murder. We're absolutely horrified that such a man, under our employ, lost control and—from what the police told us—killed your friend. Why he did it, we have no idea."

She seemed accustomed to explaining difficult things, to facing visitors who had unpleasant questions. She did it well.

"If you just want to get a sense of what we do," she said, "I really recommend you take a look at some of the materials here." Maybe she was trying to sell me something after all. She pointed to the low tables, and I picked up some colorful brochures, along with some pamphlets and news clippings. Then she walked to a wall that was covered with brightly-patterned wall hangings.

"Jack is proud of his collections," she said. "These mats are from Central America, Guatemala, mostly, each one selected by Jack in a different Indian village. Take a look. They're really exquisite."

I looked up at the wall as she stood there smiling, and I thought for a moment that she was waiting to turn over a letter, like that blond hostess on the TV game show. Then I shuffled through the materials from the tables. She watched patiently. I read through several of the newspaper stories. The company presented itself, in these writings, not

95

as a real estate and land development business, but more as a charitable enterprise or some kind of nonprofit community relations organization.

"Guess you people do a lot of volunteer work for the needy, huh?"

She seemed to like that, as if I'd cracked some kind of code. She then said she'd see if Carlton was available, and perhaps I could meet with him. She disappeared into an inner office.

Carlton came out. He was taller than me by maybe three inches, and a bit broader, though not heavy. He was probably in his late forties and in excellent shape. He moved quickly, approaching me before I could stand. He started talking as if we were continuing a conversation, shaking my hand as he did. "Meredith told me why you're here. I think we can give you what you need to take home and feel comfortable with. Why don't you come on into my office?"

On the way to his office, a collection of shiny ebony horse statues was prominently displayed on a wall facing a large spiral stairway. I stopped to look. There were about fifteen of them, each one no larger than my hand. They were sitting out there plainly for the taking. No security at all.

"I see you're taken by my collection of horses," Carlton said. "Each piece comes from the mountains of Sri Lanka. It took me five years to get them all. Go ahead, pick one up, feel it. That's what they're here for. Art is for the experiencing, not just the looking."

I never was much for experiencing art, or even looking at it. I wasn't even sure this stuff was art. I picked up one of the pieces, turned it over a few times in my hand, could see nothing significant about it, and put it back. Maybe this was the one Simon stole. Or maybe he never even made it here.

"By the way," I said to him as we went into his office, "for a building with all this expensive art everywhere, I'd say you have pretty light security."

Carlton smiled. "We're really not worried about security problems. The whole point of doing business is to make contact with the public. We don't want people feeling they're entering a jail. We welcome everyone here."

You ask a man a simple practical question and he gives you a philosophy lecture. And one that makes no sense. Clearly he was lying about the lack of security. I was curious to see what else he was selling.

He sat in a big leather chair, I sat on a couch, and Meredith came in and sat next to me. Carlton leaned back, loosened his shirt and tie, and put his feet up on a polished wood desk.

"Those stories," he said, pointing to the clips I was still holding, "are the first thing we show new customers and new employees—anyone interested in our business. They're more important than all our financial statements. Our business is selling—whether it's homes or land or development plans. Selling is about trust, nothing else. If the stories like those aren't enough to do the job, we surround them with reminders." He motioned to the walls and I noticed a series of plaques. One said, "Strive to Care." Another, larger, said, "Respect for Others Above All Else."

Meredith picked up one of the clippings. It was a story about Carlton's rescuing a boy who had threatened to jump from a rooftop.

"This article," Meredith said, "is a pale shadow of the real thing. I was there. I'll never forget that night. It was raining. Not just raining. The kind of night umbrellas are useless.

"We were here, working late that night. I had the radio on and I heard about this standoff at Saint Theresa's school that had been going on for hours. The police and fire departments were over there because a kid was on the roof, threatening to jump. The kid had a knife to keep the cops back, and he wasn't listening to anyone. As soon as I told Jack about it, he said we had to get over there. Jack went right up to the roof. Didn't hesitate. He went to the kid and talked him down."

"What I did," Carlton said, standing as if he was going to show me something physical, "was sell, which is all about trust. I told him I wasn't the cops, I wasn't the teachers, I was just a businessman. But I told him I'd had it hard, and I knew what that was like, and I'd been on the edge myself. Haven't we all?" He smiled at me.

"The kid was soaking wet and shaking, jerking his head—he was on drugs, like so many of them today—and he was flashing this knife around. He says to me, 'You don't know nothing.' " Carlton used a Hispanic accent for the kid's words, and he did it fairly well. " 'You have everything,' the kid says to me, 'and I have nothing. Only bad luck.' I figure he's going to jump, but I also figure that as long as I'm talking and he's listening, I'm doing the right thing."

"So Jack went out further on the ledge with the kid—" Meredith picked up the story, shaking her head as if she were experiencing it all over again. "There was lightning, lots of it. I really thought a bolt would strike them down. And all of us—the cops, the teachers, me—we're all trying to listen, and every minute there's a boom, and we can only hear snatches of Jack's words in the thunder. Would you believe he's telling the kid a story—about lightning?"

"That's right," Carlton said. "I ask him whether in his school they teach you about lightning. And he says no, so I figure he's still listening, he's not going to jump, and the thing is, I really felt I had something important to tell him. So I start yelling over the storm. Right behind him is the church tower, with spires, it's an old stone church. One of the spires is a tall metal pole, a lightning rod. Until that moment, I never even noticed it before, but it's like God put it there. Just what I needed. So I tell the kid. 'Two hundred years ago no church in the world had a lightning rod. Every time a church was hit by lightning it was destroyed, burned to the ground. In those days, people thought that lightning was like the angry fist of God.' And while I'm telling him, there's lightning coming down. But he's listening. So I point to the sky."

"He's pointing to the sky," Meredith said, "and yelling at the kid, and there's lightning flashing and thunder rocking the roof."

"I told the kid that Benjamin Franklin discovered the lightning rod and he was the ambassador to France at the time, and he saw the problem they had with churches getting burned down by lightning. So he offered the Archbishop of France his new invention. But the archbishop refused to use the rods, saying the lightning was sent by God to remind man of his sins, or something like that, and it strikes a church to teach humility and obedience to even his high servants, his priests. But storekeepers and homeowners and government officials start using the rods, and soon every place in France but churches has them. And that year, God's fist pounds and burns only churches, and when the priests, the local ones, see that no amount of penance and prayer stops the heavenly fire, they cry out for the rods. And the next year, the archbishop accepts Franklin's rod.

"The moral, I tell the kid, is that that moment was part of the end of superstition in the world, and the beginning of the world we know, where the gift of God's grace is ours only hand in hand with the fruits of what we do for ourselves."

PAYBACK

"By now," Meredith said, "the kid has forgotten all about the knife. He's listening to Jack, the greatest sales talk I've ever heard, and Jack says to the boy, we all hear it, 'There is no good luck, there is no bad luck. Only opportunities. And this is your lucky day, because I'm going to help you with your problems.' The boy just hands him the knife, and the two of them come back from the ledge. Believe it."

"If you understand that story," Carlton said, "then you know why we're in business. Which is to do some substantial good in the world while making money. And that's why we could never have had anything to do with your friend's terrible tragedy. Can you understand that?"

Before I left, they gave me copies of some morale-boosting videos Carlton used for his staff, and other company materials. I felt like I'd just applied for a job, and been hired. Welcome to the Carlton family.

15

As I WALKED DOWN the spiral stairs toward the big glass lobby, I juggled the tapes from hand to hand. No doubt about it, Carlton was my man—a swindler in a good suit. They always worked with mirrors and smoke, though the details varied. For Carlton it was the big windows and the openness—or the appearance of it. After they had the money and power, and they didn't need the hocus-pocus anymore, they kept on using it anyway, they just couldn't drop it.

Once in a great while, you ran into one of them who was just a pure bad, money-sucking, power-hungry, crazy-to-run-things kind of guy—but he'd be the exception. The rest of them, Carlton included, it seemed, had this thing they loved to put on display—their good-guy twin. Help the community, be a leader, offer a philosophy, talk about freedom and America, or whatever sounded like what the buyers out there wanted to hear. Give to charities, throw block parties, look good. It was probably because they had wives or kids and they liked to play it decent in front of them. Because they absolutely knew, the big rip-off artists with the nice stationery, that it was just grab it all with both fists, and hold on tight when the others come running to grab it back. You could ask them anything, and they'd have a long answer ready—and the answer was always something they'd rehearsed carefully before anyone even had any questions.

I wondered what Carlton's answer would be about the ebony horses. I intended to find out the truth and then go back to him to catch him in his lie. That would be fun.

I was reminded of the feeling I had when I first took the job as a reporter for Shannon's small newspaper in Delaware County. There is a certain kind of investigative story, the big people/small people kind. The first one I ever did was about a group of doctors and lawyers and a local judge. They'd figured out a way to get control of millions of dollars belonging to patients and clients. They ended up leaving about fifty senior citizens almost penniless.

What they did was falsify medical reports to make the old people appear much sicker, on paper, than they were. They only picked people who had little family. Then they went to court and showed that these people were incompetent to handle their own affairs, and so the lawyers and judge assigned control of their assets to a distant family member. By phonying up paperwork or making deals with distant cousins, the lawyers managed to divert all the money to themselves and the doctors. They got hold of about $6 million. It was a neat scam.

I'd been tipped to the story by an old woman, a friend of mine. The trouble was, she couldn't prove it, and at first neither could I. Meeting the old people helped—eighty-year-olds, some living in nursing homes. No one had listened much to them because they were officially incompetent. As usual, with these types, it wasn't just money the doctors and lawyers stole; it was life.

They kept some of these old people in what they called a nursing home. It was thirteen years ago, and I still remember exactly how it looked. It was on a rotted old city street, with hardly a sidewalk in front of the building. An endless run of blocks in either direction, with only dead air, no movement, and what looked like a blanket of dust. The front door to the building wasn't even a door but a shuddering, pressured, sagging frame of wood. The floor was painted with dirt, the patterns almost readable, as if time had arranged the dirt in some way. Bits of plaster were ready to fall everywhere, the long, darkened whiteness of the halls wet and musty. Along the walls were large green plastic garbage bins—the kind used outdoors or in parks to gather leaves and debris. There was an odor coming from those cans, the smells of a battlefield, of blood, of waste. In a large room were people in wheelchairs, most of them pale and thin.

I was there to talk to one woman in particular, and when we finished, and I was about to leave, she said she wanted to show me something. She took me back down the corridor. She introduced me to a black woman in her sixties, who was on a kidney machine and in obvious pain. "I never realized dialysis was painful," I said. "That's the point," the woman told me, "it's not supposed to be."

The doctors and lawyers running this clinic were cutting back in every way they could. They were taking a huge sum of federal dollars, but they weren't spending the money on the patients. They were pocketing it and barely keeping the old people alive. Some died in that place. The filters in the dialysis machines were reused dozens of times, even though they were clearly marked "single use only." What they were doing was pumping filthy blood right back into the patients. When dialysis is done right, and the filters are replaced each time after use, and the machines are properly cleaned and maintained, dialysis isn't nearly that painful, I found out.

After that visit, I went through every public record I could think of—the court cases, medical assistance records, federal contracts, federal audits, local housing records, even some financial records I managed to look at in the law offices. It became clear that the lawyers had phonied the names of some relatives of these old people, managed to get hold of their savings, then deposited the money in Swiss accounts. I could have written a great story, but I knew that wouldn't have helped enough. The D.A. would investigate, but the doctors and lawyers could leave the country and avoid prosecution, and the old people would still never see their money again.

I didn't write a story. Instead I went to the senior lawyer in the group. I told him what I'd found and gave him an ultimatum: Return the money to the ones still living, clean up the clinic, and stop the scam for good. Or else the story went in the paper and the evidence went to the D.A. I had no idea how he'd react or what he'd do. I didn't even think about it. I just did it. He could have pulled a gun or something like that. He could have threatened to expose me for blackmail. Or he could have laughed at me. But he did none of those things. Instead, he did exactly as I asked. They were glad to make a deal. They got to keep a good sum and managed to avoid a hassle.

The roughest part for me, by far, was having to face Mike Shannon— the best damn newspaper editor I'll ever meet. I couldn't explain it to him. I loved the man, respected him as much as anyone, and I hated that I was doing something that went dead against his judgment. I knew how he'd feel. I told him only that I couldn't do the story. I had the information, so the story couldn't be written without me. He was furious and hurt. I let him down. He thought I'd taken a bribe, although to this day he isn't sure. He fired me, then he used his contacts to make sure I couldn't get another job in journalism ever again. He was right to do all of it, of course.

I realized soon after he fired me that I'd stumbled onto a kind of career. There are people like those doctors and lawyers everywhere, often operating on a much bigger scale. Some are smarter and tougher and greedier. Some use violence. They act like gods in their own little worlds. They make the rules and expect others to follow obediently. They have a very low tolerance for people who question them. They have no regard for people who suffer at their hands. They often aren't even aware there are victims. But there always are.

The thing about law enforcement—they can lock you up, but someone always comes along to take your place. And the scam continues. They change the face, but not the game. What I try to do is keep the faces in place and change the game. So I make deals. Pay back the victims, stop the scam, and you can keep your job. Or else.

When it works, the little gods are forced to live in a cage—the real world. They have to give up their kingdoms and follow the rules of ordinary people. It drives them nuts. I think they'd rather be in jail.

When I threatened that lawyer, one of the first things he said was "How much do you want?" I didn't take anything, but I learned something from it. Now, when I make the deal, I take a cut. Expenses are high, because I pay a law firm and accountants to keep track of every case. My fee varies—whatever seems fair at the time.

Carlton would make a good client. My client. That's one way I was different from a private investigator. They got hired by lawyers or clients. Not me. *I* choose my clients. And the thing is, they never want me. But in the end, they pay me.

16

REIDUS SAT ON THE COUCH in his office, watching the tape of Carlton's meeting with Gray. Every room in the building was wired and constantly monitored. All the cameras were carefully concealed. Reidus left strict instructions with his men to inform him in writing of all visitors. He wasn't surprised to see Gray's name on the list. He chuckled as he listened to Carlton finishing his tale about Saint Theresa's. Reidus loved that story, although he'd often thought it should have a more dramatic ending.

He walked up the flight to Carlton's office. He knocked and let himself in. Carlton swung himself around the chair and before Reidus even spoke, he suggested they have lunch sent in.

"I'm having fresh flounder and asparagus," Carlton said. "Won't get fat on a diet like that."

"No, thanks," Reidus said.

Carlton looked at him sternly. "What's wrong?" he asked.

"Did I say something was wrong?"

"I can tell," Carlton said. "I know you, Will. You know that."

"What did that guy want?"

Carlton looked away as if he hadn't heard the question. "Nothing," he said. "What's the difference? He's a friend of the private eye who was killed. He's upset. He'll be no problem."

Reidus knew he'd have a hard time with Carlton on this. In their four years together, Reidus had established his value in handling the "field work," as they called it, with any major troubles, especially from competitors. He "induced" lower bidders for jobs to drop out, "enforced"

104

territorial rights with other competing businesses, "persuaded" reluctant property owners to sell land Carlton wanted. Carlton was aware of the outcome of Reidus's work and valued it, and he usually didn't want to know the details. But Carlton also liked to take on projects alone. Like the other night when he drove out to the warehouse to deal with Simon, for example. Carlton never should have tried to handle that situation, but he couldn't resist. Reidus knew it was a matter of pride for Carlton. He believed he could handle anything—with his words. Reidus asked Carlton if he knew anything special about Gray.

"No," said Carlton. "Should I?"

"Yes," Reidus said. "He was here one day. He's been to the newspaper in West Chester. Down to Hatley. To the stables, twice. He says he's a friend of the P.I., but he moves too quickly for that. He's not in mourning. He's an operator."

Carlton half stood, leaning toward Reidus with a supportive look. "Hatley?" he said. "You think he has an interest there? Is there some problem you haven't told me about?"

Two years ago, when Reidus realized he had to make the move on Hatley, he put together a beautifully elaborate business rationale to sell the plan to Carlton. He hired a market-research firm to prepare a report showing that Hatley was the *perfect* town to buy, house by house, and convert to a modern development. Because of the abnormally low turnover in houses in Hatley for the past hundred years, housing prices there remained ridiculously low. Better yet, the small Chester County town was surrounded by wealthy estates and new developments filled with affluent professionals. The land values in most of the area had shot up in the seventies and eighties, while Hatley remained a town with 1940s housing prices. It was a truly unique investment opportunity. Buy hundreds of houses at bargain prices, wait a few years, and develop and sell the land in the 1990s marketplace. A deal Carlton couldn't turn down. What made it better was that despite dropping prices across the country, statistics showed that real estate values in Chester County were increasing. Of course, the houses were occupied—but that was why Carlton had Reidus.

"There is absolutely no problem in Hatley," Reidus said. "What I'm telling you is that you want to look out for this guy from Philadelphia. I smell trouble."

Carlton sat back and tapped his desk with a pencil eraser. "I do trust your instincts, Will. But let's not worry for no sufficient reason. We get many operators here. All businesses do. And you handle them. So no one's a threat. If it makes you feel better, why don't you tell Meredith to check with her reporter friend at the *Tribune* and see what's known about the man."

Carlton walked over to Reidus, took his hand and patted his shoulder.

"We're partners, Will. I trust your judgment. Let's see what Meredith comes up with, okay?"

Reidus nodded.

When Reidus left, Carlton looked out the window at the formal gardens. He felt Reidus was capable of moving too strongly on things he only suspected were threats, that he liked the action too much. He'd moved too quickly in snatching the private eye. If he hadn't made that mistake, nothing would have happened at all. Now he might move too quickly with Gray, and for no good reason. Carlton had been having a nagging sense lately—one of those intuitions he'd grown to trust over the years—that Reidus was losing some of his control, that he could go too far too fast and create serious problems for the company. It was a situation Carlton hadn't yet figured out how to handle. It wouldn't be easy. Nothing with Reidus ever was.

He sat back in the recliner and stretched. He felt a tightness in his back. He often felt that tension after talking to Reidus. He wasn't used to reacting that strongly to another man. He didn't like it.

17

MEREDITH DROVE THE MERCEDES to her first appointment of the morning. Most of the men she visited liked being first on the list. They had woken up in a hotel room or in the separate apartments kept for just such occasions.

She imagined the feeling they had, the apartment a stage for their fantasies, something that got them ready. She pictured them arriving the night before with an armful of porno tapes and magazines, or whatever turned them on. Maybe they brought their favorite foods too, and got into their pajamas and played with themselves before falling asleep, excited, exhausted, and content.

Every morning visit found them the same way, coming to the door in their boxer shorts or their pajamas or their thin robes, or sometimes naked. Though she had not yet done anything for them, they were already wildly aroused, their hard organs making tents of their clothes. They would lean against her, their hands always on her breasts, their faces looking for her lips, their bodies pressing hard against her dress.

She didn't pick the men. Carlton did. Reidus sometimes made suggestions, but she never listened unless it was what Carlton wanted. The difference was she trusted Carlton to have thought it out, to have decided it was necessary or likely to pay off. And Carlton also would have thought to some extent about the risk. Wherever she went it was to bring pleasure, so generally there was no risk. At least, not the first time. If there was, well, that was why the money stakes were high.

Her client this morning was new, someone named Terrence Backman. Carlton wanted to get his help with a bid on a project, and Meredith was delivering her part of a straight reward. She always had a goal, and she kept it clear in her mind. It was an important part of what made it just business for her. The goal here was simply to do the kinds of things he wanted, and to do them well enough so he would think only of her. The apartment was in a high-rise in the Society Hill section of Philadelphia. Residential neighborhood, luxurious, and only blocks from Independence Hall. There was a doorman. Backman had told Meredith by phone to come right up. That meant the man was married. So she made a point of asking the doorman for the apartment number. Carlton had told her to stop and be remembered.

She had seen Backman's picture, and Carlton had described him. He was in his late thirties, in decent shape and wasn't bad-looking. Meredith guessed his wife probably looked pretty good, too, and he was probably having sex with her, at least occasionally. He'd either tell Meredith what he wanted, or she'd get a sense of it. Carlton said he'd never met a woman who could do that as well as Meredith. She knew that was true.

When she got out of the elevator, Backman was waiting by an open apartment door at the end of the hall. He was in a blue terry-cloth robe. Her first thought was that his thick brown hair looked better in person than in the picture. She walked toward him, knowing he wanted to watch. When she reached the door, he grabbed her before she could go in, standing there half in and half out of the apartment. His hand cupped her ass and drew her forward to a close embrace.

She had learned to trust her intuition so totally in matters like this that she rarely hesitated. He would want something that wasn't ordinary, because he was married, and the one thing that was always true about married sex was that it became ordinary.

She made a decision and stepped fully back into the corridor, holding onto him so the two of them were outside the apartment. He smiled, pressed against her, and pulled her into the apartment. He kissed her, but didn't do much else. She opened the top buttons of her red silk dress, uncovering her breasts, stepping back a bit and out of his grip so he could see what she'd done. He hadn't spoken, which was good. Sex was always easier and hotter when they didn't talk first. Not because talking was bad, especially if it was about sex. But inevitably they started to talk about something else, and that made the whole job more difficult than it needed to be.

He reached for her again, this time to stroke her breasts. She made a low noise and let him lick her there, while she stroked his thighs and groin. She followed her idea, moving away from him again and letting him follow her. The apartment door was still open, and she went back into the corridor. It was ten'o clock on a weekday morning. No one was in the hall. She stepped into the alcove leading to the stairway. When he followed her there, she closed the door and moved next to him. This time he touched her everywhere, breathing hard and taking what she offered. She knelt, separated the flaps of his robe. He had nothing on underneath. She took him in her mouth, and he guided her movements with both hands in her hair. After a minute she got up, raised the bottom of her dress and stood with one leg up on the stairs, to let him enter her that way, face to face.

They eventually went back to the apartment and she stayed for an hour, leaving before he wanted her to. The point had been to make a friend for Carlton. She believed she had.

It was lunchtime, and a good time to do another bit of business. She drove north for twenty-five minutes on I-95 to a new corporate park in Bucks County. She arrived just before one, knowing from the information Carlton had provided that the executive wouldn't return until 1:30. Carlton had told her that this man had something different in mind. She knew how to provide it.

She settled herself into the waiting area on his floor, telling the secretary she was there to see Mr. Dawson. The secretary was very good. She showed no emotional response at all. She did ask if Meredith was expected, and Meredith said no. When the secretary asked why she was there, Meredith said it was personal.

In about twenty minutes, a half-dozen executives, all male, came off the elevator, walking one by one past Meredith. It was a branch of a national bank, and she admired the restraint she saw in action. Three of the men who passed did all of their looking in a properly veiled way, without breaking stride. Two were a bit more obvious, slowing as they went by, but casual enough in their looking to go unnoticed by most people. One of them, however, stopped at the secretary's desk for no reason. Meredith changed her position so he could see more of her, and that was when he went into his office.

When Dawson finally arrived, Meredith approached him by the elevator before the secretary could tell him she was waiting. She slapped him, pushed him, called him names in a loud, hurt voice. Several men came out of their offices to see what was happening. Meredith then stormed off on the next elevator. She was very credible. She could deliver many versions of the same scene, all just as credibly.

She got in the Mercedes, feeling good about her performance. She drove the hour and twenty minutes back to Chester County, where she had a restaurant reservation with the *Tribune* reporter, Foley. This was the way she liked it. A full day of work.

Foley had been waiting at the bar when Meredith arrived. She looked in at him from outside before she entered. Foley always arrived first and she liked to see him while he waited. She had a habit, too, of always inviting him to some new restaurant he hadn't known about. He'd been in West Chester a long time and was used to thinking of the whole county as just some farmland outside Philadelphia. That had changed for good in the growth days of the eighties. But for some reason the change still made him uncomfortable.

As she looked in at Foley through a glass door, Meredith could see in him his own thoughts and feelings—not the version of him she controlled. Lately she'd been seeing something especially uncomfortable and awkward about him. She wasn't sure, but she thought it had to do with his job. For someone as bought and owned as he was, as deeply given up, it was painful for him to be near other newspaper people less faded. She knew Chris Baines made Foley uneasy. Baines functioned with conscience and competence in the same muck in which Foley dwelled. His presence probably made Foley question his sellout. Baines wouldn't know Foley was an inside source for Carlton.

She liked having access to Foley, to hear what he'd been telling Reidus. She felt secure, too, that her own name would be kept out of those reports. Reidus spooked her. He never gave a sign of being stirred by her, as other men were. Yet he seemed to envy the effect she had on men. Carlton never worried her. He was unable to see a woman as a threat, especially a woman he slept with. She didn't know much at all about Gray. He had shown almost nothing in the meeting at the office. Carlton needed to know why he was there and what he wanted. Meredith was curious for her own reasons.

She walked in and approached Foley slowly. She knew how his look would change when he saw her, she knew what he might say, even what he might think. He was revealed, stripped, and open, his ways known to her as if they were her own. Everything important was known in advance.

She could see that he was trying to appear unaffected by her, but she knew better. He was aroused just by the sight of her. She came up close to him and took his arm, stroking it. She could feel him sweat at her touch. He looked ahead, avoiding her gaze. She pressed her thighs against his hip as she kissed him lightly on the cheek. He became immobile, frozen by arousal. She moved him forward a bit like a doll, as the maître d' approached. Foley started to speak to the man, but she interrupted him.

"Something in the rear, quite private, please," she said.

Foley reddened, the maître d' smiled. Meredith and Foley were seated next to each other at a small table by a warm brick wall. They made small talk, but the important part for Meredith was arousing him. In such a state he would tell her everything. He drank water and waited nervously. That was their way together. After a waiter had come and departed with their orders, and while Foley was in the midst of some routine complaint about his job, Meredith leaned back and slipped off one of her shoes. She crossed her legs and put her stockinged foot against his ankle, then raised his pants leg with her toes, running her foot against the bare skin of his ankle and calf. She leaned closer to him, taking one of his hands in hers. She put her lips close to his face. "Have you been a good boy or have you been thinking naughty thoughts about me?" she whispered.

She could hear his barely audible moan, and his hand jerked a bit in her grasp. She pressed her fingernails into the flesh of his palm. She reached forward under the table and unzipped him. He put his hand down to stop her but she ignored that. It was weak protest. He was the kind of man who enjoyed being embarrassed a bit in this way, though the tablecloth covered them. After the waiter brought food, her hand went back under the table, touching him. She took one of his hands and moved it between her thighs. The restaurant, the table, the other diners, all these were gone from him now. He was completely focused on her, all attention and hope.

Suddenly she broke the contact, taking away her hand and her heat and her touch, and leaning back casually in her chair as if they were indeed just in conversation. She delighted in the look of him, hanging forward over the table, his clothes in disarray, his urgent need unsatisfied. Now she asked him everything she wanted to know about Gray. And hoping to keep her there, he told her all he knew.

18

I HEADED OUT TO Chris Baines's house at 7 A.M. I knew I'd be able to recognize him from the pictures, both the ones in Greenwell's dossier and the family photo at his desk at the *Tribune*. I could have telephoned him in midday but it was better this way, dirtier, more of a threat. I knew how to do this sort of thing and didn't much like how well I knew it. Especially since this guy was only a reporter who'd been trying to do his job. Those are the worst ones to blackmail: the innocents. But to get the guilty, a lot of what I did I didn't like.

I got his address from the West Chester white pages. Half the time these days I went out to look for a guy at his listed address, and what I found was the remains of a family and the guy living half an hour away in a small apartment. But in this case, I knew he'd be there. The whole point of the thing, what made it work for Greenwell and whoever else he'd been working with, was that Baines was very much a family man. Except for the woman in the pictures. Baines wouldn't much like my calling on him, but I had with me the only weapon I needed, the envelope with the photos.

I pulled onto his block. There were Victorian houses, most in good repair, set back a good distance from the street with high stone steps leading up to each outdoor porch. It was pretty, peaceful, quiet, a family kind of block. Kids would be playing on the sidewalk in a couple of hours.

I parked in front of his house, walked up the steps, and knocked. I waited a few minutes. I knocked again. I could hear the sound of slow movement inside; then a man wearing a brown bathrobe opened the

113

door. It was the guy in the pictures. He was groggy, yawning, and asked sleepily what I wanted.

"My name is Gray," I said. "I'm a friend of the private eye, Simon Griffey, who'd been helping you. I'm looking into his murder, and I need your help."

He gave me a look that door-to-door salesmen must see in their nightmares. "I don't know who you are or what you're talking about," he said. "Do me a favor and leave. I've had a tough week."

"Let's not make this any harder than it has to be," I said. "I have to see your notes on the Carlton story. Your notes and any documentation you have. Give me the stuff and I'll keep you out of it. You don't have to worry about Carlton's people."

I heard a woman's voice calling from inside. "Who's there?" she was asking.

"No one," he shouted back to her. "Just some salesman who likes to wake people up early. I'll be right in, honey." He looked back at me. "Get out of here, okay?"

I didn't want to drag this out. It was already too unpleasant. But necessary. I wasn't certain he'd seen the dossier and been through the whole thing with Greenwell. Only one way to know for sure. I took out the photo file and handed it to him. His look of disgust, but not shock, told me Greenwell had already threatened him.

"Look," I said. "I'm not one of *them*. I stole this from Greenwell. I have the pictures and the negatives. I'm ready to give it all to you and you can burn the stuff. I just want the notes and the records in return. Okay?"

He was getting nervous, visibly upset, rubbing his hands together hard. But he wasn't saying anything.

"Think it over," I said. "I'll meet you at the office tomorrow at noon. We'll make the exchange and that's it. You won't hear from me again."

He didn't respond. I took the file out of his hands and headed down the stone steps.

"Tomorrow," I said. "Noon. It'll all be over for you, and you can forget the whole thing."

I got in my car and drove away. He looked like a nice guy, someone you'd want as a friend. He was probably in the kitchen already, kissing his wife good morning. He must have felt like a rotten sleaze. That made two of us. Good morning, let me ruin your day. I drove to the courthouse.

The boy in the green polo shirt didn't seem impressed with the modern lobby at the county courthouse. He was keeping his sister occupied, and he ignored the receptionist's invitation to look at the computer console up front. The boy rolled a toy car up and down the side of the chair leg and looked over at his sister, sitting with her hands folded. She was almost in tears. He picked up a rag doll from the floor and folded its arms around his sister's hands, then talked to the doll reassuringly.

I watched the children for a half hour while waiting for the clerk to come back with the criminal court records I'd requested.

Public records. I'd always found it incredible that you could learn so much about anyone just by going to the public records. Details of almost everyone's life were compiled in those files. The records were created to serve the narrow needs of dozens of different government departments, but taken together they usually told a story. They were as good a source as any for journalists. The key was knowing that they were there (most of them in courthouses) and being willing to put in the time to sift through them. The records remained available and accurate for so long because people forgot they existed, didn't bother with them. So even if you knew nothing about, say, Jack Carlton, you could go to the records and find out things even Carlton's friends didn't know about him.

The thin young clerk finally returned, holding only the two-page form I had filled out, and offering a dull, apologetic smile.

"I'm sorry," he said. "I can't seem to find any records on Jack Carlton or William Reidus." That didn't mean their records were clear. Possibly the clerk couldn't find anything, or the records had been altered or removed. I'd have to look elsewhere. I smiled at the clerk. "Thanks," I said, and turned toward the stairs, heading for the civil court records room. You could go through the file folders in civil court on your own without having to fill out the forms and wait. You might not come up with anything, but it was better than relying on a clerk.

I started with some of the simple ones, not expecting anything. There were no local birth or marriage records for either Carlton or Reidus. Carlton was registered to vote as a Republican. He'd changed his address three years ago, the same time he changed his political affiliation from Democrat. Reidus wasn't registered to vote. Checking the alphabetical file in the long, low beige file cabinets, I did a quick run-through of civil suits, bankruptcy, divorce, and, in another room, real estate and tax liens. In a half hour, my notepad was filled with citations under Carlton's name, including the fact that he was divorced. I'd found nothing under the name William Reidus.

Most of the data on all the records was in the county's computer system, but the courthouse also kept a complete set of paper files. The clerk in the records room was a friendly-looking woman in her fifties. She didn't ask me why I was there, but I knew that in my dark blue suit and striped red tie I looked more like a lawyer than a reporter. No one else walked around these places with such ease, and reporters almost always announced their business as soon as they walked in. I asked her if I could pull the records on a divorce case, and she politely led me to a room with tall rows of thin file cabinets along one wall. She helped me find the case file, then showed me a desk and said I could use it to read and take notes. I didn't ask, but she offered to let me use the photocopier. "Only a few pages," she said, smiling. They weren't paid to do all this. Sometimes you just bumped into them, the decent ones, and it was one of those unexpected pleasant surprises. Nothing big, just unexpected kindness. I smiled and thanked her. She turned and left me alone in the quiet room.

The file was thick. Most divorce files were. There was a certain weight and heft of paper and ink needed to capture the commonplace series of accusations and countercharges that divorce actions inevitably became. The more money at stake, the more tricks the lawyers used, the more detailed the depositions, the thicker the file. If the wife and husband were angry, if the lawyers were good, if there were children, if the children were troubled—for every added element of pain, the file grew thicker. I skimmed most of the pages. Nothing extraordinary. The divorce went through nine years ago. Turned out this was his second one. His first was in Detroit. Twenty years ago.

Trails. Everything that moved left a trail. And the trails lasted forever in those records. If most people were aware of the records, they'd probably try to change them. When reporters pointed out to the subjects of their stories what it said in the record about them, people usually said that the record version wasn't what really happened, that things weren't the way it said they were in the folder, on the paper. They always had an explanation, a way to get around the facts.

I put the divorce folder back in its place. I walked to the end of the long wall of files, followed the curve of the smooth off-white cement column that led to the next room. There was no door, just the large column, and when I made it fully around, I saw what appeared to be an endless series of neatly aligned gray steel horizontal shelves running side by side from one end of the big room to the other. There were little numbers and letters at the head of each narrow passageway, and I flipped through my notebook to find docket numbers and dates for the civil suits filed against Carlton. I tracked the numbers on the thin gray shelves halfway across the room until I reached the right file. The first wasn't very thick. I pulled a half-dozen more before going back to the desk.

In case after case, Carlton had been sued by local residents, many of them elderly customers of Carlton's real estate company. The complaints were specific and local, because it was state court, but many had numbers cross-referenced to federal suits. Carlton's people had enough energy to work the locals, and customers in plenty of other states. The howls of silent protest erupted in these files. Snake-oil salesmen on the move. Many of the complainants said Reidus had done the business with them. It took a certain desperation to describe in detail the way one's possessions had been stripped and to say, for all the world to know, that you'd been taken for a sucker. But they had had nowhere else to turn.

Carlton had managed to get thousands of local folks to put their savings into vaguely worded land-development deals. At the same time, he and four other men, named in several of the complaints, invested only tiny amounts of money but served as the executive officers in the limited partnership that owned the commercial developments. By the time Carlton's real estate salesmen had bled the local people dry, the development was worth over eight million dollars. But there was no development. Carlton and his four friends sold the land rights to another company, which they also owned. They then paid out two million dollars to each of the four men as "profits and bonuses." And the small investors were left holding worthless deeds to barren land in the blighted city of Chester. I sat way back in the wooden chair and looked at the folders on the table. The volume of each of these files was slight compared to the divorce records. But they contained more truths.

I went out and walked the half mile to the Federal Building. The sky was a dark mix of overcast haze and afternoon clouds. It was hot and sticky, and I realized why everyone else was in a car, windows closed, cold air flowing. By the time I had walked into the Federal Building I was soaked with sweat. I went straight for the FBI office, where I asked for an annual publication called "Organized Crime Directory." What I was looking for were the names of the four investors who went in with Carlton. They might be in the book. A lot of people are. Two of them were. The book said the two had "ties to crime families—Detroit."

I went back to the chilled lobby, feeling the clothes dry on my skin. The setup was common enough. This is one way they launder mob money. Detroit was probably sending cash or cashier's checks as their token investments in the land-development deals. Then, when the land company sent them their checks, they could legitimately claim the income as business profits. The mob money thus became tax accountable, or "clean." One of the ironies was that the IRS then collected millions in taxes on money from prostitution, gambling, and illegal drug sales.

I went back upstairs and filled out two Freedom of Information Act request forms for FBI files on Carlton and Reidus. I assumed there were some. I knew the procedure required written approval by the two men, and part of the form was a notice to each that I was requesting their file. Even if they gave their approval, the FBI could still withhold the files if there was an ongoing investigation. It was the sort of request that usually made people angry, a rude invasion of their privacy. But it wouldn't hurt, and it might bring something in return.

I drove the four blocks to the registry of deeds. In the main reception area, a computer console was open for public use. It had a simple program with instructions printed on a piece of cardboard. For sales this month, push "One." For sales this year, push "Two." For purchases this month, push "Three." And so on, with twenty-five different choices, by date, year, name, location, purchaser, purchasee. Once you hit a key, the little console hummed its computer music, then the screen welcomed you and offered a series of more detailed choices. After a half hour at the machine, I found dozens of transactions in several categories under Carlton's name. I found nothing listed for Reidus.

The property records themselves were on another floor. They were in a room with a high ceiling and a stepladder leading to a second level. The deeds were kept in large hardcover black vinyl binders. They were arranged by date and alphabetized, and stored in narrow bins, sitting atop small wooden wheels that creaked against a metal rod as I pulled out the heavy casings. It took me close to three hours, moving up and down on the two levels, to locate all the deeds and write down the information. In that time, only two other people came into the room. One was a young intern from a title company, searching a deed on a condominium that had been built three years ago. The other was a construction worker, looking for the office where you could ask questions about your property taxes.

The real estate records showed that Carlton had purchased hundreds of properties in the last two years, mostly homes in the town of Hatley. I went to bankruptcy court on a hunch. In bankruptcy court, I headed straight for the wooden drawers with the index cards listing names and dates. I went down my list from the Hatley property sales, and cross-referencing with the bankruptcies, I found dozens of names that matched. The date of the property sale and date of bankruptcy were usually within a month of each other. What it meant, I guessed, was that most of these property purchases by Carlton were from families that had been unable to make mortgage payments and were about to be foreclosed.

I went into the back room and started pulling bankruptcy case files. In affidavits filed with the legal papers, several of the homeowners said they thought they were receiving loans, or "second mortgages," from Carlton. In many cases, the families said they had made the deals with Reidus, and some explained in detail how Reidus had promised to "help them out" with their financial problems. But when the papers were signed, the Carlton company took control of the properties and the families were evicted.

I had only about an hour before the building closed for the day. I headed upstairs to the law library.

Why Carlton and Reidus had bought the land in Hatley wasn't clear.

119

The land in and around Hatley had no obvious value. What was clear was that Carlton and Reidus had gotten a lot of people out of their homes. They probably hadn't gone easily. People usually hold on to their homes as best and as long as they can. There isn't anything living that doesn't want a home of its own. Somehow Carlton and Reidus had found a way to separate people from their shelters. How they did it wouldn't be in public files.

At the library I was able to use a VCR monitor, but had only enough time to watch parts of the video tapes they gave me at Carlton's office. Carlton had made the tapes for distribution to his sales managers. Most were standard inspirational speeches about how to turn problems into opportunities. In one of them, Carlton referred to a negative article about his company in a national financial magazine. He talked about business and white-collar crime.

"I've done things in business that made me lose sleep. I've talked up the size of my collateral to get loans, I've fudged the size of my inventory to make a financial report look good, I've exaggerated my prospects to close a deal. I did these things to make money and build business. In everyday life, those are lies. In business, they're not lies. Because in the end I make good on my loans, I pay fair dividends to my stockholders, and everyone makes money.

"Something's a crime only if Party A complains to the law about Party B. That will never happen to me because there is no profit in complaining. Criminal court doesn't get you your money back."

I was driving back through the mushroom farm country just after sunset when a police car came speeding from behind. Neither the siren nor the flashing lights were on when it passed me, then abruptly cut in my lane, forcing me to hit the brake hard and swerve onto the dirt shoulder of the narrow road. The police car stopped in front of me. The driver got out and walked slowly back to my car. He was tall and thin, good shoulders and a big grin. The black pin under his badge displayed the word "Marksman," and under that was a name plate that said "Hayes."

He put his hands palm down on my door and leaned over.

"You weren't speeding," he said matter-of-factly.

"And you're a Wakefield cop ten miles out of Wakefield," I said.

"Get out of the car," the cop said.

I thought for a moment about driving on, but there was no point to that. The most deceptive thing about cops was that they were in uniform. It was in some ways the least important thing about them, because it told you absolutely nothing. When gang members wore colors, it told you about a commitment they'd made, a need they had, and a way they solved the age-old puzzle about how to belong to something in the world. The first time I'd ever seen a teenager in colors I thought it had something to do with the kid's family. With cops, on the other hand, as with soldiers, the uniform was nothing but a show for the outsiders. It protected the bad cops and sometimes tarnished the good ones. It told people who needed to know that the individual cop was a part of a gang that had, say five thousand members in a big city, or, in the case of a Wakefield, maybe fifty, but it said absolutely nothing about the state of need in the heart of the man or about what one had to do to get whole. For that reason, many of the good cops I knew wanted badly to make plainclothes, to get out of the uniform. In plain clothes they retained the authority and the purpose, but didn't have to stand up in the spotlight and advertise their power with the badge.

I'd had a run lately of getting through things without violence, of walking one cliff after another as if there were nothing below but soft cotton and no hard edges in the world. It was the kind of run of luck that lulled me into feeling I could do anything at no risk. Someone else had died, but I was still alive, lucky dog. I got out of the car.

Hayes and his partner, Officer Evans, told me to walk around behind a low gray cinder-block building on the edge of a mushroom farm. I could see a few Mexican workers off in the field, but they ignored us, probably wanted to stay as far from the police as they could. Hayes and Evans didn't seem to care one way or the other. Hayes told me to stand with my back against the cinder block. As soon as I did, I got a strong whiff of the fertilizer that must have been stored in the small building. The smell was coming down from the wood ceiling, with a vent just above the brick. It was awful.

The two cops stood about five feet in front of me. Neither had drawn a gun, and it appeared I was in for a beating. Evans stepped back, then took out his gun, but pointed it at the ground. Hayes moved in closer.

I saw the leg coming at me in time, but I took the blow directly on the shin. It stung. I decided to do nothing. Let Hayes take a few whacks and that would be the end of it. Message delivered. Who had sent it, I wasn't exactly sure. I'd find out sooner or later.

Hayes rammed his knee at my stomach. I moved slightly so the impact was taken by my hip, but he was fast and his kick was hard. He punched me in the ribs, then the jaw, and that kicked off the horrible stinging inside, that feeling you can't control. Like when you hit a foul tip off your toe. The sudden pain drives you absolutely crazy and for about ten seconds you just want to scream or drop to the ground or die. Dying would be the easiest. The last thing in the world you want is to be hit again.

He stepped back. His grin never faded. He was enjoying himself and he looked back at Evans. "Maybe you better help out," he said. "Guess I don't hit hard enough to get this guy to fight back." Hayes took out a blackjack. They wanted me to fight. That was all right with me. I couldn't take any more this way.

I needed a few seconds to get my head clear, and I was lucky that Hayes was having a good time laughing. It gave me time to prepare. I had learned to fight the same way I learned to hit fastballs. It was mostly a matter of concentration. For one thing, I had convinced myself there was no such thing as the direct experience of seeing an object as it came at you, whether it was a baseball or a fist. Everything was changed by the way you wanted to see it or feel it or think about it. The great hitters say a baseball looks the size of a basketball when it's coming in; the bad hitters say it's as small as a golf ball. And the speed of a punch partly depends on how much of it you pay attention to. Some people decide they're getting hit the minute the other guy throws the blow. They don't want to see it coming, and can't wait for it to be over. For them, a punch, any punch, is instant. It's delivered, in effect, the moment it's thrown, and distance doesn't matter. You have to concentrate and watch a thing to slow it down.

When Hayes came at me with the blackjack, I watched it like that, with absolute concentration. And when it slowed down, slowed down enough so I could duck right under it, I got all the way to one knee. And then, feeling the ground solid under my knee, I turned and drove a hard left up and through the tall man's gut. It was enough to make the cop's legs empty sticks, the small hard tool flew from his hand, and as Hayes fell, gasping for breath, I got up to take the full weight of him in a fireman's carry. In one motion I came up like a weight lifter jerking iron, and thrust Hayes's body at Evans. Evans struggled to stay up as his partner crashed into him. I was flat on my stomach with the effort. Evans started to topple, and I was ready to roll away and run off to my car. But Evans managed to push Hayes off his side before the two of them went down. He was on me before I could move.

With his free hand Evans caught the back of my head and pushed down hard as my nose and mouth ate gravel and dirt. With the butt end of the gun he hacked away at my back and shoulders. The pounding and the grinding became an unstopping rhythm, and at a certain point I no longer felt pain, just rhythm. There was a buzzing in my head, low and steady like a faraway siren riding the back roads but never getting closer. The wheels kept turning and digging up dirt, spraying sand, and the distant engine roar was as steady as the siren. The sounds didn't fade.

It seemed like I'd gone ten minutes without breathing in anything but dirt. Then I realized his hand was no longer on the back of my head and no one was taking chops at my back. I slowly lifted my head, then my hands, then got to my knees and used the bottom of my shirt to wipe blood and dirt from my face. Then I started checking all the parts— the teeth, nose, tongue, elbows, knees, shoulders—still there, moving—slowly. And hurting like hell.

The two cops were gone. I didn't remember them leaving.

A couple of farm workers walked cautiously toward me, a very thin teenage boy with long black hair and a darkly tanned, rough-skinned older man in a straw hat. They didn't say anything, just looked at me, maybe checking to see if I was alive. Maybe I'd been lying there looking dead. Maybe I was dead. I felt that way, anyway. I got up.

"*Buenas noches,*" I said, and they kept looking at me, silent. "Okay," I said. "*Hasta luego.*" And I limped back to my car. Guess my run of luck had run out.

19

I WAS WAY PAST counting sheep. I tossed and turned on the sheets, making them wet with sweat and crumpled with movement. I fell into brief sleep and startled myself out of it, woken by the throbbing of parts of me where my skin had turned dark from the beating. I sat up with a jolt and realized that the loud, persistent thumping I heard was not in my head, but someone knocking at the door. I looked at the digital motel clock: 1:47 A.M. I threw on pants, walked slowly to the front of the room and looked through the shades by the window. I opened the door before she could knock again. It was Meredith McDowell, from Carlton's place.

She was wearing a thin purple dress. It wasn't transparent but it came close. She had a silver necklace with small violet stones that sat nicely against the tan of her chest and the tops of her breasts. They inflict the wounds, they heal them, I thought.

"I know it's late," she said in a small, contrite kind of voice. "I called a dozen places before I found you. Do you mind?"

I wasn't blocking the door, but she didn't come in. Her restrained manner was just the right contrast to the way she looked and the time and the place.

"You can come in," I said, feeling exhausted and empty, and probably sounding that way. She didn't seem to notice.

I expected to smell perfume and I thought she'd find a way to make contact as she passed. I didn't smell a thing. She ignored the chair, and sat down on the edge of the bed. She said nothing, just let me look at her. I sat on an uncomfortable chair next to a plastic desk. I'd never seen anyone so at ease while undergoing inspection. She had long legs that softened her height. Everything about her looked soft. Soft black hair. Soft pretty face. Soft skin. I wondered if she could take on a multitude of looks, and if soft was the main thing she thought I needed right now. If so, she was reading me right.

"You look like you could use some rest," Meredith said.

"So you came over to put me to bed?"

"Would that be so bad?" she asked. She stood up, clearing the way for me to move to the bed, taking it for granted I was going there. I got to my feet and she closed the gap between us. She fitted herself in to the way I was standing so that every part of me was close up against a part of her. She had a hand on each side of my head, stroking my hair. She kissed me, but not hard enough to expect me to kiss her. When she stepped back, I took a breath and felt the settling of bones and the stretch of flesh. The pain from the beating was less noticeable.

I pushed her away. I meant to do it lightly but it didn't work out that way. She fell back onto the bed. She stayed there and didn't look upset or even surprised. She looked prepared, expectant. The dress fell away from her legs and she left it that way, her bare thighs exposed. She bent one knee and showed some more of herself. This woman walked around fully dressed and fully available.

She was Carlton's partial offering for my troubles. It was a gentle approach, as these things went, and it was smart. Carlton could use Meredith like a net, cast out to all the men who drifted into his waters. A man might have services or information Carlton wanted and wouldn't mind this kind of trade. In my case, the cops in a mushroom field were the first approach. The hard and the soft.

Two impulses were pounding away in me, and they couldn't live together much longer. One was the way it felt to have a woman who looked like this so close. That was good. The other was that a friend had ended up soaking the dirt with his blood at Carlton Stables—and she worked for the people who did it. That was bad.

I sat down next to her on the bed. She edged a bit closer, but that was all. She seemed to sense my concern and to respond to it.

"What?" she asked softly. "What is it you want?"

"There *is* something you can do for me," I said.

"Yes," she said. "Tell me what it is."

"Go over to the office and get me copies of every record on the deposits and payments in the past three years for Gates and Morgan in Detroit."

She didn't laugh or get angry or look away, but her expression shifted to neutral.

"I need all the correspondence that goes with the financial files, and most importantly I need documentation of the form of payment they used when they first transferred their money to Carlton. Form of payment—cash, cashier's check, whatever. That's very important."

She didn't bother to cover her legs, but she sat up.

"And I need everything I can get on the Hatley project. Market surveys, cost projections, break-even estimates. In particular, I'd like to see the start-up files, the ones that would give a clear explanation of why they chose Hatley."

She moved her legs to the floor and stood up. "I don't know what you're talking about," she said.

"And I'd like to see Carlton's own portfolio," I continued. "Especially the profits he made on the real estate transactions last year in the city of Chester. That would probably be cross-referenced with the Gates and Morgan files."

"You're crazy," she told me and headed toward the door. I got up from the bed and stepped into her path.

"Let me go," she said. But I wasn't holding her. I guess the words were.

"Why don't you let me help you?" I said.

She laughed, just a little. "Help me?"

"Sure," I told her. "Maybe you don't see it now, but you're in trouble. You're living on the edge. Take a look at the people you work with. Look at what they did to Simon Griffey. Better yet, look what they did to Greenwell—he was one of their own. Torn to shreds by dogs. You're not immune."

She tried to go around me. I grabbed her arms and held her still.

"This isn't going to end until I've made an arrangement with Carlton," I said. "And that arrangement will cut into his business. What do you think that'll mean for you?"

She kicked me, and she had decent strength. The condition I was in helped her out. She bruised my shins. I held her as still as I could and farther away from me.

"There's something else to worry about, too."

She stopped struggling for a second.

"Reidus. Has he ever shown any interest in you?"

"Never."

"Aren't you curious about why? Did you ever think about what would happen if things went sour at Carlton Associates? Do you suppose Reidus would just ignore a woman like you?"

She didn't answer.

"You know what he does," I said. "What if he does it to you?"

I let go of her and she just stood there.

"Carlton can't stop Reidus," I told her. "Even if he wants to. Work with me to put the case together now, and I'll help you. It's your best chance."

She walked to the door, smoothed her hair, and straightened her dress.

"Think about it," I said. "Think about what these guys do."

She was gone.

20

WHEN I GOT TO the *Tribune* building, Baines was waiting for me in the lobby. He was wearing a gray suit with a red tie, and a downcast face. I had the photos and negatives. He came up to me but managed to avoid my eyes, then led me out of the building without saying a word. We walked a half block to his car, where he opened the trunk and took out a large manila envelope filled with notebooks and documents. I handed him the dossier. He gave me the envelope. I stepped back because he looked like he needed the room.

"I'm sorry," I said. "I'll return your notes as soon as I'm done."

He took in a deep breath. "Sure." That's all he said.

I took the stuff to my car and drove to Hatley. As always, the rolling pastures and horse land was beautiful. I didn't give a damn.

There were enough flowers in George Howard's hospital room to start a garden. His head was propped up, the rest of him tucked in to limit mobility. His face was bandaged, but he could speak and see. He was a big man, and I thought about how many men it would take to beat him. I pulled up a chair and introduced myself.

"I'm here because of Chris Baines," I said. "He's the reporter who talked to you just before the beating."

"That's right," Howard said. "I remember him. Good man. You work with him? You another reporter?"

"No. Kind of a friend."

Howard didn't know about the two dead bodies found at Carlton Stables. When I told him about Simon and Greenwell, he paled and

128

coughed. I thought I might have to call a nurse. When Howard calmed down, I told him that Baines was sick and might be out of action for a while. "I'm looking into Carlton's business, some of the things Chris was working on. I thought you could help me."

"If you're serious about it, then I'll help," Howard said. "But you've already lost a friend. And look at me. You sure you want to get into this mess?"

"I'm already in it. I know some of what Carlton is doing to Hatley. What I don't understand is, Why? Do you know?"

"I keep turning it around in my head and I still have no idea," Howard said. "Maybe I'll never know. There's absolutely nothing special, in terms of making money, about this land. No gold or oil that I know about. Nothing like that. Just houses and people. It makes no sense." He stopped to take a breath and closed his eyes for a moment.

I gave him some time, then asked, "Do you know if he has any specific plans for the land?"

"Firsthand, I don't know anything for sure. I can tell you what your friend the reporter told me. He said he'd seen records that showed that Carlton Associates planned to turn the land into some kind of private community, with a giant mall and all sorts of special luxuries. But only for his friends or people who could afford it. Not that I believe any of that, or understand it. But that's what he said the records show."

"Why Hatley?"

"No idea," Howard said. "I've lived in Hatley all my life and never planned to leave. My family and my neighbors' families built this town. Barfield. Wilson. Griffin. Howard. Every one of those families is still here, lots of others, original residents. Some date back to before the Revolution. This little town goes way back, almost three hundred years, even before they had the names for the thirteen states. For some of us, it's like a different world. Quiet, friendly town. Boring, if you come from Philadelphia or New York, the kind of place some young people would never come to. But we've sustained it. Original families, that's why. I can see the world turning outside, I know what's going on with the new developments and the prefabricated suburbs. But we want no part of that. We're happy with the little piece we have."

I nodded my understanding, which was totally sincere and meant to be encouraging. It was clear that the people of Hatley had managed to preserve age-old values that were dying elsewhere. Why would Carlton want to take that away?

"We've never had any major trouble here," Howard went on. "Then, about two years ago, the town got jinxed. First, a few people had bad luck. Warner Marshall couldn't make his mortgage payments, next thing we knew, he's out of his house. An out-of-town real estate company shuts down the property. No "For Sale" sign. Nothing. Sits there. Vacant. Same thing happens with the Duncans. The Williamses. Then we have this thing where several local kids are sexually assaulted—raped, fooled around with—it's unbelievable—in one of our neighbors' houses when the family is away. We're all in shock. The kids swore that Jim Brenley, a family man who's never before been in any kind of trouble, hurt them. There were things they found in the house—Brenley's personal items. Brenley denied it, and most of us believed him. But the experts tell us kids don't lie about these things, and that made sense too. It never got to court or anything. To protect the kids somehow. But the kids' families wanted to kill Jim and anyone who sided with him. Then Brenley's house caught fire and burned down. Tore the town apart."

Howard stopped to drink some water. He looked tired.

"Everywhere you live you get differences. Here too. But we're a town of relatives and friends. Always, always, we've worked things out. Then these things come up, out of nowhere, and all at the same time. We hardly get a chance to handle one thing when there's another. Like we were cursed."

At the same time all this was happening, Howard said, out-of-town real estate brokerages started buying homes from people who had any kind of money problems. "And everyone does, sometimes," he said. "When the problems hit, like with Brenley, the brokers used it. Sales pressure, hard sells, good offers, and at least one of the brokers actually made threats, by telephone. I know it. I can't prove it, but I know it.

"The connection between the brokers' buying and the troubles in the town seemed obvious to me—but I'm a contractor. Most people didn't see it that way. It's hard to believe, right? That real estate brokers would be involved in something as horrible as assaulting children? And why? None of it made any sense.

"People got scared. People who'd lived their lives here were willing to sell. Blocks were abandoned, houses were vacant, some boarded up. It was panic that did it."

Six weeks ago, Howard said, he'd gotten together with a local real estate agent and pulled property records. It was then they found that all the brokerages were owned by Carlton Associates. Howard and a couple of friends had tried to get help. They went to the police, FBI, newspapers, local television.

"They weren't interested," Howard said. "They thought we were kooks. It's hard to explain. To them, our complaints sounded like sour grapes, like I'm a contractor and I lost business to Carlton. No proof of anything. So what if Carlton was buying land. That's what they do, right? They're in real estate. We couldn't tie the other stuff to them. That's when I met up with your reporter friend at the planning-board meeting. I told him. I know he believed me, probably because he knew other stuff about Carlton, right?" He looked at me and I nodded.

The night after Howard had met with Baines, he was attacked on the way home. It was only one man, he said. "The guy was an animal," Howard said. "I'm in pretty good shape and I never had a chance. I never even saw his face."

I asked Howard if he knew a man named Reidus, and Howard said he didn't. I described him, but Howard said he didn't sound familiar. I tried to picture Reidus next to Howard, and kept coming up with Reidus being the smaller man. I knew you could learn to fight, and it wasn't just size that mattered; Reidus was capable of *anything*.

"It's crazy," Howard said. "Land's so available around here, why destroy our town? Whatever his reasons, we can't stop him. If he killed a private detective and got away with that, what can *we* do?"

"I have an idea," I said. "I'll tell you what I've been doing. I'm pretty sure there's no way to make a legal case on the murder. In all likelihood, it's probably hopeless to try for a direct trail to the killer, although I'm sure it was Carlton or his people who did it. But there's another approach. I've basically been gathering information about Carlton's operations. Not looking for evidence in the killing, but pulling together every string that's out there on all his other dealings. What's been going on in Hatley might be the key. No matter what we end up doing, it'll take some kind of evidence, and that's one thing you and your friends in the town already have plenty of."

131

"What do you mean?" Howard said. "We couldn't get the FBI to believe us, and we don't have any real evidence. No pictures. No documents or anything."

"You have more than you think," I said. "Not all cases rest on documents or pictures. In some cases all you need is a lot of credible testimony about what's going on. One of you going to the FBI is just someone from a small town with a gripe. Two hundred consistent and corroborating statements is another story, the kind that gets authorities rolling. But we'd need cooperation from everyone who's lost a home to Carlton, everyone who's been threatened or worse. It won't take much money or much time. It'll take courage and staying power. The people from the town will have to stick together again. Carlton's people might come back at all of you with pressure, but this time we'll be ready. Some of you will be offered money to drop out of this. There might be threats. But if everyone sticks it out, it would be possible to build a case strong enough to get Carlton to change his plans."

"What would we have to do?"

"I'd get some lawyers to come down. People would have to give statements to them. Make formal complaints. Sign affidavits, be willing to testify. Party A against Party B. That's all. I'll take it from there. But people have to be willing to talk and sign papers."

"The problem with going to court, though," Howard said, concerned, "is that the damn thing takes so long."

I smiled. "The goal is not to have to go to court. The goal is to make a deal." Making a deal was an easier concept for most people to swallow than blackmail.

As I drove out of Hatley, I noticed how the back of almost every house touched woods or low grass, as if bordering on a natural commons. I pictured crowds of children and pets being let out of the houses in the cool autumn evenings to wander at will over the land. There was a remarkable lack of commercial development. It wasn't a place where one could congregate at the Pizza Hut. I could see Howard's point about a very low turnover in a town like this. Moving to Hatley had to be a more limited and personal decision than people usually made when they were filling out their lists for what they wanted in a place. The local school must be great. Probably old-fashioned, not at all innovative.

PAYBACK

Hatley was the kind of place you could love only if you had low expectations for excitement and little personal ambition. That, and a strong desire for decency. I felt like moving right in.

I was driving fast now on the narrow roads that ran through woods and breakout patches of green land. As soon as I got out of Hatley town limits, a Wakefield patrol car appeared behind me. This time the lights were going, the siren was on and there were two different cops. They arrested me—on charges of assaulting officers Hayes and Evans—and treated me the usual way. They frisked me, cuffed me, read me my rights, put me in the back of the police car, and drove to the Wakefield jail.

21

As THE SUN CAME UP, the streets outside the police station slowly grew brighter, one perfect notch after another, as if the world's steadiest hand were turning up the juice. Up above, clouds and sidestream fog and the occasional airplanes cloaked the spreading light in tiny patches, but still the light came on.

In the twenty-six hours I spent in the jail, I saw several people sleep and wake, and not one of them had the rhythm of the outside world right. Guys in the cells had stayed up long past sundown and woke in the hours before the sun rose, responding to their internal calls to roll and stretch, feeling the pokes and eddies of strong poisons coil and spring and ebb, each one marked and sullied by the alcohol and drugs that had led them here.

It was dark again when one of the sheriffs came back to tell me I'd been bailed out. That was as much a surprise as anything I'd seen or heard in the cell. I hadn't spoken to anyone since they'd locked me up. They hadn't let me make a phone call or talk to the captain or anyone else who might have been in charge. The man with the bail money was Steve Foley.

Foley took me to his car. He told me that the newspaper had gone along with putting up the bail, a courtesy for a visiting reporter, sort of. Although, he said, looking glad about it, he'd had to prod them a bit about their sense of duty. He felt that I had been there to help Baines, and it was the right thing to do. Foley told me he also had something else in mind.

He said a woman had called the *Tribune* anonymously, asking for

Baines. Foley was given the call and he'd convinced her to meet with him, but she was nervous because of the murders. She'd agreed to see him that night at a building just outside Kennett Square.

"I told her you'd be with me," Foley explained in the car as we drove to meet her.

The sun had set hours ago, but it was still much too hot, and Foley's air conditioner wasn't very good. All this movement made no sense. First they beat me up, then they send me a woman; they lock me up, then they take me out for a ride with a messenger whose explanations are as flimsy as toilet paper. Either more than one guy was calling the shots, I thought, or someone doesn't know what he's doing. Or he knows, but isn't using the same logic the rest of the world follows.

Foley was pathetic. He kept chattering about the declining quality of newspapers in America. I found myself listening not to the words but to the cadence of his complaints, and the occasional energy born of his bitterness.

"Newspapers aren't run by editors and reporters, but by circulation and advertising executives," he was saying. "The high-level meetings are between the company president, who's a businessman, and the circulation and advertising people. No journalists in the room. They chart population shifts and reader trends. And the trends have nothing to do with hard news. It's special feature sections, advertising, comics, local sports—so-called 'mass appeal.' "

I'd heard reporters talk like that before. Usually the tone was more muted, accepting. Most reporters were decent and managed to do a good job despite the problems. Foley had given up.

We turned off Cedar Spring Road and drove a short distance on a dirt road. The area was mostly weeds and tall grass. We came to a large building with lettering on the side that said "South County Depot Company." Foley stopped the car and turned off the lights. It was dark and the stars were hidden by a haze.

What was waiting in the warehouse? It certainly wasn't a new source on the story as Foley had said. It couldn't be more Wakefield cops, could it?

Foley got out of the car, evidently planning to enter the warehouse with me. He had no real idea what he was involved in. I had no idea myself, but at least I knew it was dangerous. Foley didn't seem to comprehend that. I didn't want him there. He could get in my way, probably would.

I grabbed him by the back of his shirt and turned him around. "You can't go in there," I said.

The reporter was startled. "What's got into you?"

"Whoever's in there," I said, "it's not the same businessmen you work for. I know you were only paid to keep an eye on Baines. Then when I came along, they only asked you to pass along a few messages."

Foley remained silent. I told him to get back in the car. He hesitated, then got in. He had the look on his face of a pinch runner who'd just been picked off first base: embarrassed. He drove off. I guessed someone else would provide a ride back for me.

I walked slowly toward the warehouse. The building was long and low. I circled, found a back entrance with an open window, and entered with what I hoped was no noise. It was one enormous room filled with wooden crates and stacks of cardboard boxes. The only light came from the harsh glare of an auto mechanic's lamp, which was facing the main door about forty feet away. Two men were waiting, partly hidden by crates about twenty feet back on either side of the door, expecting us to enter there. One was an older man in his sixties, with a rifle. The other was younger, with a pistol.

I crouched along silently until I was able to lie on my stomach in the shadow of a crate near the older man. I was motionless and therefore invisible in darkness. The older man looked nervous. He was sweating heavily, and he kept glancing over to the other guy.

One of them would do the talking, the other would be the silent backup, the muscle—probably the younger one. He looked slick, in a suit and black shoes. He was out of place here. The old man was dressed in faded jeans and work pants. He looked like he worked at the warehouse. It seemed odd he had the rifle. A rifle was more suited as a backup piece, and should be held by the one covering. A check of public records would undoubtedly show that South County Depot Company was owned by one of Carlton's corporate progeny. Perhaps the old man was the warehouse watchman. Maybe he owed Carlton a favor. Maybe he thought he owed Carlton his life. Perhaps Carlton had once pulled his son down off a ledge somewhere.

Then I realized with a chill why the old man was sweating. This was a kill. Despite myself, I was shocked.

I'd expected violence, but not a kill. Two murders? Foley and me? And that coming within days of Simon and Greenwell? It made no sense, so it wasn't Carlton's doing, I thought. His style was control, and this setup was out of control. It could mean only one thing. There was a wild card, someone irrationally willing to raise the stakes. It had to be Reidus, acting on his own. But why?

I looked at the younger man. He was calm. The professional. That meant trained well enough not to make mistakes. I'd have to force their errors.

I searched for something to throw and found a few heavy, rusty bolts on the floor. It took me two throws before I knocked out the lamp. On the first throw—which struck the cement floor just in front of the light— the old man jumped forward, lifting the rifle. I took the mental snapshot just as I threw the second bolt. As soon as it struck, I made a run at where I envisioned the old man was standing. I reached in the darkness to where I thought the rifle would be. My right hand was a couple of inches high. I yanked the rifle down with my left hand, and the old man got a shot off just before I pulled the weapon away. He groped in the dark, knocking the rifle to the ground before I rolled off to the left toward some crates.

I heard two quick pistol shots and the thud of a body going down over splintering wood. The old man had paid back whatever debt he owed Jack Carlton. I could hear the other man moving in the darkness. He probably realized he had killed his partner and not me, but he wasn't waiting for his night vision to improve to make sure. He was coming for me now.

The warehouse was an enormous square, one hundred by one hundred yards. Endless rows of crates stacked on pallets mostly in parallel lines from wall to wall. It sounded like the man was edging his way down the far side of the building toward the window I had come in through. He was disoriented. He'd seen the place only with a light on. The darkness worked in my favor. I'd have the man from behind when he got to the window.

I moved slowly down an aisle. I was taking a more direct route, and would get there before the gunman. I heard the footsteps moving slowly behind me, along the side of the building. The man was lost, uncertain, looking for an exit.

Then I heard a gunshot, and right after that the sound of a man moaning. The overhead lights came on. I was staring at the young gunman, who was bent over, grabbing his foot where about a half inch of shoe was missing at the heel. His gun was on the floor a few feet in front of him. He didn't seem interested in the gun or me. I didn't see anyone else. Whoever had fired wasn't showing himself.

"Just stay where you are." I spoke loudly, as if the unseen marksman were my partner. The gunman hobbled to his feet and said nothing. He was tall and thin with curly brown hair and dark brown eyes. And he was in obvious pain, but he managed to keep quiet. I walked over in his direction and picked up the pistol.

"No need for that," said a woman's voice.

I shouldn't have been surprised. At least I didn't show it when Sara stepped out from behind some crates and walked toward me. In a long-sleeved dark shirt and black pants she looked like a man at first. Her long hair was coiled under a cap. She passed within inches of the dead guy and didn't even glance at the body.

"Who are you?" I asked the gunman, ignoring Sara. "Who's the old man, and who sent you here?"

He said nothing.

"Don't bother," Sara said. "He was working for Reidus. So was the old man. I saw them both meeting with him this afternoon."

"Have you been in here the whole time?" I asked her.

"No. I just came in. I was outside dealing with a guy who was planning on eliminating the guy who drove you here—Foley, he said his name was."

"How did you know to come here?"

"I was following Reidus and when I saw him with these two guys earlier, I decided to see what they were up to. Then I saw you drive up with Foley. When the two of you split up, I had to choose, and I chose Foley. I figured he couldn't handle himself as well as you could."

So it was a Reidus setup. But why? One of his games? A test, maybe, to see if I was a worthy opponent? Or to see if Sara could keep up?

"Let me guess," I said to Sara. "There's no way this guy would testify against Reidus. That's what you were about to say next, right?"

"Not if he cares about his future," she said.

I turned to the gunman. "Okay. Go find yourself a doctor."

When he was gone, I walked over to the old man on the floor. I knelt down and checked the body, just in case. No pulse. I felt a hand on my shoulder. "Come on," Sara said. "Leave him."

She drove me back to West Chester, where my Civic had been parked in a spot behind the police station. The town was asleep at 2:30 A.M., so we drove our cars to an all-night diner just off 202. I hadn't eaten a decent meal in two days. No sleep and no food were having an effect. My thoughts were racing. My mind was making lots of connections. Some made sense; others didn't. When the waitress brought the coffee and rolls, I picked up the cup and was suddenly aware that the last thing I'd touched was the throat of a dead man. Too many bodies were dropping.

The point of my deals was always to get things handled without pain. Reporters leave things unfinished. My job was to finish them—and neatly. But it wasn't working out that way.

Simon was dead. The old man was dead. Greenwell was dead. She didn't show much feeling, but it had to be harder on her than on me. She was new at this, and her father had died only months ago. She had made herself good at fighting, no doubt about that. She had a chance to survive. But that was all she had—a chance. I'd never met anyone like Reidus.

If she took Carlton and Reidus to the kill, she'd have no way out. If they won, she'd be killed. If she won, she'd be a killer. I liked her, but killing changes people. It didn't matter what fine distinctions she made, calling this bad and that good. It would come out the same in the end. You can't just stroll away. You take it with you, and usually permanently. One of my friends was a cop who shot someone to death during a robbery ten years ago. He never recovered from it. He quit the force. Then he went crazy.

I liked her, but it bothered me that she didn't say much about her father's death. She knew she was angry and that she wanted revenge.

139

But she needed more than that. You can't fix the fact that your father is dead by killing. You can't fix it by ignoring it. You have to face it, and face what it means.

I hadn't felt her particular brand of loss, but I'd had one of my own. It wasn't as dramatic, but it was hard enough, and it was mine. I decided to tell her about it. Maybe it would help.

"My father had a plan for me when I was a kid," I told her, after we ordered. "He was a minor league baseball player who never made it to the majors. I was going to be everything my father wasn't; that was the plan. At eighteen, it looked like I had a terrific career ahead of me. I put up great numbers in Double A. Then I got injured and couldn't play anymore."

She put her hands on the bench and pressed her back higher up, stretching against the black vinyl seat cover.

"I was sure my father was crushed when I left baseball, and I thought he'd never forgive me. I took a job as a newspaper reporter, but on the side I still scouted high school baseball players and wrote a baseball column—as if somehow I could make it up to him if I stayed near the game. Then, when I was twenty-two, my father died of a heart attack. At first, I hardly had a reaction; I didn't really believe he was gone. I didn't cry at his funeral, just listened to lots of old baseball stories with the guys from the leagues who showed up. After that, I stayed close to the game for a while, to stay close to him. Pursuing his dream even though he wasn't there."

She put a finger on the side of her coffee cup and lightly traced a circle on the rim. Her eyes were focused on me and she was listening intently.

"About six months after he died," I continued, "I was visiting my mother and I went up to the attic to help pack things and put away the old uniforms and equipment. One minute I was packing items one by one, folding everything neatly, and making a travel pack, the way you do it on the road in the minors when you're taking buses every few days. One of his uniforms stuck out of the trunk. I tried to force it in but it wouldn't fit. And the next thing I knew I was slamming the clothes into the trunk, then I hit the uniform to make it fit and it still wouldn't go in. I stood up and pulled the thing out of there, and then I pulled everything out and threw it around. And I slammed the trunk itself up

140

and over my head and into a wall. That wasn't enough. I took one of his old bats and started smacking the walls with it. Finally, after I broke the big attic fan and a window, I stopped mid-swing and got calm enough to ask myself: What the hell am I doing? And I realized I was angry about his dying because I was still leaning on him, living partly his way. His dying was like having something taken away, and that made me mad. And all I really wanted to do was miss him, and not be thinking about what was robbed from me.

"The next day I stopped writing the column for *Baseball America*, then I stopped scouting for a while. I could just miss him and it wasn't all mixed up. A short while later, I changed my name. My father had given me the first and middle name of the Babe—George Herman Ruth. When I first came up, the players kidded me a lot, but I didn't mind. Once I left baseball, though, I dropped it entirely, and only answered to my last name, Gray. When you consider what I do, I guess the name's appropriate."

She stopped playing with the coffee cup and let her hands rest on the table. She didn't say anything, but she looked different, as if maybe she wasn't thinking about her crusade for the moment. I thought I could see some relief in her look, a realization, maybe, that life does go on, that there's something out there other than Carlton or Reidus or revenge. All she'd been going on was tunnel vision: her father to her to Reidus. She'd resisted broadening the scope, but for a moment now, she let herself wander.

I didn't mind that Sara didn't say anything. All I wanted was to get her to start thinking that she wasn't unique. And that she wasn't alone.

22

MEREDITH TOOK A LONG ROUTE to Carlton's office, looking in downstairs first, as she usually did, to check on Reidus. She noted with relief he was in his office, which meant she'd be alone with Carlton. She felt comfortable with that, no matter why he'd called her. Reidus was another story, she thought. A wild card.

She came into Carlton's office with her usual assurance. He was seated when she entered, his head back and resting on the tall slope of his chair, eyes casually on her as he spoke on the phone. Everything here is rife with presentation, she thought, taking in the room. She was always conscious of the room as a display, a setting for the king, though he was other than that to her. He looked pleased with himself. It might be the phone call. Or maybe he assumed she'd slept with Gray, but had come back with no information. And Gray was still in town, seemingly ignoring any attempts to make him leave, almost as if he had inside information on what was coming next. Was he onto Meredith, somehow? Was she holding back? Carlton wouldn't ask her anything at first, she knew, but he'd bring it up when he was ready. That was his style. He always looked for signs of continuing loyalty. She could provide that, she thought, and she had answers ready. She kissed his cheek, then stepped away.

She'd met Carlton seven years ago at a conference in Washington. She had been working for a mid-sized consulting firm at the time, doing pretty much the same thing she did now, but for less pay. She'd been looking to move up. She'd always wanted to move up, since she was a little kid, an army brat, drifting from town to town each time her father was transferred. She wanted a place of her own, a house, a good car, maybe some land, and the right man. Traditional desires in an unconventional woman.

What she liked about Carlton, the first day she saw him, was that he was so smooth in the midst of all the sharks. The purpose of the conference was to teach businesses how to get government contracts—expert con artists teaching amateurs. People were hustling in every corner, or learning how to, and Carlton seemed so calm, above it all, taking in the scene as if for pleasure and no more. She liked the fact that he was there with his then wife, an attractive woman, who didn't seem to realize that Carlton was using her to win over some of the businessmen. Meredith recognized what he was doing with his wife, and when the time was right, she mentioned it to him. To her surprise, he responded by saying that she was correct, and he liked the fact that she was so insightful and direct. He said he was looking for someone new at his company. Eventually he offered her a job at twice the pay she was making, and one reason she felt so comfortable in taking it was that she knew he wasn't coming on to her sexually with the offer, that he really wanted her for the job. For him, money came first.

When Carlton divorced the following year, Meredith slept with him for the first time, and it seemed natural to both of them. They liked each other and felt good together. They knew they'd both have other lovers, and that was fine. As time went on, they realized they had something special, and it was even nicer because it came as a surprise. They'd never planned to stay together, but it had been seven years now, and she didn't mind at all.

Carlton was still on the phone, and he motioned Meredith into one of the armchairs across from his desk, then clicked on the speakerphone so she could listen to the call.

He had a yellow legal pad on his lap. He looked at his notes, smiling with anticipation. This was the way he always looked when he began one of his personal deals, Meredith realized. He enjoyed it so much because it was just him, like the old days when he sold things on his own. No meetings, no opinions, no staff asking questions. Just Jack Carlton, entrepreneur.

"How are you, Mr. Carlton?" she heard the man on the other end say in a warm and pleased tone.

"Fine, Matt, just fine. Sorry to keep you holding for so long," Carlton said. He reminded the man they had met at a charity conference last year. He asked how business was.

"Very, very promising. I just got off the phone a little while ago with a hospital in Wilmington. If everything goes smoothly—and I know it will—we'll have a major contract signed in a few weeks."

"Sounds great," Carlton said with enthusiasm.

"Oh, yes," the man said. "We've got two or three deals that should be completed by October. You know, I'm surprised you're interested in our business. But I appreciate it, of course. What can I do for you?"

"I've always been interested in Medisystems." Meredith knew that Carlton was lying. In fact, he had never heard of the company before yesterday morning when he'd spoken to a friend at a bank in Philadelphia. "Your company's not doing well at all, though, Matt. You've got debt up your ass. You're near bankruptcy. You know it."

"I don't understand, Mr. Carlton," the man said, now wary. "You want to invest? Is that it?"

"Invest?" said Carlton. "Don't you think I have better ways to write off my losses than by investing in your failing company? No, not investment. But I'll solve your problems. I'd like to buy Medisystems."

"Interesting," the man said. "Well, let's talk. We may be able to work something out. This is a great time to take over this company, Mr. Carlton."

"I already have a figure in mind, Matt," Carlton said. "I'll buy your company for nothing." Meredith looked over and saw him doodle a dollar sign and an arrow pointing down on his pad. She dropped back deep into the leather chair, resting her head, closing her eyes, knowing what was coming. "That's not a bad deal, Matt," Carlton said. "I take the company for nothing, but I'll take care of the debts. I happen to know that comes to about two million. You've got an interesting failure of a business. It needs energy and capital. I've got that, you don't. What do you say?"

Carlton knew Matt Randolph wanted to unload the company, even for nothing, just to get rid of the headache. For over a year, he had managed to do nothing more successful than to borrow money to pay

144

off debts. That was the position of many of the small companies Carlton managed to swallow. They survived long enough to take the five-year tax write-off for new businesses and to depreciate and sell their more concrete assets. While this was going on, they played the gambler's game of hoping for a shift in the weather, a sudden growth of demand— like the sudden surges in land development sales Carlton could generate. That was one reason the company was worth acquiring. There were also tax advantages a new buyer could reap, and at the least, the business was a legitimate shell Carlton could offer to his Detroit contacts who were looking for ways to conceal dirty money.

On the other hand, without either a business of his own or a buyout price, Randolph would have nothing: no money, no prospects.

"I've got to say no to your offer, Mr. Carlton," Randolph said somberly. Then he roused himself, still hoping to turn things around somehow. "I'm not unwilling to sell, but frankly your offer—which really is no offer—it's insulting, and you've got a mistaken idea about our debt load."

"Oh, I don't think so," Carlton said. "Your best sources of financing in the past have dried up. You managed to stay afloat last month by borrowing against a fifty-thousand-dollar inventory you didn't even own. Now I'm the last person who'd drop that anywhere—we all hate the Feds on our necks."

Randolph understood the threat clearly. His voice was strained. "Why do business like this?"

"Look, Matt," Carlton said, "you avoid bankruptcy, your debt nightmares are over. You get a night's sleep."

"Uh huh," said Randolph dully.

"Think about it. Because it's your only choice."

"My only choice? To be left with no job?"

"What do you mean, no job?" Carlton asked, laughing. "Didn't I tell you? I'm keeping you on as president of Medisystems. For the next year, anyway. You know the company better than anyone. I need you. At a salary of one hundred thousand dollars. And no worries. What do you say?"

Meredith was taking it all in, smiling. She'd seen this game before. Take a desperate businessman, split him open, seal him again, light him up, save him.

145

The man managed an unintelligible murmur. Carlton took it as a yes.

"Great," said Carlton. "You're a smart man, Matt. I'll have my lawyers work out the details. They'll contact you."

Meredith was silent as he clicked off the phone and came over to her. When he put his hands around her, and cupped her buttocks, pressing her hips and thighs against him and letting her feel him hard, her mood lightened. She'd been right. Whatever he'd thought about her meeting with Gray wasn't instantly damaging. Still, she wanted him to know what happened.

"This'll make you laugh," she said. "Gray is gathering a case against us. Would you believe—he tried to get me to give him records from our files?"

"I know, I know," Carlton said softly, rubbing her back with his hands and rolling his chin on her hair. "I know what he's up to. It's nothing. I'll handle him."

She took the weight of him without having to step back and without putting more pressure on the desk. She let their bodies come close without putting her hands on him, because he didn't like that. He liked to be the one to do things. He touched her in the same ways, the same order, every time. All he did at first was loosen her hair, putting his hands under it and letting it fall. She leaned her head back and he kissed her softly. She pressed forward, opening his lips and breathing into him. He moved his hands down to her blouse, opening it, touching her breasts. She felt his hardness through his pants, but not pushing against her. This was Carlton the way she really thought of him, not doing things to others, not aggressive at all, but—she searched for a word—protective, maybe just of her. The idea was a nice one. Everything he did was right, at least for her. Her legs felt warm, she opened them a bit. She reached behind to open her bra, letting her bare skin adjust to the air-conditioning, her nipples hardening, so he began rolling them between two fingers, with gentle pressure.

They kissed and he moved his hands down to her stomach, then kissed her neck. She wanted to be with him, liked the feeling of being naked when he was still dressed, and as always when she was with him, found herself more excited than he, unlike with most other men. That alone aroused her, the sense that she was unable to wait.

She pulled down the zipper at the side of her skirt so that as he moved

146

his hand under the waist, the pressure of his hands made the skirt fall. She could feel her legs getting hotter and she put her hands at his hips, holding on, slumping back a bit against the desk. He put his hands on either side of her and pulled down her remaining underclothes, rolling them down with slow motions of his palms against her hips and bending as he did. She could feel the warmth in the chilled air, his face moving against her body, licking from her navel to her thighs, his hands now behind her. Instead of leaning on the desk, she was cradled in his hands, and he was pulling her gently forward. At the moment she felt his tongue between her thighs, and his warm mouth, the breath and tongue of him, inside her, she made a sound of pleasure, a grunting, but low, and pressed forward again to feel more of him. She was no longer standing, really, but just held by him, and when she got even hotter, she was no longer standing at all. He stood up in one motion, the full weight of her in his arms, one shoe off, the other on, and he walked to the couch and put her down. She lay there, moving a bit to get comfortable, and watching as he took everything off, not hurried, but not slow either. He moved next to her and put a hand between her legs, and now she touched him as well, thinking to herself not about the excitement, which she did feel, and not at all of the times over the years she'd seen him grab at things and win, but instead about how gentle he was, and it stayed that way while they made love.

He was still on the couch when she left the office twenty minutes later. Carlton dressed slowly, then walked to the big picture window.

He was so good with people, he thought, and he'd never find anyone more valuable than Meredith—though finding new people, good personnel, was something he always looked forward to. One of the joys of moving to Pennsylvania had been finding Reidus, and he regarded the big man with the genuine affection he had felt toward any of the thoroughbreds he had once owned on his land in Michigan. There was nothing so advantageous as having the most talented horse in a race. Finding personnel was the key, and it was one of the reasons he was usually a step ahead. Within weeks of setting up a new location, he was able to attract the people he needed.

At the beginning, he himself had gone to bars and restaurants in the business district and had made contact with people he liked one by one. He'd made a few false starts at first, choosing men who had lost jobs for what it turned out were cosmically good reasons—they were bad salesmen, losers. Then he had come upon Billy Barrett, a find who was still covering tracks for him and keeping some boiler-room operations going in Detroit. Billy had bought and sold real estate so well and so illegally that the U.S. Attorney had made deals in which budding investigations were settled out of court, with one of the riders being that Billy be put out of business. Without a broker's license, he'd been unable to sell when Carlton had found him. What Carlton had known how to do—and this had never occurred to Billy, for all his talent with finding ways around regulations—was set Billy up with a new name and do the same old business.

The key was in having a boss who could certify that you were no longer actually buying or selling real estate, but simply doing, say, public relations, or operations like personnel management. You get one of those job titles, but then you go on selling land. No one at the U.S. Attorney's office ever even looks your way. Billy had been grateful, and had brought other men in similar situations to Carlton, men he'd been able to use to build up the business.

Eventually, Carlton always had to move. The number of victims who complained got too large, the number of agencies interested grew, and the increasing numbers of officials with hands out became prohibitive. When he did move, he traveled light. The only thing he needed on arriving in a new area was the basic account, which kept growing, and Meredith. Arriving in Chester County, as at any other place, the key was in knowing who else was operating in the same territory and getting to know them and their operations. And there was nobody better at doing that than Meredith.

Not all were willing to involve themselves, but there were always a few. And the information they provided her was usually enough to allow Carlton to move in on a few of the holdouts. Once in a while, a victim fell in love with Meredith. Carlton worried about those few, and always had someone like Reidus provide her with protection. No use losing a good associate to random passion. You never knew what could happen. The passions she stirred were sometimes unpredictable. He appreciated that, understood it. He'd be reluctant to let her go.

23

I RENTED A FORD and sat in it across the street from the Wakefield police station. Hayes and Evans were due in by six, and from what I'd already seen in the couple of days I had been following them, they were usually prompt. At 6:05, the two cops drove up in the patrol car, parked at the side of the building, and walked in at the front entrance. They seemed to be enjoying themselves, as usual. I could see through a large side window that they were joking with the desk sergeant.

A few minutes later, a young, sprightly-looking woman came from Captain Brock's office, and as soon as she saw Hayes, she punched him. He laughed, but it looked as though she had hit him as hard as she could. I could see Hayes take her arms for a minute, holding her at a distance; then he let her go and backed away, putting up his arms as if for protection. He had a broad smile. The woman looked upset. She brushed past Hayes, walked out, then drove away.

At 6:30, Hayes and Evans came out the front door, both wearing jackets and ties. They got into their patrol car. I followed. I'd seen this routine once before.

Cops break rules regularly. I've never known a cop who believed you could actually live a life obeying the law. It was obviously ridiculous. People had to have their own ways of working things out, and only when they didn't work them out very well did a cop need to get involved. Cops considered themselves some kind of backup for when the things ordinary people did failed, but in most cases they saw themselves as having to deal with people who weren't ordinary, who didn't belong in

149

the world, and who, if the cops had their way, should be taken out and killed.

After a few years of being a cop, one became convinced that constructive solutions of any kind were impossible. All that mattered was keeping the peace, and you did it for a while as you put in your time, and after you did it, another generation of cops would take over, and so on down the line. It was an endless war, and one that could never end, because the enemy was actually part of the neighborhood, part of the citizenry, a dark part of the self that could never be peeled away or isolated. And that was the great dream most cops had, that they could get to someplace, someday, where the sleaze was actually on the other side of some fence, kept away and observable across the distance as a definable "other." It was why every cop I'd ever known wanted to live in a television town, wanted to dwell in a storybook neighborhood, was a sucker for a home in the 'burbs, and why, when they retired, they always ran off to Oconomowoc and Wackatuck, places with Indian names and fish-stocked lakes in the Midwest, or places where the enemies were restricted to some other part of town.

Hayes and Evans drove slowly along Walnut Street in the small downtown, as if they were on duty, then pulled up to a sporting-goods store. Hayes stayed in the car and Evans walked into the shop. A few minutes later, Evans came out, apparently not having bought anything, unless it was small enough to put in a pocket. They drove away, and turned left on Packer Street.

The squad car parked in front of a men's clothing store. Again Evans went in, and a few minutes later came out with nothing in hand. The rush-hour traffic was pretty much gone, and I wondered how much longer I could follow the cops before they'd spot me. Just the fact that I was driving a rental, and not the car they'd stopped me in a few days ago, seemed to be enough protection—that and the fact that they were so casual about everything and would never expect to be followed. They pulled up to another shop. This time Hayes went in.

The cops' little protection scheme had the feel of a scaled-down Carlton operation. Maybe Carlton had inspired them. The notes and records from Baines helped fill out the Carlton picure. Baines was a pretty good reporter. He had interviewed dozens of people who'd worked for Carlton, then quit. They had described a small-time con operating big-time stakes. They described Carlton's methods for buying and selling real estate—basic boiler room with massive phone campaigns, workers reading phony scripts to customers. Worthless land became golden opportunities; brokers ignored requests from customers as Carlton manipulated the value of his phony land developments; they bought and sold land for customers without informing them of the transactions, getting them to sign papers the customers couldn't possibly understand. Everything described was in violation of a federal or state law or regulation, but none of it on its own was the sort of thing the government went after too vigorously.

Carlton seemed to get a special pleasure out of his more creative gambits, some ex-employees said. In one case, they described how a Carlton subsidiary won a $500,000 consulting contract from the U.S. Department of Commerce to study the effectiveness of federal auditors investigating real estate fraud. Every other week the company mailed two checks for $1,500 each to consultants named Boone and Kennedy. But Baines's efforts to turn up Boone and Kennedy had led him to the conclusion they didn't exist, that the names had been made up, and the checks were being picked up by Carlton or a messenger at a post-office box in West Chester. The nonexistent consultants' signatures were then forged and the money was deposited in Carlton's personal checking account. In its report to the Commerce Department, the Carlton subsidiary concluded that the government was doing an excellent job in detecting real estate fraud.

As for the Hatley plan, Baines had been able to get company documents that showed Carlton and Reidus were taking over that town's mortgages because they planned to rebuild it as a private community centering on a huge regional mall, a Carlton monument. It meant displacing hundreds of families and destroying a town that had quietly existed for generations with little change.

There were two major sources of funding for the new development, both dirty. One was money stolen from investment accounts Carlton handled for about thirty larger companies interested in Chester County property. Each month Carlton skimmed 5 percent of their interest profits. Records were doctored by changing the interest rates for all the portfolios

151

whenever money was stolen from some. It would take a great auditor to figure out what was wrong—and an honest and independent auditor to report it.

The other source of funding the ex-employees described was considerably larger and fit with what I'd found in public records. Baines had concluded that drug syndicates from Detroit were sending millions in untraceable funds to Carlton as investments in land and getting "proceeds" sent to phony corporate bank accounts in the Cayman Islands or Panama. It made little difference to the mob folks in Detroit that Carlton was relatively small, by their standards, because all they wanted was clean money. Carlton could provide that.

Hayes finally came out of the shop and got back into the police car. The two cops chatted with a woman who was leaning over the passenger window, her loose-fitting blouse keeping Hayes and Evans interested. After ten more minutes, the two cops drove off, slowly motoring down the street as if on patrol, then they pulled into a small shopping center. They stopped in front of a TV-and-appliance store. Hayes got out again. I parked in a cluster of cars and watched through the crowded parking lot.

Evans stayed in the patrol car, looking bored. I glanced around at the stores in the shopping center. Most were neat boxes, equally sized square parcels, all glass fronts, clean straight lines, the earth-toned steel framing the glass so that each store itself seemed a purchasable package. People walked by, many more pedestrians here than on the sidewalk off Walnut Street. People in suburbs didn't seem to like walking on sidewalks these days. They stayed in their cars or they went into malls.

I noticed a young man and woman standing by the nose of a small sports car. The guy was strong-looking, short, dark-haired, shirt open. On his arm, the pretty, long-haired woman with tough features was talking a lot, throwing her head back, laughing and doing a lot of work for a date. I noticed the guy's face; he was barely watching her antics.

It was more than five minutes, and Hayes was still in the shop. Evans seemed to be napping. I wondered what Reidus was doing. I'd heard enough of Sara's tales to begin to understand her obsession with Reidus. Howard and the rest of Hatley could understand as well. Carlton liked to think of his world of business dealings as a neat, orderly kind of place. But he had gone out into the woods and found a helpmate—brought something untamed into the house and called it a pet. He and I will get to a point, I thought, where we will want to do neat and orderly business. But we'll have to deal with the beast. Sara had said she'd call if Reidus roamed again in Hatley, but there were others who concerned me as well.

I'd managed to track down the last place Simon had been seen after he left Carlton Associates with the stolen statue. I'd tried forty bars on every road within ten miles of the Carlton headquarters. Simon would have had several hours to kill after he'd been to Carlton's and before we were supposed to meet for dinner. And he was the kind of guy who'd choose a local little bar to spend his time in. Most of the people I spoke to had nothing to say when I showed them a picture of Simon. But there was a place on 842 near Upland, a little motel with a bar up front, where a teenage girl said she recognized him. She said it was hard to forget because of the way he left: he was literally picked up off the ground near his car in the parking lot and pushed into another car in broad daylight. The man who took him was big, strong. I'd described Reidus to her as best I could, and she said that sounded like the man who'd taken Simon. That would have to do for the time being; I had no picture of Reidus to show the girl.

The fact that he took Simon so blatantly and in the open only confirmed what Sara had said about Reidus: he seemed to enjoy his exploits and he liked to have an audience. It was probably only a matter of time, I knew, before Reidus would visit the girl from the bar. After all, she was an eyewitness—maybe the only eyewitness—in what could become a case of murder. Reidus knew that. He'd assume she'd keep quiet. But if and when he learned she'd talked to me—and I knew he probably would—he might decide to further influence her decision not to talk to the police.

I could see that Evans had grown tired of waiting. He got out of the patrol car and went into the TV store. I walked to the window of the store.

Inside, in the back, Hayes was arguing with a heavyset man in his forties. I couldn't hear the words. Hayes slapped the man a couple of times, then pushed him against a wall. Evans rushed up and pulled Hayes back. The two cops exchanged words for a moment, then Evans walked over to the older man. The man said something, pointed at Hayes, then walked into a back room with Evans. A minute later Evans came out alone. He and Hayes started for the front of the shop, when the man came out of the room and yelled something to the cops. I was able to make out the response from Evans.

"No," he said. "Get that idea out of your head. Hayes is still the man, and next time, if you don't cooperate, he deals with you alone, and I stay in the car."

The cops drove out of the shopping center. I stopped following them. I'd seen enough. I'd have no problem getting them to drop their assault charges against me. I had what I needed to make a deal.

24

AT THE REAR of the guest house of Carlton Stables, Reidus stood alert in a large bedroom, listening carefully for the frenzied low growl of the animal prowling in the corridor outside. Dogs were easy to arouse, and persistent through the kill. He'd trained this animal for a year for the hunt today.

He looked out the window. In the shaded path not far from the house he could barely see the red-haired woman in her car, apparently watching. He liked that. Let her watch, he thought.

The hunt itself would only take minutes. Out in the yard he'd given the dog some rags with his scent, along with the command: kill Reidus. The dog was in magnificent shape, he'd observed happily, an expensive full-blooded German shepherd. It was intelligent and had strong emotions. Reidus had killed its mate in front of it while it was chained. He'd left the female alive to hunt because it was the more dangerous foe. Now the dog was stalking him.

He'd left clothing with his scent scattered throughout the house, which kept the dog in wild pursuit. He quietly raised the bottom sash of the bedroom's storm window now, and poked his head briefly out. He had several seconds' lead, as much as he could expect. He gripped the sash with both hands, raised his legs in a smooth lift and went out the window. He swung his body around to face the wall and raised his legs over his head in one motion so that he lay upside down against the wall of the house. He held his weight up by the pressure of his thighs and feet on the wall, taking the entire weight of his body on his palms and fingers. From below he would have looked like a huge spider pressed against the red brick. The roof was about two feet above. He heard the sound of paws clawing on the wood floor inside, the slow whisk and pad of the animal's feet as it moved from room to room. He dropped back down to the sill, then climbed the two-foot distance onto the roof. His landing made a slight noise, the thud of contact as he took a solid stance and raised himself to full height. He picked up a small bag filled with rocks and covered with the scent of his own sweat and hurled it down to the yard below.

In seconds he heard the harsh growl of the large dog as it charged out a side door at full run, its paws digging furrows when it stopped to attack the bag. In one motion, it snatched the sack in its jaws, tore at it, then jerked her head from left to right in a frenzy, so the rocks went flying off. It dropped what was left of the bag, turned, and headed back for the house. It was whining as if hurt, growling at the same time, teeth pushed out for attack, lips back. Reidus leaned over the roof and yelled. The dog raced inside the house, taking two flights of interior stairs in seconds. It was in the bedroom instantly. It reached its head out the window, as Reidus had minutes before, looking up to the roof, barking wildly, its front legs up on the wall.

Parked in her car down the road, Sara heard the loud and furious barking, but saw only glimpses of the dog in the yard and then at the window. She saw Reidus on the roof; he was clearly working at something, and very intensely. But what was it? Was he hunting? She got out of the car and walked toward the house.

She could see Reidus scurrying on the roof as the dog wailed inside. He was indeed hunting. With the dog. But was he chasing or being chased? He paid no attention to Sara, though she stood in front of the house with her rifle. His inattention to her, she concluded, meant only one thing: he was being hunted. That meant he had no time for her.

If he was suicidal enough to fight a shepherd and give it an unchained chance, then maybe this was her chance too. She went back to her car to get a short, shiny tire iron and her gun. She headed for the house.

The door was all wood, with no metal sides or layering. It was unlocked. She went in. If she was right about the hunt, the dog would be focused only on Reidus and would ignore her. She'd be able to get as close to Reidus as she wanted, and he couldn't do much about it because the dog would be after him. If she was wrong, she still had the gun.

The ground floor was empty, and she went up the stairway, crouching by the top stair. She waited for three or four minutes, hearing the noises still above her. All at once a wooden bedroom door opened fast and slammed shut, and Reidus came quickly out, running full stride. Sara rose up and swung the tire iron into his legs. He turned into the blow, catching it on his calves, and not the bony shins, but he fell. She brought the gun up, but before she could say a word or get off a shot, he rolled straight into her. She heard the high whine and angry growl of the huge dog thrashing its claws against the closed bedroom door. Reidus grabbed her wrist and slammed the gun and it bounced down the stairs. Sara swung the straight end of the tire iron up at his body, aiming for the throat, but catching him instead at the shoulder. She felt the iron penetrate and blood slicked her hand, but she knew it wasn't enough. He grabbed both her hands and stretched her out so that she lay next to him on the floor. They were face to face. He twisted her wrists hard, numbing her hands. She was certain he would break her wrists and arms.

"If you want to kill me," he said softly, "you've got to hold onto your gun. Otherwise, there's no chance." Then he let her go. She understood. He was inviting her to make it interesting. She got up. The tire iron was at her feet. She was sure she could get to it. He might even let her. But she could hardly feel her hands, and she was badly bruised from the fall. She reached down for the iron but instead kicked a foot into the bedroom door. It cracked open. The growling shepherd came through at full speed, heading straight for Reidus. He was already up and running around a corner. She didn't follow. She limped down the stairs and back out to her car.

Reidus made it back to the roof, jumping a vertical gap the dog couldn't make. He looked at the shepherd from six feet up as it leaned out the window again. He knew the dog was practically rabid, wanting the kill. He also knew that dogs have almost no depth vision, and that was why there were virtually no accidents in which dogs went out windows, while cats, with better perception, frequently did. Ignorance

157

kept one cautious. To a dog, it was impossible to tell whether the space outside the window was two stories down to the yard, two miles down, or a bottomless abyss. Such a leap was unriskable.

The dog jackknifed back from the window to search wildly for another way to the roof. The only access was a short ladder leading to a light wooden sun-roof door. It had been latched from the roof side, so Reidus unhooked the lock. The dog charged the ladder, but its weight and momentum tore a piece of the ladder's first wood step off and the animal crashed on its side into the corridor wall. It scampered to its feet and jumped several times again until it caught the top ladder step with its front paws and clawed with its back legs for a supporting foothold. Stable momentarily on the ladder, it pushed its head against the thin roof door, opening it, then jumped up, too fast, onto the roof, skidding on the tar paper. Reidus was waiting behind a short brick chimney. He'd left scraps of clothing with his scent all across the rooftop. The dog ran furiously from one piece of scrap to another, snarling and snatching, gritting its teeth. Suddenly Reidus flung a small heavy object right in front of the angry animal. The object trailed liquid as it traveled and the liquid came across the dog's face like a comet's tail. As it did, the dog went crazy, foaming, snapping at the air, and running madly in fast circles. The dog smelled Reidus's scent on the package but also smelled something else. It was the scent of its mate, the one Reidus had killed earlier. The animal ripped open the package and in it, wrapped and tied, was the dead dog's foreleg.

Reidus emerged from behind the chimney, while the dog was still in a rage over its dead mate's limb. Reidus knew that in seconds the dog would sort out the smells, ignore what was death's reminder, and attack. He set himself. He suddenly ran for the roof edge. The dog immediately took off after him in a race the dog would surely win if it had more than a few seconds. Reidus threw himself off the roof, catching the edge at the last moment with both hands and flipping himself over the side. The dog skidded to a stop right at the edge, snarling and barking wildly.

The dog peered cautiously over the ledge. Reidus was holding onto the slightly raised wood beveling just below the roof's surface, his feet braced against the top of the window ledge of the house's second story. To the dog, he had disappeared. He'd thrown himself into the void. Its prey had escaped into another universe. There was still his scent but nothing else. Reidus braced himself stiffly and looked up. The dog, eager for the kill, leaned out, looking down. To Reidus, the edge of its snout made a dark circle over the clean line of the roof. With extreme speed, Reidus stabbed his right hand upward, fingers spread fully, and grabbed the entire lower jaw and part of the furred throat of the giant animal. He put enough pressure into his grip to break blood vessels in the loose skin and slacken the dog's clenched jaws and drawn lips. He then pulled the dog's face slowly forward over the line of the roof. It tried to wrench its head free from the vise hand, while snapping its top jaw futilely at Reidus's fingers. At the same time, it dug its legs into the roof to keep from moving forward.

Reidus knew the dog was trapped by its own conflicting forces: the instinct to keep from going over the edge, and the drive to complete the hunt. With a final surge of strength in one arm, Reidus suddenly propelled the animal out into space. He watched it fall the twenty-five feet to the hard bare dirt of the yard. It hit the ground head first, bones breaking from face to neck with full impact, loud enough for Reidus to hear its spine breaking cleanly before it convulsed and died.

Calmly, Reidus lowered himself back into the window of the house. He catalogued the damage. Both dogs were dead, but he'd planned on that. There were some scratches and marks in and out of the house, but at the stable that was acceptable. There were the bodies to dispose of. Carlton sometimes came in the evenings to ride. Reidus had time for everything. The red-haired woman was of great interest. She hadn't followed form; this time she'd approached him. Why? Was she working with Gray? He'd find out later. Filled with feeling, he raised both hands, stretching and touching the ceiling of the room. He thrust his head up and screamed for several seconds.

Sara hadn't seen anything happen for five minutes. There was only the still heaviness of the midday heat and the dust. Then she heard the sound from inside the house, the howling of an animal. It wasn't a dog, she knew. It was Reidus. The howl frightened her more than she ever would have imagined. She was bruised and numb, and now she realized that it wasn't the injury that was making her numb. It was fear—fear of Reidus.

She tried everything she'd learned about how to relax—closing her eyes; shaking her head; slowing her breathing; focusing on her limbs one at a time, imagining them tight, then trying to let them loosen. Nothing worked. She was physically panicked and she knew it.

The fight had been the least of it, she realized, though almost losing to him, almost dying, was unbearable. What shook her more was the ritual he'd been engaged in with the dogs before she arrived. In all her weeks of preparing, she'd come to see Reidus as a man who wanted attention, who performed his deeds for the effect they had on others. Someone who needed an audience. But the fatal game with the dogs had nothing to do with that. He did it on his own territory with no one watching, at least no one he invited or expected. It wasn't for the attention and it wasn't performance. It was something he did in private for his own pleasure.

Being so close to him and seeing, even in the moments that he might die, that he enjoyed what he was doing, and that he had no fear: that scared her.

She asked herself for the first time if she could really handle him. Until today she'd been certain that she could. She knew now, and admitted for the first time, that she needed help if she had any chance of stopping Reidus.

25

CARLTON'S DRIVEWAY was one of those winding affairs, wide, hidden from the road, landscaped to the hilt. Carlton answered the door wearing gym shorts and sneakers, a towel around his neck. His face was dripping with sweat. He gave a warm hello, then apologized for his attire. "Too much to do and not enough time to do it," he said. "But you got to get your exercise in every day, right?" He laughed.

He asked me to wait in the den while he showered and changed.

I looked around. I'd been in a number of houses over the years where people born with a lot of money, or who'd had the will to acquire it, had the chance to express themselves a bit, to carve out from the surrounding random lands the cut and jib and nooks and niches they thought of as their home. Especially the ones who'd made the money through some version of taking it with both hands stretched out and grabbing it from less aggressive or dishonest men and women. I'd been interested to see what they created for themselves, and what I'd seen hadn't been surprising. When people either didn't have much money or at least hadn't stolen what they had, their homes were almost always an inevitable mixture of the things they brought in new and the things their families and communities provided. I think it has something to do with continuity, with keeping in check the shifting way we all tend to be.

Carlton's home was nothing more or less than the kind of suburban ranch they piled end to end in places like Long Island in the East and Tarzana and Northridge in the West. Long, low, inviting. Homes had messages, and this one said, I am perfectly friendly and open and your

161

kind of guy. It was the kind of house you'd expect someone to have if they had no secrets, if they owned a local store, had kids doing well on the local high school teams. A family, neighborly kind of place.

When Carlton came into the den, he perched himself on a small wooden bar stool. I sat on a wide, comfortable recliner. We looked at each other for a few seconds before either of us said anything.

"You think I'm a thief, don't you?" Carlton let his opening line sit for a moment, looking at me for a reaction. Getting none, he went on. "A clever thief, of course. You figure I cover everything with good paperwork, and great lawyers and accountants. But the bottom line is, you think I don't know truth from lies."

I stretched, putting one hand behind my neck. Then I sat forward. "You called me out here to ask me that?"

"No," he said. "I have a deal for you. We want you to drop what you're doing and go home. The police will solve your friend's murder. If they don't, we will. The point is, I want you to understand what's going on, so you and I can do business. You see, you and I are similar."

"We're similar," I repeated.

"Yes," he said, with enthusiasm. Then he stood up and began pacing. "Don't you see it? I do. You operate in the open, so do I. You say you do good deeds, so do I. But you're a blackmailer. We've looked at your background. Our company has good staff, good connections. The way you work is, you get dirt on prominent businessmen, you come on to them as an aggrieved party, make a kind of deal not to go to the authorities, then take a fat cut for yourself. You count on the gimmick that you're helping other people by what you do, and that it's a personal matter to protect yourself, your morals, ethics—whatever you call it to yourself. And you take your little fee as if it were an afterthought. Do I have it right?"

I pushed back in the recliner without bothering to answer.

"We've put together a good file on one of your cases," Carlton went on. "A hospital in Hartford was profiting from fatal experimentation with cancer drugs on patients. Then you showed up. Shortly after that, they stopped the drug project. Take a look at this." He took an envelope from an attaché case and tossed it to me.

As I read, Carlton continued.

"Whatever your motives, it's blackmail. Or, in legal terms, extortion."

I found the documents fascinating. I looked up at Carlton.

"In this hospital case, you had evidence there were deaths, probably homicides, right? But you didn't go to the police. You made your deal, took your cut, got out. That's concealing evidence. Maybe even accessory to the crime. Do I have a point?"

I remained silent. They had done a good job of gathering specifics and guessing the rest. Some details were inaccurate, and there were no dollar figures, but it was clear that with more research they could fill in the gaps.

"You leave and we'll sit on the file," Carlton said. "You stay, and the files—this one, and some others we're preparing—go to a district attorney. And you can believe we'll pay whatever it costs to ensure the case doesn't get lost in local politics."

Carlton's voice was sweet reason, his expression benign. "Look at it this way. We had nothing to do with your friend's murder, you must know that. We'd like it to be solved. Leaving the case open is bad for our image. Maybe we'll bring in some good private investigators, the best. And then this whole thing will finally be cleared up."

Most people would think that the guy Sandy Koufax feared above all others was Willie Mays. Or Hank Aaron. But the veteran pitchers I knew, the smartest ones, had always told me it wasn't the great hitters that gave them fits. It was the rookies, the dumb kids, like me in the minors, the ones who didn't know enough to think. You stand up there on the mound, with all your experience and wisdom, and you stare down the batter after firing two fastballs over the outside part of the plate. You know the hitter's thinking curve ball, maybe change-up. The catcher's thinking off-speed stuff. You're thinking breaking ball. Everyone's guessing. So you fool him and throw another fastball right over the inside corner. Mays and Aaron just stand there, frozen, stunned, disbelieving: You'd throw me three fastballs in a row? You crazy? Damn straight I'd do that. Because I knew you'd never expect it. Strike three. You're out. But the dumb rookie isn't fooled by anything. He isn't even thinking, just swinging fastball all the way. And pulling it down the left field line and over the fence. The fool. He probably couldn't even hit a curveball.

That was Carlton, the rookie. He thought he belonged in the big leagues, but he couldn't tell a curveball from a slider. The thing is, he was going to take his swings. And that could end up being trouble.

I got up out of the chair and picked up a short black metal poking rod from the fireplace. I tapped it against my thigh rhythmically, looking at Carlton and the rolling pastureland beyond his wide backyard.

I walked around the room, then put the fireplace tool back in its holder. I looked at the pictures on the wall. There was Carlton, the businessman, the athlete, the good citizen. And there were his associates including Meredith, who looked great even in a dusty 8½-by-11. But no Reidus. Somehow he'd managed to escape the shutter every time it clicked.

"All right," I said, "let's talk about this for a minute. You take your evidence to a grand jury, to the D.A. I'll admit I'm the person who did all those things. But I won't ever end up in jail, no matter how solid your facts. Let me tell you how it'll work. For one thing, the criminal statute of limitations has run out on that hospital case. As for the other crimes, prosecutors will bring charges every time when it comes to a mugging or a bank robbery. But white-collar crime—that's what you'd consider my cases—that's when they slow down.

"Because, first of all, they have to prove intent, that is, prove to a jury beyond a reasonable doubt that the defendant meant to break the law. How can they show that with me? I'm certainly not going to say I intended to break the law. My purpose was to stop a scam, right? So then, who will they pull into court? The Hartford doctors who were doing the drug experiments? Remember, I'm still holding the evidence against them.

"Where does that leave the prosecutor? The next thing he considers is something they call jury appeal. That's very subjective. Like let's say a grandmother pocketed a hundred dollars a week from the cash register in the local hardware store. But then she spends the money to feed poor kids in the neighborhood. No jury's going to convict her, even with a confession. The D.A. knows that. He won't even bring the case.

"Okay, so I take money in exchange for silence. But who are my victims? Who have I hurt? And who have I helped? What kind of jury would convict me? The prosecutor goes over all these things before he brings charges. And how would it look—we're talking about public image here—for the district attorney to bring a case against a man who goes after swindlers?

"Are the cases against me solid on facts? Yes. Do you have your specifics right? Yes. Would I be charged or convicted? I doubt it. Anyway, I'm willing to take that risk. And even if you go ahead, there's no possibility any of these things would come to court for months—and I'm finished here by then and long gone. So why waste your time?"

Carlton didn't answer. He walked over to his desk, sat down, then quickly got up. "Hold on one goddamned second," he said in a stronger voice than he'd meant to use. Then he calmed himself and lowered his voice. "Isn't there some business you want to take up with me?"

I thought about it. The timing wasn't perfect for me to lay out my case against him now, but it wasn't too far off either. He seemed eager to make a deal, to compromise on something, anything, and that's pretty much the way I wanted him. But I wasn't quite ready. I needed a little more information, and the lawyers in Hatley weren't done yet taking depositions. He'd have to wait before we could deal. I looked at him with a relaxed smile.

"No," I said. "Not now, anyway." Then I walked out and drove off.

Carlton liked to feel the heat of her. She was lying with her back to him and he put his hand at the place the long legs turned into the soft tuck of her bottom and she moved her legs apart and opened herself to him. He cupped her in his hand and felt like he was up close to a fire. There was something about the image of holding his hand on a fire without burning that he liked. She pressed back, more to see if he wanted her than to start the loving. He kissed the back of her neck, lifted her thick hair up and let it fall. She put her hands over her head and let him take them in his own. He felt the softness of her hands stroking his, felt the softness of the rest of her with his body, and knew again how easy it was to forget everything when he was with her.

In the seven years Carlton and Meredith had been together, the account grew, and the comfort—when he needed it—stayed reliable, available, perfect. She took the care of herself that he imagined a world-class athlete would, and he allowed her the money and the time. The looks were the raw talent on which the whole thing rested, and it was useful as hell. It gave him the ability to be smooth as well as ruthless, to add image to the checklist of ingredients one needed to succeed.

She stirred and half turned to him, managing somehow not to move them apart.

"So where do we go from here?" she asked, her voice curious but at the same time calm and contented. It seemed more like a matter of idle interest to her, or anticipation, than a concern about what might await them.

He put his arms around her and turned her to him fully. He looked at her face, intelligent but not demanding—an illusion, he knew, for she had the purely human and inevitable interest in her own fate and its protection. He considered ignoring the question for a moment, and moving into her, losing himself in the busy thighs and the beckoning heat. There was only a gap of an inch between them now. But he'd been thinking about the very thing she'd raised, and she was entitled to some reassurance. What was, after all, the risk at this point? None, he'd concluded, and he told her so.

"The fact is," he said, the tone the one in which he occasionally told his temporary associates to correct some false idea they had, "we don't have to go anywhere else, because absolutely nothing's happened." He laughed out loud. "A man is running around town and thinking about me, and it means nothing."

He hesitated. He couldn't help but recall he'd often thought of himself in just that way: one man, alone, making his way successfully through a world of complicated and ultimately weak and empty challenges. It wasn't impossible, he knew, for one man to succeed, but whatever it was that Gray had found out about the murder, there was certainly nothing that could end up in court, and therefore nothing he could really do. That there had been a recent distasteful run of events he was willing to acknowledge. He hadn't been able to get Gray away from the area, and he'd achieved nothing in dealing with him personally. Maybe it was one of those currents he'd have to go with. He'd certainly lived with unpleasant realities before. The important thing was that none of them lasted or mattered in the end. The basic account grew, and, if need be, he moved along. He decided to share the thought with Meredith.

"But you know," he said, "if we have to leave, so what? I've actually been thinking about Santa Fe. It's gorgeous there. And there's the two of us, that's all we need, right?"

She smiled. The smile glowed at him.

"The only thing a bit hard to replace will be Reidus, but his kind of stock can be replenished. I'm sure Santa Fe will provide," he told her.

PAYBACK

The thing is, he thought, for those of us who have the money, we always survive. You get immune, you live in the stratosphere, you make it to this promised land, and nothing bad ever happens after that. Because there are no consequences after a while, and nothing you do ever really gets you in hopeless trouble, and even the places they put you when you get caught breaking their rules are different, and easy, and fine. It's work to get to the top, sure, but once you arrive, you never have to leave.

She hadn't spoken. Carlton had never given her a bad moment in all the years. It was something close to love, he thought, and he wondered for a moment if that was the way she saw it. He closed the gap between them and rolled on top of her. She had a strength for sex that seemed everlasting. Everlasting—an appropriate word for him.

26

IT WAS LATE AFTERNOON, and the girl who'd seen Reidus take the private detective in the motel parking lot was working at the reservation desk, near the entrance to the bar and lounge, and just across from the corridor leading to the guest rooms. She was young, no older than seventeen, and wearing a white cotton blouse and black jeans. Reidus had decided to pay her a visit as soon as he found out Gray had been to the motel. He was glad he'd had one of his men keep track of the girl.

There was nothing about her as a person he needed to know. She was a loose end, period. Whatever she did or didn't tell Gray was of no consequence now. The first act of telling someone a secret takes courage. But it is only the beginning. In almost all cases, telling a secret once is meaningless. It has to become a career, a commitment, a process of telling the same secret, with all its embellishments, varying each time according to the audience, over and over. If she ended up talking to the police and courts, the girl would have to tell her story to lawyers and judges, under oath and under cross-examination. So far she'd only told it once, and in an informal setting. Could she do it over and over? It was easy to interrupt the process at any point along the line, which was why the rules of the law meant nothing. Only violence mattered, and there law was inept.

He'd read once somewhere that Bobby Kennedy used to tell people that the mob could kill anyone, that the only safety lay in everyone's acting against the mob at once, so that no one killing could stop the wheel of justice. That was surely a truth, Reidus believed. Whenever something rested on the contribution of just one person, it was vulnerable. That was another part of why he never worried about the police. Because ultimately everything rested on people, just people, the weakest, most vulnerable link in any chain. Gray couldn't be naive enough to believe that this girl was a foundation on which to unravel a case.

He walked into the small lobby and sat in one of several armchairs. There was no decor to speak of, but it was a comfortable enough place. He was overdressed a bit in a black suit with blue pinstripes, white shirt and red tie. The girl looked at him right away, but there was no recognition. He expected that. He'd been wearing khakis and a polo shirt when he'd snatched Griffey.

The girl was no longer looking his way. He realized she had found a category to put him in—a guy waiting for a friend who was registered in one of the rooms. She had a nice face. The long blond hairstyle was simple, pretty. She'd been wearing the same outfit the last time he saw her. White and black. She looked good in it. He got up.

As he approached the desk, he saw her studying the register as if preparing to check a room number. There were a few customers at the bar for "happy hour," but no one else was in the lobby. He reached forward over the counter and put his hands under her arms. She started to pull away, and kept trying, but she didn't have anywhere near the weight for that. He bent back a bit, taking her up on his forearms, lifting her up and over the counter like a baby. She tried to scream, but he moved his hands down a bit and pressed both palms in and down on her rib cage, squeezing out the air. No breath. No screaming. He held her a few inches off the ground, so that only her toes reached the floor. She could barely breathe. Actually, in that position, she could do absolutely nothing, and the predictable—always the predictable, he thought—occurred. She appealed to him with her eyes. As usual, he saw pleading and the puzzled wondering, open-eyed, slack-jawed, stunned and questioning kind of look. Why me, why me? She did it well.

Reidus met her eyes with his own, which were empty. It was only justice, he thought, as he carried the weight of her back toward the corridor. Was it any more than she herself had done after seeing him with the detective? Had she questioned what she'd seen? People never

169

did. They saw what they wanted to see—the expected, predictable occurrences of the day—nothing more. So he was not concerned whether anyone appeared now and observed him carrying her out.

"There's no reason you have to die," Reidus whispered in her ear. Then he put her down. She didn't say a word, didn't move. He tried the doorknob to an exit leading to the parking lot. It was the easiest route to his car. He jiggled the knob, but it was locked. He looked around, saw no one, then stepped back and planted himself. He was able to build up tremendous speed in a small space by rotating his body in a half turn. He smashed his foot against the door. It burst open. The girl's eyes were wide. She'd learned something, hadn't known you could open one of her precious portals like that. The doors were nothing much, Reidus thought. People were nothing much.

He grabbed the girl by the arm and pushed her ahead of him. They got to his car with no trouble, and he drove off.

Sara had stayed in the background as she'd promised. She and Gray had an agreement. Gray wanted innocents protected if possible. In the case of that girl at the motel, Gray himself had exposed her to a possible Reidus assault simply by talking to her. He felt responsible. Sara was following Reidus anyway, so she could keep an eye on the girl if Reidus came calling there. She promised Gray she'd do nothing, only watch, until he got to the scene. Then they'd act together. That was the agreement. She called him from a pay phone, but he was out so she left a message on a machine that he had hooked up in his motel room. She knew he checked it every hour.

No one's life could be protected with Reidus around, she thought as she followed them out of the parking lot. At best, you might be able to protect only yourself, if you were prepared. She didn't like the situation. Protecting the girl might mean her only option would be taking Reidus out long distance, the one thing she didn't want to do. She needed him up close, aware of her before he died.

They drove east on 82, then north on Route 1 until Reidus took a back road into Brandywine Battlefield Park. The park was empty in the late afternoon. Sara waited for Reidus to stop, then parked her car a good distance behind his, stopping first at a nearby garage to leave Gray another message, giving him her location, and walked the rest of the way. Reidus must have known she was following him, but he showed no sign of noticing—either that or he just didn't care. She moved up slowly through the trees and spotted them in a clearing halfway up a hill.

Reidus was pushing the girl ahead of him. She suddenly turned around and the face she showed him was defiant. She threw her hair back over her head, a gesture that must have calmed her a bit, provided energy. It was a motion she might have used with a boyfriend who'd made her angry. It reaffirmed her looks, and Reidus respected that. Attractiveness was a potent strength, and she had that. But attractiveness alone wasn't much.

"What this is about," he said, "is that you have the idea that when someone comes around looking for information, you're supposed to tell them what you've seen, just as if you'd taken a civics lesson. In reality, what it means is that whatever it is you've seen, you've become a part of."

He then said, in a very quiet and polite voice, that she shouldn't have told Gray she had seen him and Simon Griffey together. She immediately agreed that she would never say so again if only he let her go. Whatever defiance she had managed to tap into for a moment, it was short-lived. She had no resistance at all. She wanted him to release her, a reasonable desire. He told her to take off her clothes.

He didn't bother reassuring her that nothing sexual was intended. If she thought so, fine. She didn't take her clothes off. He opened a box and took out a stun gun.

"This is increasingly becoming the weapon of choice for the average citizen in our larger cities," Reidus explained. "It's basically a portable battery, about as powerful as the ones in cars, but smaller because it doesn't have to recharge itself. When it's empty you take it home and plug it into any outlet. Of course, you couldn't buy this one—it's modified. The commercial models have some real problems. I've eliminated them." He smiled at her. "New and improved."

She was staring at him, following his words, focusing more on the weapon than on him, but she still hadn't moved to undress. He held up the box—a six-inch mold of brown plastic and metal dials—and turned it on in front of her. A small yellow light glowed on one side of the box.

The girl jumped back when the light came on, and at the same moment she let out a short yelp. Then she lifted her hand to cover her mouth, as if to silence herself.

He smiled. "You see these small knobs that look like tiny arrowheads?" He pointed to the two small front end parts of the box. She nodded. "These are attached to two thin lengths of wire, about ten feet or so. When I press this button it fires the little arrows out and they attach themselves to whatever they reach. They're shaped like little burrs, so what they're best at attaching themselves to is clothes. If they're fired at skin they may or may not actually stick in, and if they do, they're easy to pull out. You just grab them, like the body of a tick, and pull them out."

She blinked, and he could see that telltale film of moisture in her eyes. Sometimes even the men got that way. It was interesting. He liked the sight of it.

"Of course," he continued, "what might stop you from doing that is that the person with the box might meanwhile have pressed the same button a bit deeper." He showed her the button again. "In that case, the box fires an electrical charge through the wires, hundreds of volts, enough to temporarily shut down muscular control. The very first thing that happens is that a person loses control of his bowels." He again smiled at her. "Understand what I'm saying?"

He pointed the box toward her, shaking it a bit so that the small arrowheads reflected the light.

"What you need to do is to start taking your clothes off. The more parts of you that become nude, the less likely that I'll fire this thing and that if I do the burrs will stick. The quicker you take your clothes off, the better your odds."

He could see by her face she'd already lost all control, but she was responding nonetheless, her fingers unbuttoning the two small white buttons at the throat of her blouse, then quickly lifting it over her head. She removed her jeans next, then her shoes and socks, moving fairly quickly. Reidus felt no need to fire; she was fully cooperative. Then she hesitated and Reidus could see she needed reminding to take off

172

her bra and her panties. Reidus considered the targets her nipples made, but the spurs weren't positioned well enough apart to make that possible. He felt a brief flush of interest. He loved the outdoors as a setting for sex, but there was the matter of Gray and Sara—surely they were somewhere near, if not watching already, and he didn't want to begin a defense with that much of a handicap. He glanced at his watch. He'd already had a half hour. They were holding back, he reasoned, perhaps because he hadn't really done that much yet. He could have killed the girl any time. What made them think he wouldn't?

She was barely managing to speak, but she started talking anyway. "Please," she begged. "I won't tell anybody anything, not about today, nothing, please. . . ." She was practically dancing as she spoke. Whenever the breeze wafted into her, brushing her thighs, for instance, she squeezed her legs together, or turned slightly in the wind. She was afraid to change her posture in any way, apparently feeling she had to keep facing him, looking at him. He fingered the box, waiting for the impulse to strike. He could practically put the thing on automatic pilot and not even make a decision to fire or not, but just let the motion of his fingers respond to the wind, as the girl's body was doing. He could wet his finger, say, and if the wind struck and he felt a sudden chill, he could fire for just that reason and no other. He looked at the girl and said nothing. There was still no sign of Gray or Sara. But soon, soon.

"Go ahead," he said to the girl in a soft voice. "Cry. Maybe I'll just let you run away. Let's see what happens."

The girl was already at the edge, but he'd extend it a while, maybe use the gun on her to make absolutely sure she'd keep the pain in mind, never tell any more secrets. Perhaps Gray and the red-haired woman would want to play. It was his place, his play. Time for him to draw it to a close. He pushed the girl down onto the grass. Her back was near a tree.

Suddenly he spotted the redhead. She must have decided she couldn't let him take it any farther. But where was Gray? He wanted them both. He felt deprived.

She stepped out from the woods, making herself visible to him. The range was about thirty feet. She aimed the rifle his way; it was the same one she'd had in Hatley, and he knew she was good with it. When she was mid-stride and unlikely to squeeze off a shot, he grabbed the girl's

173

wrist and twisted her around between himself and the redhead. He twisted the girl's wrist slowly, letting her body move like a puppet in response to each twist. Buttons, just pushing buttons, Reidus thought.

He twisted again, first one way then the other, letting the girl's legs rise and plant, her thighs and buttocks turning each time he moved her wrist. Then he began to slow down the motion, his eyes on the mouth of the rifle. The redhead could shoot his leg, then perhaps put a bullet through his lung. She might get his head, but he had quicker movement in all the extremities, including the head. You really had to go for the trunk. But she didn't want to kill, did she? He hoped not. He enjoyed the play of it.

There was a breeze coming through the woods, stirring up the dust and ash at the base of the tree. There was a swatch of red leaves and charcoal dirt, like a path running between Reidus and the redhead, the ash the residue of small fires people had set in the park late at night. There was no sign of litter, no aluminum cans, but the natural beauty of the woods was organized, nonetheless, into patches of color.

He let the girl's weight rest now. She was positioned perfectly, the stance itself taking her weight. If she could only appreciate it, she'd realize she might never have stood as perfectly as this on her own. Her posture was superb. He noticed the straightness of her spine. This was what dance instructors and karate trainers took years of practice to achieve, the totally relaxed surrender of the self's usual physical stiffness and restraint. She was nude and had lost all self-consciousness. It was egoless perfection, letting someone else do everything. It was a perfection of the physical without consciousness, a talent, like that of the retarded child who can do complex calculations.

"Look at this," he called out. "Isn't this great?"

"You sick son of a bitch," Sara said. "Let her go right now or I put one in you. This time for real."

"The thing I've noticed about you," Reidus said, "is that you never seem to rush into anything, never panic. Look at all the opportunities you've already had for decent shots—you haven't taken any."

"I'm going to tell you who I am first."

"Oh, no," Reidus said, "let's not do that yet. Besides, I'd have to kill the girl. Don't you have orders or something to keep her alive? Where's your friend, anyway?"

He noticed at that moment the appearance of a squirrel at the base of the tree to his left, the small shaking of the bush signaling its arrival. He suddenly squeezed the box in his right hand in a smooth motion and the twin wires shot out, pinning the animal back to the tree. He pressed down on the trigger at the top of the box. The voltage effect was instantaneous, the squirrel surged back. He held the button down and convulsed the animal over and over, killing it. He held the girl in one hand and kept the animal tethered with his other, then looked up at Sara and smiled. He pulled the wires back from the animal, pushed the girl in front of him and aimed the stun gun at her. It was while Reidus was juggling, keeping the girl between himself and Sara, and at the same time whipping the wires back and forth to free them from the dead animal, that Gray showed up.

I came at them cautiously, seeing that Reidus and Sara were frozen in some kind of preamble to a fight, noticing the naked girl was caught in the middle. I recognized the stun gun in Reidus's hand—I'd seen them in the hands of police in several cities. They were the newest technology for torture, and they left no permanent marks. It looked as if he hadn't used it yet on the girl.

Sara and Reidus were faced off, posturing. I had only one objective: to get the girl out. I wanted Sara to survive, but, as she had endlessly reminded me, she would choose her own way, and didn't want rescuing. At the moment, she certainly seemed in no danger. She was the one with the rifle.

The main thing was the stun gun. They usually weren't all that reliable. The lag time between the planting of the burrs and the firing of the charge varied from shot to shot by as much as several seconds. It was also often true that the wires themselves were not in good shape and didn't carry the juice well. Sometimes, merely shifting position, or forcing one of the burrs out of position, weakened the charge. Long shots. Expectations were the key. And physical momentum was the way out. If you could just commit yourself to a certain motion, start it before the charge hit, then manage to stay aware when the electrical burst occurred, it was possible to avoid being hurt.

I measured the distance between Reidus and me. Reidus didn't have any other kind of gun so there was no way he could stop me from at least closing the distance. The girl would probably have to take some pain. But if she was breakable, she was broken already. If she was going to make it, she'd make it, even with that extra blow. I spared a last glance for Sara. She was showing absolutely nothing.

Reidus suddenly gestured toward the girl. Then there was the metallic pop and click of the stun gun. The wires landed on the girl's back. The electrical charge surged immediately and the girl began to dance, without collapsing, held up momentarily by the spasming of muscles. Sara kept the rifle aimed at Reidus but did not shoot.

I ran out and toward Reidus in a zigzag, closing the forty feet or so as fast as I could. Reidus backed against a tree, ready to take my attack, but I changed direction. I threw myself into the air, aiming at the space between Reidus and the girl. In the seconds before I connected with the thin glare of the charged wires, I readied myself, but it was more mental than physical. There is no way to prepare the body for a jolt of electricity. At best, you can keep the fear down. Maybe not. You take all your plans, thoughts, feelings, memories, everything you've got, and you put them in an envelope of flesh. Scatter it to the wind. You wrap it in cellophane, stake it on tissue paper, put it out, perfectly positioned to be torn up. You ought to be able to wrap it in a cylinder of steel, put it behind layers of bulletproof metal and bury it under the ground, do something better than tool it around in the most fragile thing there is.

At first it was one sudden sizzle, a hard line, a taut rope, something between a tickle and a sledgehammer joining every nerve. Even as the pain hit, my last sensation was the weight of the girl under me, and the thought—before all thoughts fled—that the girl, at least for the moment, was safe. It was true only for that particular second because there was no more than that. I'd worry about the next second if it ever came.

Given a choice, you back away from current automatically, like taking a hand off fire. But I had given my body no options. It was only a matter of falling. Gravity, not choice. The follow-through was out of my control.

I hit the ground like an apple falling from a high branch. Then the pain came, waves of it like trees blown down in a windstorm. I felt nothing for moments at a time, then the crashing again. When I felt nothing, I was able to see. The girl was free. The burrs had torn out of her when the weight of me hit. Reidus was pressing over and over on the charge trigger.

Information was meaningless. You can't make a deal, can't do anything, can't tie your shoes or sign a check. Where was that body anyway, and why couldn't it do anything? And then another wave of pain hit. My head just happened to be facing Reidus, and while I looked at him, something wonderful happened, and I realized it was my own plan. I'd been on the wire for only seconds, though it seemed like minutes, and the weight of my body rolling had jerked at the wires until the box itself flew out of Reidus's hand.

Now Reidus was unarmed and exposed. But even as the charges stopped, my hand just wouldn't obey my order to grab the box—it wouldn't move at all. I couldn't move, but I could hear, still slowed— as everything seemed to be—and there was a giant explosion behind my head. Only after I saw bark leap off the tree, did I realize that Sara had squeezed off a shot. I felt grateful for all explosions everywhere, and felt exultant about rifles, and women who could shoot, and all manner of foolish things. In another moment or so I came to my senses, sat up and looked around. The naked girl was curled up near me on the ground, and Sara was walking toward us. I saw woods, grass, leaves, and the ashen light of the forest.

I did not see Reidus. He was gone. Sara said she didn't know if he'd been hit.

27

IN THE SILENCE, the snaps and clicks the gun parts made filled the air as she moved through her collection. Sara was unloading harnesses and holsters of all kinds from a large leather bag and rolling out small, sleek packages of black and silver metal. Rolls of ammunition were tucked into fabric and I heard the solid clunks of heavy metal. One by one, she moved each weapon through the air, throwing the smooth weight of them from one strong, quick hand to the other. There was a silent music guns made when they were handled without being fired.

We were in Sara's motel room, one of a long series of places she'd stayed in the past few weeks. The room was a half hour from Carlton Stables.

We handled the girl as best we could. She had been in a panic. She'd clearly been grateful for us getting her away from Reidus, but she was numb and at the same time almost out of her mind with fear. After we calmed her a bit, her first words were that she wanted to go to the police. We started to explain to her that the local police were already bought off, but before we could even finish dissuading her, she'd changed her mind. She wanted to forget the whole thing. All she had to do, she said, was forget she'd ever talked to me, just as Reidus said, and never mention it to anyone again, and everything would be all right. We took her home and said we'd keep an eye on her. She told us not to, to go away, to leave her alone. And we did.

"Don't you think Reidus might go after the girl again?" Sara asked.

"No," I said. "He got his message across. There's no need to deal with her anymore. He won't bother."

She stopped loading one of her .38s, went to a dresser drawer, and took out a gray lead box. Then she went back to fixing the guns.

"He'll come now," Sara said. "For both of us, but one at a time."

I wanted to disagree, but I couldn't.

"You're right," I said. "It's no small thing that Reidus was willing to take the girl and hurt her in front of us so openly. But maybe we can handle him without the violence. A guy like Reidus isn't unique. There have been unsolved murders everywhere, serial murders. Reidus has probably been responsible for some of them. We could find a way to involve one of the serial-murder task forces—focus them on him, get them some of the evidence they need."

She glared at me. "And then what? Cut a deal with him? Reidus?"

"No. Just get the proper authorities involved and let them go after him. I don't know if cops have ever gone after him before. He seems to think he can elude them forever. He can't."

She got up, grabbed me by both arms and looked into my eyes. "No strike force, okay? Just me." She hesitated. "And if I don't—you will."

I said nothing.

"You," she said. "Not a strike force, not the courts."

She went back to her preparations. "He'd never get to court, anyway," she said. "He'd never let it happen. I should have shot him in the woods. I had justification when he was torturing the girl. I should have done it." She dropped both arms and shuddered. "It's just that I have to tell him why before I do it. I have to tell him."

She took a minute to gather herself. "He's out of control," she went on. "I keep half expecting him to kill himself, just on impulse. Take others with him if he can." She paused and looked at me. "I know I'm sick. Because I don't want him to do it himself. I want to do it."

I was watching her get more involved as she talked, and I thought she was going down herself, physically, the shoulders dropping. The usual stride she had, that went directly here and there with no hesitation, was slowing down. I wondered for a moment if she'd be able to get back from the edge she'd already crossed. I sat down. I admired her passion and knew I couldn't change her plans in any way.

"Well, maybe you can just listen for a minute to our other problem," I said. "I'm close to moving on Carlton."

I told her what I had so far, filling in details on the Hatley scheme, the laundering of mob money, and everything else from the public records and the Baines notes. When I finished, she sighed.

"I'm not sure I understand," she said. "You've got all those files and records and statements. What exactly are you waiting for? Don't you have enough for the Feds to get indictments? Enough to put him away?"

"Yes, that's pretty certain. A U.S. attorney could bring solid fraud charges in scores of real estate transactions. He'd have a good case of theft by fraud in the handling of several hundred federally insured home mortgages, and an even better embezzlement case involving about three hundred thousand a month, conservatively, from the real estate holding divisions.

"The clincher by far would be the illegal cash transfers from corporate investment accounts—millions. Carlton's company isn't big by any standards, but he manages to steal more than a lot of the big guys. It's as simple as bank robbery. Federal investigators like that. They know what to do with it in court."

"You put all that together in a week, huh? Are you that good?"

"Reporting in my line of work is a lot easier than when you have to write for a newspaper. I can fill in the gaps with guesses and I don't have to play 'connect the dots' with every paper trail. I just have to convince one person that I have the goods, and I don't really have too much to lose if I guess wrong."

Sara shook her head. "You've got plenty to lose. But you don't guess wrong, do you?"

She was done with the weapons and put them in a large bag, a leather carry-on. Then she went to the bathroom to wash her hands and face, and came out ready to leave. I was staring out the window at some kids playing in the parking lot.

"As much as I like you," she said, "I get mad when you talk about these deals. You lost someone, a friend—he was murdered. The cops aren't doing anything and you know it. Revenge—it's so clear. It's the only thing we have."

My back had been to her as she talked. I turned. "If I believed that," I said, "in my line of work, I'd have nothing but a trail of bodies behind me. That's not how I want to live, Sara. It's not a matter of mercy or righteousness. It's more practical than that. I deal with these kinds of people a lot. I don't want to become one of them. Call it a career choice. I don't want to make a living as a killer."

She looked at me, maybe as if she understood, maybe not. "And what if you can't prove Carlton or Reidus killed Simon? Then where are you?"

"That's what this is all about," I said. "I never will prove they did it. It can't be proved, not in court, anyway. So I have to take another route. You stop trying to solve the murder—that's a blind alley. Instead, you go after the murderer. Not to prove he killed Simon, but to look down every trail he's ever left, and eventually find a whole lot of evidence on things that could take him into criminal court on something else. That's when you can make a deal. That's the payback. Blackmail. You end up calling the shots, telling them what to do and making them pay you. They hate it more than any jail."

She picked up her bag, flung it over her shoulder, and opened the door. "I'll leave you to get the bars ready on your cages."

I watched from the window as she put the bag in the passenger seat, strapped herself in and gunned the black Z out onto the road, disappearing behind a curve and a cluster of dusty brown trees.

28

SHE WAS MILES from Carlton Stables when she noticed Reidus in the rearview mirror. He'd had that sense about things before. At times when she was following, and there was no chance he could have seen her, she'd observe his behavior change, the way someone adjusts when they realize there's an audience. She'd think at first that he'd spotted her, and was preparing a defense. But then she'd realize it was some ineffable instinct. He didn't know where someone was, but he knew someone was there. It was the same instinct that had put him into his car, heading in her direction, at the moment she'd been planning to arrive at his home and kill him.

He was moving up on her. She stepped up the engine on the Z. There was no chance of outgunning him on the wooded road; he'd use the Jaguar's engine and bulk to shove her off. What she needed were a few more obstacles or vehicles, something that would allow her to turn the advantage around.

He was coming up fast. She tried to stay out of her side mirror. That was the one Reidus could see, and she wasn't sure her face showed what she wanted it to: confidence. She gunned the Z and raced the three miles to the highway, climbing the entrance ramp to 202. As she squeezed on at high speed, a small van shot its horn in protest and hit squealing brakes to avoid her. She cut to the middle lane and zoomed ahead.

In her rearview mirror she could see Reidus make a similar entrance. He came up behind the same van, and the driver was so shaken, he

182

pulled over. She took the Z up to 75. Reidus was still advancing. She took it to 85, then 95. He continued to gain on her.

Up ahead in her lane was a truck carrying cars, econo-boxes, small American knockoffs. She pulled up tight behind it, as if she were one of the cars on the rig. Reidus closed in fast. She swerved off around the truck, then in front of it. Reidus pulled up in the passing lane next to her. Other drivers began to notice their dance, and moved away. She and Reidus weaved in and out as if they were actually enfolding the other cars in the skein of their movements. One or two of the drivers seemed oblivious, but most pulled aside or dropped back, disappearing into the whirling highway.

Reidus again pulled up next to her, this time on the passenger side, and opened his window. He leaned out toward her with both hands showing. It was a grand gesture. A bump in the road could have shot him across her front or off into space. It was a total surrender to the happenstance of road and fate. She dropped back so that she was behind him, but he wouldn't have that, and he switched lanes, slowing down, so she sped ahead. At their speed, all movement was relative. The patches of cars they passed seemed to stand still. Trees at the side of the road were moving backward. Clouds were approachable, active bulks that shook and jittered, rolled over and disappeared. Sara and Reidus were linked, twins, moving together through the world, a relationship only of iron boxes.

He came up behind her. Ahead was a truck, huge and riding heavy to the ground. Its dull slate back stood up like the bow of a ship, the tall wall sloping up to heaven. As she approached it, Reidus sacrificed his chrome fender guard's outer layer to push her forward.

She tried braking, but it was useless; she felt literally no effect, despite practically standing on the brake. He was pushing her up, slowly, into the solid slab of truck. She knew as soon as she made contact, that he would rock her side to side, and she and the truck would fall out of control, dancing one last rhythm before crashing off the road.

She grabbed the gearshift with two hands, forgetting the steering wheel, trusting that Reidus's intent to kill and the hard thrust of the Jag would keep her frozen straight. She grabbed the shift lever as if it were an arm-wrestler's hand and wrenched the protesting engine into neutral. The danger was that, without her engine being engaged, he could speed her up and push her into the truck directly. But from neutral she could shove the shift into reverse, and that was what she wanted. She popped the shift, and there was a scream of rending metal, and a plume of smoke at the hood, as if someone had tossed a match on straw. The car became dead weight and stopped helping the Jaguar along. She floored the accelerator, shoving the car at high speed into full reverse, which did no more than bump him back from her for a second by the resistance of the sudden gear burnout. Then, in the second or two he was a few feet back, she brought both hands to the wheel, throwing it to the side in one motion, taking her car off the track and into the side lane, leaving Reidus heading into the truck at one hundred miles per hour.

As she veered away, she noticed him beginning to handle the danger. She hoped the Jaguar would take a lot of damage. She headed for an exit, the Z still smoking, but moving at about seventy. There was a mall just beyond the highway exit. She'd be able to get there, and perhaps get inside, before Reidus caught up. It was all she needed.

She left her car near the entrance to the lot, ran to the mall entrance, and headed straight for the hotel lobby inside the mall. She registered for a room, went up to check it out, then came down to wait in the mall for Reidus.

Her plan was simple. She'd greet him, tell him what it was about, then kill him. Simple, except that when dealing with Reidus the word "simple" had no meaning.

The mall had five corridors on each of four levels, all running off a center display area, and two rings of benches around umbrella-type fountains. The upper fountain had stone animals in a cavelike pen, the kind that housed seals in a zoo. Twenty-three stories above, a huge skylight let in the sun.

A group of teenagers was playing with a large computer information board, getting some laughs. She spotted Reidus behind them. He looked calm, satisfied, in no hurry, as if out on an ordinary jaunt. Sara moved up quickly behind him and pressed the nub of a large bore revolver to his side through the thin leather of her handbag. At first, he didn't seem to react at all; then he laughed.

184

"Don't kill me," he said. "I'd still like to get to know you. I like you already. You don't need the gun. I won't hurt you."

He was incredible, she thought, absolutely confident he could turn the thing around. He would know just by looking at her face that she seriously intended to kill. Either he believed he couldn't be killed or he didn't care.

She told him to be quiet, and he was. He followed her directions through the mall and to the elevators.

"You're a fun gal," Reidus said, "and here I was beginning to think you were all business."

"I'm a lot of fun," she said, pushing him ahead into an empty elevator.

"Let me guess," Reidus said on the way up. "You and Gray work for someone in New York. What is it they want? Our accounts? Carlton's Detroit business? No, something better, right? More intricate. But you know me. Better make sure you kill me today, otherwise you get nothing, and I take what I want; or maybe you die. One more possibility: Tell them I might be available for hire. Don't waste this opportunity. What does Gray think? Why do you do all the dirty work, not him?"

"You want to know what Gray thinks?" said Sara. "I'll tell you. He wants me to stay away from you. He says vengeance and violence won't do me any good. That's what he thinks."

Reidus chuckled.

"But I disagree," Sara said. "I think vengeance will be sweet. My name is Sara Mitchell. Four years ago you framed a man for rape, Ben Mitchell. You and Jack Carlton. You ruined his life. Last month, he killed himself. But before my father died, I learned a few things about guns. When we get to my room, I'll show you what I learned, you sick son of a bitch."

"So that's what it's about." Reidus slapped his forehead. "Some adolescent revenge thing. Shit, I had this pegged bigger than that. By the way, I have no idea who your father was. You've got the wrong guy."

The elevator stopped and she prodded him out. They walked to her room. Just as they entered, she yanked the gun out stock first and slammed it full force on the back of his head. He staggered forward, his hands catching the corner of a dresser, and he managed to stay up. She came at him fast, swinging the metal in short powerful strokes at his side just under the heart. He went down on one knee, his arms

185

clutching his chest. She kept on him with fully extended blows to his head and neck, then just as quickly slid to his side and unleashed a rapid staccato of straight-up kicks into his gut. He was unable to stop the blows. His arms dropped, he let out a ragged gasp and fell flat on the floor. Blood flowed from his neck, face, and arms, and he didn't move.

. She reached in her bag for the tube silencer. Her hand was wet with sweat and some blood, and as she tried to screw the tube onto the gun, it slipped to the floor. She quickly dried her hand on her pants and bent to pick up the silencer. This time she screwed it on tight, then stepped back to aim. Even as she took position, she sensed movement. She glanced around quickly to see if someone else was in the room. She saw nothing. By the time she looked back to Reidus, he was standing in front of her. She reeled back in surprise, then recovered and fired.

It was too late. At the precise moment she pulled the trigger, he knocked her hand aside. The bullet slammed into the bureau, spraying wooden chips to the floor. He twisted her wrist with a thumb on the pressure point, numbing her hand. The gun dropped. She began another attack but he blocked her with his arms, then swung an elbow hard under her chin. He pushed at her shoulder and pulled at her hips, turned her around, and threw her face forward into the wall. She got her hands in front of her, but momentum took her face into the wall. She managed to turn toward him, dazed and bleeding. He was holding the gun.

She moved in his direction, not caring if she died, willing to take any chance to kill him first. Then she realized there was no chance, not now, but there might yet be one if she lived. She stopped. He smiled at her, then sat down on the bed.

Reidus laughed. He got up again and paced the room with great energy. His face was still bleeding, and he did nothing to stop that. "Combat skills are the most important thing, don't let anyone fool you about that," he said. "The greatest skill, though, is being prepared for the unexpected. I always am. You have to be ready to improvise. Take this thing, for example: being beaten for revenge by someone with a gun. That's a new category. I just filed it away. What you do is, you block only the blows that can cause serious injury—blows to the throat, the nose, anything that might cut off breathing. But you don't look like you're doing it; you just look like you're lost in panic. The moment each blow arrives, you push out, kind of explode out, but you stop moving when contact is made. You have to time it. It hurts a lot, but that's really nothing if you know you'll survive. It's also important to bleed, but harmlessly, get bruised, but not seriously. That way the attacker is satisfied. You were, weren't you?"

She stepped back again and leaned on the wall.

He looked quickly into the bathroom, then around the room again. He was taking some kind of inventory: ". . . tub, towels, water. . . ." He was talking to himself as well as to her. "Your mistake was using so much energy to strike me on the wrong parts of my body. The shoulders and the back of the head are the least vulnerable—they can take a tremendous beating and remain virtually unharmed if you take the blows right. That's been documented. So I took a reasonable amount of your pounding and then kind of gradually fell unconscious. An unconscious man is invisible, right? You stopped noticing me. I stood up. *Voilà!*" He was joyous.

Damn. She'd already known everything he said. But she let her anger get in the way. *Fucking emotions.* She had had him when they first walked into the room. He was dead at that moment. But she had to punish him first, beat him before she shot him. *You idiot! You blew it.*

He kept the gun loosely on her, rubbed his bloody face with one hand, then looked up, enthused, as if he'd solved a problem.

"I got it," he said. "You'll love this. Back in the forties and fifties, there were no psychiatric medications like Thorazine. There were tens of thousands of people in mental hospitals, most of them wild a lot of the time. Of course they were supposed to be wild, since they didn't know in those days that psychotics could be quiet. We've got quieter psychotics today, not just because of the drugs, but because we expect them to be. Ah, expectations."

He sounds wistful, Sara thought, and also expert. Maybe he'd once been a patient himself.

"In those years before the medications," he continued, "the staff of the hospitals needed ways to restrain patients, to deal with them when they went berserk. Everything that was a restraint was also considered

187

a treatment. So there were lobotomies—psychosurgery, induced convulsions, use of electricity and insulin, and they also had this beautiful thing, let me tell you about it."

He was moving around the room, stripping the bedspread off one of the two double beds in one swift motion. Then he removed the white sheets. He threw the bedspread on the floor but held onto the sheets. He tucked the gun into his belt, carefully folded the sheets, then repeated the procedure with the other bed. When he was done he reached out a hand to Sara.

"Please," he said. "Come."

He pulled and guided her to the bed. She noticed his arm was loose, a good defensive posture; she couldn't pull him off balance. When he bent, his legs were spread for stability of body, and his thighs were tight. She couldn't have kicked him in the groin. He was so effortlessly defended, yet she felt sure she could, at least, bring him down, maybe grab the gun. But this wasn't the time. She was still too weak, and he was too ready.

"The beautiful restraint thing they did," he said, "was called the wet pack. I'll show you how it's done. Take off your clothes."

She hesitated.

"Take them off, please, or I'll have to do it for you. Don't take this wrong. I won't hurt you."

Like the girl in the woods. Was that all she could manage? Sara thought. No better than a young motel receptionist?

But there was no safe response at this point, she realized. So she unbuttoned her blouse. Moving slowly, as if she were shy, she took off her shirt and then her bra. She pulled off her shoes and socks, loosened the buckle of her jeans.

"You're beautiful," Reidus said, looking at her with open appreciation.

She pulled off the rest of her clothes.

"To be honest," he said, "I expected a fight."

"I want to live," she said.

"You know it's not just you I'm after," he said. "I want Gray, too. So let's get him involved now." He picked up the phone, dialed, and apparently got his machine. "Gray, this is your friend from the woods. I'm at your girl's room at the Mayfair Hotel in Exton. Come get her and I'll meet you on the roof. Take your time, she's in no danger."

He turned to Sara. "Your friend'll be here soon if he checks his messages often. I'm sure we can entertain ourselves until then."

Reidus motioned Sara ahead of him into the bathroom, bringing the bedding along. He turned on the cold water in the tub, then soaked the sheets. He told Sara to stand with her feet together and her arms around her chest. She obeyed. He took one of the wet sheets and held the edge of it firmly against her bare right shoulder. He pulled the sheet around her body three times, then yanked it tight at the top and bottom and tied knots at the ends with the excess cloth.

"This was considered a humane way to bind patients who were wild, and also a kind of therapy. The idea was that patients would feel secure and calm if they couldn't move. The shock of the cold water was also supposed to help, put the patient into a different state of mind somehow. They didn't know how it worked, from what I read, but it calmed the patients for hours, even after they were released."

He sounded like a professor. "You've been through a lot today," he said. "Maybe this'll help you feel better."

He ripped a second wet sheet into strips and tied each strip tightly around her, top to bottom. Then, with a third wet sheet, he wrapped her again three times, tying the knots securely.

Then he laid her on the floor and left the bathroom for a minute. She heard him go out but was totally unable to move. He returned several times with buckets of ice from the hallway machine and dumped them in the tub.

"Now, let's get you comfortable," he said. He picked her up and lowered her body into the tub, her feet at the faucet, burying her in the ice so that only her head was above it. He turned the faucet to a light stream. The white sheets were soft as silk, tight as rubber. Reidus knelt down at the side of the tub and ran his hands over the smooth sheets, lightly tracing her thighs, groin, hips, stomach, breasts. Her nipples were erect to his touch from the cold. He pinched them lightly, seemed to consider lingering, then cupped her cheeks in his hands gently. "Any other woman would be crying or fighting by now," he said. "Mostly crying. You're as tough as I've met or you're numb. You sure you didn't die when your father did?"

She was trying to keep still, saving her energy for the effort to escape, hoping he'd leave the room before the water rose too much. "I thought you didn't remember my father," she said.

"I remember him," Reidus said. "He was as straight as they come. No imagination. A rock. A dinosaur. He could only handle totally predictable things. He wasn't creative enough to be bad. Did he love you? How routine. I let you keep him for four years, didn't I? And he didn't really deserve to live. His greatest wish was to keep Carlton's business boring, aboveboard. But he couldn't hope to stop us. His big idea was to ruin things for everybody. It was my pleasure, framing him for the rape. Thanks for telling me he killed himself. That shows me I was right about him. A loser."

He stood up, then noticed her face. "That's good," he said softly. "Now you're crying. Predictable, toughie, just like your dad."

He reached over to the faucet, turned the water up full, gagged her, and left.

29

THE SMALL ICE CUBES began melting quickly, and Sara's body was fully under water only minutes after Reidus left. She knew she could survive longer by remaining completely still. She let herself sink to save energy, poking her head up just long enough to take a deep breath. This went on for about ten minutes. It seemed like hours to her.

Each attempt to bring up her head was more difficult, and she was quickly growing weaker. Death seemed inevitable, but she refused to panic. Each time she came up she listened for sounds of someone in the hallway. That was her best chance, and even that couldn't work if Reidus hadn't left the door open. But he had. Maybe he'd wanted to make it easy for Gray to find her body.

Finally she heard voices in the corridor, and she yelled as loudly as possible through the gag. At first she heard no response. Then she heard a young boy's voice at the door. "Is someone in there?" he asked. She made as much noise as she could before sinking, her energy spent, lungs empty. In a futile effort to surface again, she sucked water in through her nose, became lightheaded, dizzy.

When she came to there were two boys standing over her on the bathroom floor. They'd removed her gag while she was still unconscious, and she was spitting up now. She hadn't taken in much water. Her words were mostly incoherent, but the boys seemed to understand enough, and they unwrapped her. They seemed amazed, as if staring at a strange animal in the zoo, and they whispered to each other. She finished unwrapping the sheets herself, and then she sat up slowly, still a little faint, and the boys tried to look as if they weren't looking, but their eyes kept returning to her naked body. When she got up, she covered herself in a towel and gave them all the money in her purse. Then she dressed quickly, got a gun from her luggage, and ran up to the roof.

When I arrived at the hotel, I got the room number from the front desk, rushed upstairs and found Sara's door unlocked. I ran to the bathroom. The tub was filled with ice and water and some of it had spilled over into the room. Torn and knotted shreds of sheets were on the sink, the floor, and the tub rim. I headed up to the roof.

The roof had two enormous sloping wedges in a steely silver hue that could be seen for miles in every direction. Inside those wedges was a large flat square surrounding the prism-like skylight that towered over the mall. The skylight was set down about three stories below roof level and was accessible by ladders and walkways on all four sides. It looked like a glass-bottomed swimming pool with no water.

Reidus was out in the open on the far side of the square. I stayed near the stairway and yelled across to him.

"Tell me what you want, Reidus, and where to find Sara."

"Come out," Reidus said in a friendly, cajoling voice. "You could have saved her, you were just too slow."

I looked around the roof, saying nothing in response.

"Be honest," Reidus said. "You found her body in the tub. You feel guilty. But there's no need to feel guilty. She drowned long before you had any chance of arriving. Have you seen wet packing before? She probably tried rocking in the water or pulling out the drain stopper with her feet, to keep the water level low. What she couldn't have anticipated about wet packing was the way the cold, soaked sheets pull tighter with every movement and slowly squeeze out breath. There wasn't any way to keep moving, wrapped like that, and keep her head above water. I probably couldn't have done it myself. Struggling to keep your head up only makes the sheets tighter. She drowned in minutes. Even the professionals—the shrinks and their workers—used to lose patients before they got the technique of tying the wet pack right. I used the original killing version." He laughed. I had no idea if he believed what he was saying. He sounded as if he did. But Sara had not drowned, or if she had, he'd taken her body away.

"Still," he said, "it was an awful waste. She was a great woman, a good survivor, and beautiful, clothed or in sheets."

In looking around the roof, I saw plenty of walls and columns for cover, and picked one out.

"You do lose a lot of friends," Reidus said. "And you bring me this girl whose father killed himself. Why don't you come out in the open so you and I can entertain ourselves?"

I made a dash for a spot behind part of the cement wall surrounding the opening for the skylight. Reidus stepped into a clearing about thirty feet away.

"Here's the deal," Reidus said. "I'll put my gun out here on the skylight ledge."

He walked the interior edge, laying the gun at a point on the square, then walked back to where he was before. The gun was now halfway between us. He turned his head slightly and looked down at the mall parking lot twenty-three stories below. I hoped he would produce Sara as an incentive for whatever he had in mind.

"Let's see which of us can get to the gun first," he said.

"Where's Sara?" I asked.

"The worst that can happen," said Reidus, ignoring my question, "is that one of us trips while running around that edge and falls through the skylight. A dramatic way to go, wouldn't you agree?"

"Where's Sara?"

"I'm an easy target now, Gray." Reidus laughed. "That's why I know you won't shoot me. Not your style."

"I'd stay here for something important," I said. "But not for this game."

I turned and slowly walked back toward the entrance. Reidus was too crazy to fathom, but he seemed to want me alive, so he might not stop me from leaving. Then, as I turned, I saw Sara, and the sight stopped me. She was kneeling, out of Reidus's sight, in a doorway behind the roof entrance. She had a gun up and was resting on one arm, squinting with a marksman's gaze toward Reidus. What I also saw was that she was soaked and trembling. I didn't know all of what she'd been through, but whatever it was had affected her badly. She had no chance of making the shot, and trying to do so would expose her. She'd be dead as soon as Reidus reached the gun. He could probably even get to her and kill her with his bare hands. If I kept walking, she was dead. Reidus hadn't seen her yet.

I'd ruined my shoulder in the minor leagues, but there was nothing wrong with my legs. I turned quickly and sprinted for the skylight. My rush forward almost put me over the small ledge. I saw the bright glass opening beckon for an instant before I got my balance back, then ran, crouching, along the narrow stone ledge. Reidus was only a few seconds away. He'd started running as soon as he saw me move. He's damn good, I thought, as I ran my ass off, but I can beat him to the gun. I have to.

I beat him by a fraction of a second and grabbed the gun before he could. As soon as he saw I had it, he moved back toward the outer edge of the roof. I held the gun loosely, not pointed at Reidus. Sara half kneeled, half fell from her hiding place, and aimed to fire.

Reidus saw her clearly, a flicker of surprise in his eyes, then nothing. In an instant, before she could shoot or I could move, he ran, staying low to the far side of the inner skylight square. Then he leaped atop its ledge. Sara fired. The shot missed. Before she could get off another, Reidus threw himself headlong over the edge. Sara and I looked at each other, uncertain. Then we heard the sound of crashing glass. We both ran toward the ledge. We could see the crystal ceiling that had shattered, the large glass chunks falling downward, following Reidus in his final descent to the mall floor. We heard another crash as the crystal landed in the zoolike pen where the fountains kept spraying water. Then there was silence, as the fallen objects lay there, still as the stone seals.

Sara walked toward me. She stared at me for a moment as if she didn't know who I was. She yelled Reidus's name like a curse, then said some things I couldn't make out. Maybe they were words you said when you'd almost died in violence. I looked down at the commotion in the mall. Reidus had found the thought of death at her hands intolerable and had decided to take his own life. Sick. Sad. She closed her eyes. Then she told me what had happened in the room.

"But it was worth it," she concluded. "Every second was worth it. He's dead. I don't care how it happened, he's dead. And that makes me happy."

She headed for the stairs, moving quickly. "I want to see him," she said.

I caught up to her at the elevator and we rode down in silence. When we reached the ground floor, we saw the large crowd pressed close to the fountains, directly beneath the broken skylight. Sara surged forward, shoving people out of her way, frantically pushing, swinging her arms. I followed in her wake.

There were several uniformed mall guards near the fountain. Sara looked around at the broken glass, then grabbed one of the guards. "Where is he?"

Another guard pulled her by the arm, but Sara shook him off. "Where is he?" she shouted.

We looked at each other, then at the fountains. No Reidus. Just broken glass and a cinder block that had apparently crashed through the skylight. She stood there, dazed, hanging on to the guard's arm, until I took her hand and pulled her away.

We went back to her room. It didn't seem like the right place to go. We could see traces of her battle with Reidus everywhere. Blood on the wall and carpet. The track of a bullet through the dresser. Water and a mess in the bathroom. Ripped sheets. I pictured her drowning, and then rising up from the water, wrapped in the sheets, the plume of water behind her as she broke the surface. She didn't seem to notice the room. I sat on the bed. I found myself wanting to comfort her, though she gave no sign of a similar urge.

She was furious about Reidus. She wanted to go hunting for him right away. But she was in no shape now, and I tried to get her to see that. She was moving around the room, readying the few things she had with her, looking for weapons in her bag. It was as if she were on automatic, and I felt I had to say something to turn off the motor.

"You've accomplished a lot today, Sara," I told her. "You stood him off, took him down, made him run away. He won't be back in a hurry. I have a feeling he'll be gone for a while, maybe even go into hiding. So you've got a chance to slow down, at least just for now. Okay?"

"He's still alive," she said. "That's all that matters. You seem to forget the important things. He could have killed dozens of people with that stunt, smashing all that glass over a crowded mall. And he did it not just to survive, but to play a mind game. How sick does it have to get before you see he has to die?"

"I've been through these situations," I said. "All the bad ones are like him in one way. They tempt you to become like them, act like them, get involved in their games. They like that. When they see you play along, they get off on it. Don't you get it? Reidus probably likes you. He seems to like us both."

"I know you want to help," she said. "But the only thing that can help me is his death. I wanted him to know what it was about before I killed him. I let my feelings get in the way. That was my mistake."

I listened to her make more vows about killing. I tried to imagine what it might take, aside from Reidus's dying, for her to let go. Reidus's death couldn't be guaranteed. He was simply too good.

She was trying to rouse herself, shaking her head, punching her legs with clenched fists. She sat down on the bed for a minute, next to me, then rocked forward. She was still very shaky. I took her arms.

"Stop," I said. "Stop. Listen to me." I turned her toward me. "Please. You've just been through some hellish thing. You almost died. You came face to face with this monster you've been hunting." Her head was down. She was taking deep breaths. I couldn't read her expression.

"I'm not trying to talk you out of anything anymore," I said. "I'm just talking about the way it feels right now. Just for a minute, let it go. Slow down. Just for a minute. You've got to keep yourself alive."

She looked at me and took a deeper breath. "I've been going at this alone for a long time," she said. Her voice was softer. "It's hard for me to hear that someone else feels anything about me, or about all this. I want some peace. I want it all the time. It means a lot to me that you want it for me. When I saw you run out onto that ledge after the gun I thought to myself that I really did have an ally, and it felt great. I was never sure until then that you were with me. Now I know."

She put a hand on my shoulder. "My life's on a shelf," she said. "It's hard not to get numb. Sometimes I think parts of me have died. Maybe when it's all over, when he's dead . . . ." She put the gun down on the bed, then sank her face into my shoulder. "I don't know. It's so strange that now, as close to getting that bastard as I've come, I should meet you. There's no sense to it."

I put my arms around her. We leaned our heads together. She closed her eyes. It was more like resting on each other than an embrace. We let it last for a while.

196

30

WHEN I GOT TO THE HOSPITAL, George Howard's room was full of family, friends, and lawyers. The room was set up more like a workplace than a sickroom. Bridge tables were in the corners, papers were spread everywhere, and lawyers were directing clusters of people into action over the papers.

I kept myself busy for a few minutes reading through the files I'd brought along. They contained some answers; Howard might provide a few more. Finally, a little after ten o'clock at night, the room began to clear and I pulled a chair closer to the bed.

"It appears you have things in good order," I said.

Howard puffed on a fat Jamaican cigar, then laughed. "Not me. You. You and the lawyers. Like a machine. They've got about two hundred signed statements. Everyone wants to help. Great, isn't it?" The big smile called for the kind of broad gestures he wasn't yet able to make, but the cigar conveyed the right touch of grim satisfaction and pleasure.

"So tell me what those files are about," Howard said.

I bent over and picked up a manila envelope from the pile I had placed on the floor. I took out a picture and showed it to Howard. Sara had taken the photo for me while she'd been following Reidus a few days earlier. It wasn't a terrific picture, but you could see his face. "This man look familiar?"

Howard stared at it. Then he slapped his hand on the bedsheet. "That's him! That's the man who tried to attack Laura Thompson."

"When was that?"

"About two years ago," he said. "It was a holiday weekend. Memorial

197

Day. That was one of the first weird things that happened in the town. Hard to forget. Who is it? Do you know?"

"His name is William Reidus. He works for Carlton."

"Jesus Christ!"

"Tell me about the incident. We need to start somewhere."

Howard said he was home that morning, up at 6:30, as he was every day. He was in the kitchen with the coffee and some bills, waiting for one of the kids to interrupt him and begin the day. He noticed when the newspaper boy came and left, then heard a truck stop at the Thompson house. He went to the front window for a look. The truck was a Dodge step-in van, white, no lettering. He saw the worker, a big man, at least six feet tall. He was doing something at the front of Laura Thompson's house, maybe some repairs to the door.

At first he gave it little thought, but when he saw Laura staring at the man from her front window, he had a feeling something was wrong. He called a neighbor, who said he'd already noticed and called Laura and she said she hadn't ordered any work.

"That's the way we are in Hatley," Howard said. "I told you. We look out for each other. We had a feeling something was wrong. It was just a feeling, but we all had it at the same time."

"It seemed like one isolated incident at first. Then, when the other strange things happened, I figured they were somehow related. Are you saying that was what started it all?"

"I know it sounds crazy, but I think that's the answer," I told him. "It's the kind of thing that only makes sense to someone like Reidus. He's psychotic. When he attacked Thompson he genuinely believed that was his right, his privilege. That's the way he thinks. You challenged him, the group of you, and drove him off. But it wasn't finished for him. The mortgage thing was his way of making it right."

Howard put his cigar in a saucer and reached for a glass of water. He sighed. He rubbed his face, then closed his eyes for a moment.

"But why Hatley? Why not some other town? Aside from the willingness to chop people up for their money, it still must have occurred to them that they could just buy land outright easier and cheaper where the people wanted to sell. Why would Carlton go along with it? He's a millionaire. This damn thing hurt a lot of people. And probably lost him some money. He'd have a hundred better ways to invest his money. Is he crazy too?"

I shook my head. "No, not like Reidus. But to understand Carlton, you have to realize that he thinks everything he does helps people. He was helping you poor people out with your mortgage problems, sending you on the road to greater opportunity. Also, Reidus makes him a lot of money in other ways, and I think Carlton's afraid of him. Humoring him, even to this extent, might have seemed appealing compared to the alternative of getting him angry. And Carlton also believes he's got a Midas touch, that he can make anything pay. He probably convinced himself he liked the challenge of buying and selling worthless land. Those are the ways Carlton sees the world."

Howard seemed to understand. "What about the murders?" he asked. "Any chance they'll get charged?"

"No. They did them, all right. I'm convinced of that. The problem is, none of the witnesses would be any good in a courtroom. There's a girl who works at a motel, she saw Reidus taking the private detective away. But in court her testimony doesn't add up to much, and besides she's so terrified of Reidus I don't think she'd ever talk. Then there's a friend of mine, Sara, who can link Reidus with the death of one of his own men, and can provide a motive for why Reidus would go after Simon. Again, it's pretty indirect stuff in court. And, truth is, if she came forward, she'd probably get herself in more trouble with the law than Reidus or Carlton. Not that she'd ever agree to testify, anyway. The only other witnesses are Reidus and Carlton."

"So what happens?"

"That's what I'm about to find out. I'm on my way to Carlton now."

199

31

IT WAS RAINING. The base of Carlton's low-lying main building weathered a steady assault of large drops. I thought about what Carlton would do if Reidus died, or never returned. Carlton would quickly have to replace his function in the organization. There'd be many applicants. That was one of the things Carlton and I had to discuss. I wanted the job left unfilled.

Carlton came out to meet me in the hallway. It was a cool hello.

He didn't seem to expect me to say anything, and he simply turned, letting me follow him down the hallway, past the collection of ebony horses and into his private office. The rug was one continuous surface from the corridor to the inside floor, short-weaved and thick. It seemed to absorb all sound.

The walls of the secluded office were covered with objects. I hadn't even noticed them the last time I was there. Three small silver elephants—a mother and two matched babies—sat on a cedar shelf. The babies faced forward. Nearby were two gold-and-ivory envelope openers, ornate slashes of expensive material. Each had a small elephant carved onto the top of its handle. The trunks on all the elephants faced down. I recalled having heard somewhere that that was a sign of bad luck. Carlton probably didn't believe in bad luck. Or maybe he thought the bad luck belonged to whomever he'd stolen the elephants from.

I still hadn't said anything since Carlton had greeted me. Now Carlton said impatiently, "Well, did you want something or not?"

"Where's Reidus?"

"I haven't seen him in days," Carlton said. "I don't know where he is. Something tells me he's not coming back."

"Let's do some business," I said.

I took out a manila envelope from my inside jacket pocket. It contained a sheaf of reduced-sized copies, neatly stacked. I gave them to Carlton.

"All you have to do is read that. Then we can talk."

Carlton sat at his desk and studied the papers for five minutes. Then he dropped the last page on the floor beside his chair.

"These papers—that's it?"

"Those papers could probably bring indictments on a dozen different federal fraud charges. You know that. And there are enough documents and witnesses at this point to get some convictions."

"So why talk to me? The U.S. attorney's office is easy to find."

"I don't want to see the U.S. attorney. What we're talking about here is thousands of people who lost money and hundreds who lost homes. You don't do them any good in jail. But you *can* do a lot of good for them right here."

Carlton looked curious.

"Here's the deal," I said. "I don't take my evidence to anybody, ever. In return, you take this list." I handed him another sheet of paper. "It has names, addresses, and dollar amounts next to each name. Most of them, you can see, about five or ten thousand. Plus the mortgage values. The total shopping price for paybacks is about a half million. Nothing much to you. You pay the money out. You close down the extortion and mortgage-seizing operations completely—never to be reopened, not by you, not by anyone else for you. You pay special consideration to the town of Hatley. Everyone gets his home back, mortgage paid off one hundred percent. Then you become the real estate protector for the citizens of Hatley, the guarantor of neighborhood stability. You set up a trust fund that ensures the community stays solid until the last person on this list, and you and I, have died. That's what I'm offering."

Carlton was grinning. "You're really crazy," he said.

"If you don't do business with me, I'll take this stuff to the Feds, and you'll be indicted. That wouldn't make me unhappy. But I'd prefer to make a deal."

"You're assuming I'm some kind of criminal," Carlton said. "Your problem is with Reidus. That's got nothing to do with me."

"Either you don't get it or you get it and don't care," I said. "Reidus does damage, all right. But what you do hurts many more people. It's not only his violence that guts towns and keeps ordinary people in despair. You've created this slick, empty vacuum here where people do business any way at all, where guys like Reidus come knowing they've found a home. You're the one responsible for Reidus."

If Carlton didn't go along with my deal, it was bad for everyone. Whether Carlton believed it or not, his refusal to deal meant he would be gone. Somebody else would, of course, come in and take over the operation, and go on doing the same thing. Anyone could do Carlton's job. Whatever Carlton believed, it didn't require charisma. All that stuff—his videotapes, his art collections, his remembering employees' birthdays, his games with Meredith—had nothing to do with the operation. Operations like Carlton's had done just fine for centuries, whether in shabby storefronts or tents on desert sands, as well as in landscaped buildings of glass. The frills made no difference. It just took someone willing to keep the operation intact, someone to protect the turf, and always to be willing to commit all the crimes, big and small, necessary to keep things running.

I wanted Carlton to take the deal. I gave him another pitch.

"Okay," I said. "No deal? Here's what happens. A lawyer and accountant I work with have all the evidence I've put together so far, the documents and about two hundred depositions. They'll have more soon because they have people in Hatley now. They'll be dealing with a guy I know at the Federal Organized Crime Strike Force in New York. He's one of those who can't be bought, gets more aggressive when someone— especially his boss—tries to steer him away from the goods. If my lawyers don't hear from me by Monday, five P.M., they'll bring the files to New York. That Strike Force guy's been itching to get you since your Detroit days, and nothing would make him happier than jumping on top of this. He's had the RICO statute details sitting in files with your name on them for some time now, but you weren't a priority. The new evidence from Hatley is all they need to move you way up on the list."

Nothing from Carlton. No expression, not even a blink. I went on.

"They'd have enough live cases and names to bring the whole damn thing against you from their office, Carlton. Your connections in Detroit wouldn't be worth squat. I'm sure you can pull some strings in D.C. to slow the works down, but it wouldn't stop them.

"On those tapes of yours you said there's no such thing as a crime if Party A doesn't bring charges against Party B—no matter how much money was stolen. But you're Party B, and we've got Parties A through Z ten times over—all of them aching to testify against you. When you deal with other businessmen, the only concern on both sides is money. You screw somebody and they come crawling to you for a chance to get some of it back. But the people whose houses you took away, they're not just looking for their money. You damaged their lives. You shamed them. These people are angry at you personally. It's more emotional than financial. They make lousy businessmen, but they're going to be great witnesses in a courtroom. You don't hold anything over these people—that's a position you're not used to being in. You can intimidate, buy off, or arrange accidents for them. But two hundred of them? Forget it.

"Then there's the simple issue of your real estate license. Lose it—even for only a few months—and it'll cost a lot more than the half million I'm asking for. And I haven't even mentioned the newspapers."

Carlton got up and opened a window, though the room was comfortably air-conditioned. He sat back down. Still he said nothing.

"If everything I've covered doesn't do it for you," I finished, "then there's this. You know as well as I do that once the Federal Strike Force picks up the case, your Detroit partners will wonder if you're talking to the Feds about them. Rumors spread quickly. And the Detroit folks have only one way to deal with people talking to the Feds."

Carlton took in a deep breath. His face was getting red. He had no choice but to agree. Because people like him used only one thing as their guideline—money. It was all that really mattered. He didn't do things for love, or pride, or loyalty. Nothing else was relevant. So I watched his mounting anger with a degree of surprise. I kept waiting for the anger to ebb, to reveal itself as what it surely was, a strategy, a performance for my benefit, a prelude to compromise. I thought the idea was that I was supposed to get uncomfortable watching this and start saying things designed to calm Carlton down a bit, either because I was afraid of losing the deal or just because I was afraid. That's how men in this position normally acted. But that wasn't what was happening.

Carlton was leaning forward over the desk, arms flat down, fists closed, looking up at me with a reddened face and dull eyes. His head was practically on the desk, the neck still, low, like a turtle's. He opened his hands, and I thought maybe here was the signal the performance was over. But then Carlton pushed the palms of his hands at the base of the desk and with a swift, smooth motion he swung it up on its side, not just turning it over, but moving through it, pushing it forward, aiming for me.

I stood still as Carlton approached, then ducked to the side as he lunged at my head. Before I could put up a block, he grabbed me by the throat. In the slowest speed of watching another man's fury build, I had not realized that Carlton had been deciding how to kill me.

My breathing almost stopped as Carlton began to twist the nape of my neck. I slid my back against the wall, pulling a tapestry down with me. I put my two hundred pounds into two fists, joining as low as I could extend them, then swinging them up together, full force, feeling something crack as I broke Carlton's chin. The tall man stood frozen, his hands falling slack.

I braced against the wall, bent my knees, then put a straight flat fist into his face, feeling his lip split, seeing the blood rush out. I jumped at him, kicking him hard in the gut, then braced myself for a full-force chop to the chin with my elbow.

He fell back, catching an arm on the upended desk, supporting himself so that he could crawl to a chair. He didn't seem to notice he was bleeding. He didn't seem to notice anything.

I walked to the door. "I'll be in town just one more day," I said. "Call me if you want the deal."

"Wait," Carlton managed to say.

"You've got until Monday at five to settle on my terms," I said. "And if you take the deal, I'll let you know later what my fee comes to."

"Fee?" Carlton said. He half stood, wiping his lip. "So for you this is just another little case of blackmail?"

"Yes," I said. "That's all it is."

Before I left I opened a door that I guessed led to a closet. It had what I wanted. I filled the small box with all the ebony horses. I'd forgotten to tell Carlton about that part of the deal.

PAYBACK

. . .

The building was dark and empty when Reidus came in that night. He hadn't planned on returning to the office, but when his men told him Gray had been with Carlton earlier, he decided to see what had happened.

As he watched the tape, he became convinced, finally, that Carlton would no longer do. In the end, the man was ordinary, weak, predictable. To be pushed around by an operator like Gray, to be caught, to be trapped—all because he wanted to keep his little company. And keep his woman. Keeping doesn't matter. Taking is what counts—taking things to places no one ever imagined.

It was time to take something from Carlton. Something important.

32

MEREDITH WAS HOME. She was secure there. She'd bought the place three years ago, one of twenty new houses in a development in West Marlboro. It was pretty land, and private. She'd used a sizable chunk of her personal savings—although she had much more—and she'd congratulated herself on getting Carlton to spend a good deal from his own funds to buy the house.

It was past midnight. She'd gone to bed earlier, but was unable to sleep, so she'd gotten up for a drink. She was wearing a peach-colored silk robe and now sitting on her leather couch. She looked around her living room at the three glass breakfronts, each filled with different objects of ceramic and brass and silver. The collection made her feel good, like the Mercedes. Something substantial.

She also valued her privacy. That was the main reason she had wanted a home of her own. She often needed to be alone after the work she did, and Carlton understood that. Each street in her development was a short cul-de-sac, and the houses were designed so that the front entrances faced away from each other. Still, in her years there, she'd had several visits from men in the neighborhood. She always turned them away, preferring to keep her home a place to relax and not work.

The exceptions to the rule were the cocktail parties she hosted for Carlton. She didn't like them. For one thing, Reidus had often been present. His visits bothered her. She was painfully aware of Carlton's reliance on the man. She believed, as Carlton did, that without Reidus—or someone just like him—Carlton's money and power would be terribly diminished. She accepted the reality and the need for what Reidus did.

There was violence in the world, and the important thing was to have it go your way, not the other guy's. That was Carlton's philosophy, and she shared it.

Now, at least, that was over. Reidus had somehow been driven away by Gray, and by his partner, the woman. Meredith didn't know how that could happen. But he'd been gone for a week—he'd never been away that long without explanation—and Carlton believed he wasn't coming back. She guessed that Reidus had decided on his own that it was time to get out. Certainly he'd survived. She wondered if he could be killed at all. Violence was his element, as much as sensuality was hers. How long could a man live? Eighty years? That meant another forty-five years or so of Reidus on the earth. A lot of pain still to come. It was good, then, that he'd been driven away. Let him go somewhere else, away from here. Things had not gone well lately. She felt unsettled. Part of it was due to Reidus; part of it was something else.

She'd woken up unable to get out of her mind a scene she'd done the night before with a woman from a competitor's firm. The sex had been ordinary, even loving, though with a woman—but she'd had no special problem with that. In fact, she'd enjoyed the sensations it provided, the more knowledgeable touches of fingers and tongue, the softer skin, the cleaner smells and slower rhythms. But the woman's reaction afterward had been very strong and upsetting. There was the realization that she'd opened up to someone like Meredith, who was just working. She understood the chance she'd taken because she'd given in to her feelings. And then, because she was smart, she figured out that photos had surely been taken—and they had—which meant that everything she'd worked for was probably lost. This had made her tremble and cry. It got to Meredith. She never thought much about her limits before. This time she decided she'd gone too far.

There was a knock at the door. She wasn't expecting anyone. It must be Carlton. When he wanted to see her, he didn't call. He just showed up.

Her door had two rectangular panels, top to bottom, on either side, glass cinder blocks with decorative etchings. The only things you could see through them were shades of color or heavily blurred visions of objects on the other side. The distortions the glass provided sometimes spooked her. The glass enlarged things. Boys who came to collect for the paper route loomed adult-size through the glass. Opening the door was a process of visually shrinking things to their proper perspective. Carlton was a big man, and when he was at the door, only a bit of light shone through at the top, making a white halo for him. Now, as she approached the door, there was nothing to either side but full darkness clouding the blocks. Reidus, she thought, without hesitation. She controlled herself with great effort. She could do this, she reminded herself; she could keep herself from feeling. She emptied herself of everything. I must greet him casually, she thought. As if nothing is wrong.

She opened the door.

"I knew you'd come to see me," she said. "I didn't think you would just leave with no good-bys. I'm glad. Come in." She hoped her tone was friendly and mild, but with a little excitement.

He walked past her into the house, looking at her only briefly, stepping into the middle of the entry hall before stopping. He remained silent for a moment.

"We're alone, I see," he then said. It wasn't a question, she realized. It was as if in that moment of silence, he'd reached out into the house, with hearing and sight and smell, and simply determined that in a house with three floors and eight rooms and a dozen crannies and closets and corners, there were no other people. And he wants us alone. I'm not going to live, she thought. She took small breaths, closed the outside door without hesitation—she did not think of running; she couldn't get away—and moved next to him.

He was looking at her again. She began to experience a sense of relief so strong that she broke into a sweat, and her breathing deepened without awareness or will. It was as if she'd been swimming in deeper and deeper water, and rough waves were reaching to take her farther and under and down, and suddenly there was land. He was looking at her and she understood his look.

She thought about touching him, but stopped before she did, the instinct she had about these things determining her actions. She turned from him instead, starting to move away, her back to him. Within a step or two, he grabbed her, pulling her back to him, one hand almost around her waist, turning her toward him with his strength so that the motion was as smooth as if it had been her idea. Her robe covered her fully and was tied with a bow in the front. Her long black hair sprawled out over the robe and down her back. He opened her robe just by slowly drawing his hand down the front of it, touching her skin. He was wearing a good wool suit, as he usually did, and as he exposed her skin and pressed against her, she felt the soft, smooth texture rubbing her. He bent down so that his lips were against her ear. Her robe was completely open and with his right hand he casually touched her body, moving his palm over her neck and breasts and belly, pushing her legs apart with his fingers.

She moaned and spread herself for him, letting him do whatever he wanted.

"Do you think about sex when you're alone?" he whispered. She wondered whether or not to answer him. He moved his right hand under her so that she was practically sitting on his hand. He wants to do it for me, she thought. She made herself respond.

"I've thought about sex with you," she said, and concentrated on turning discomfort into pleasure. She moved herself on his finger so the pressure would be right. She opened her mouth and kissed him on the lips, putting her hands on his face. He had a light beard. She dropped her hands and shook the robe off her shoulders. He took his hands away from her and let her stand unsupported. She moved up against him, wanting to feel him hard. He let her touch him. He wasn't aroused.

They moved slowly into the living room. She sat on the couch. He remained standing, facing her. She lay back, no longer knowing what he wanted her to do or what might excite him, if anything. I don't have a chance, she thought.

"Maybe I need you to do something else," he said, his tone as ordinary as if they were working in the office.

"Reidus, I can do anything you want," she said. "Anything at all. And it'll make me hot to do it. Let me."

"You can do all the things other men want," Reidus said. "But I don't want any of those things. What do *you* want?"

He touched her face, trailed a finger across her mouth, then pushed the thick finger in and out of her mouth, letting her wet it. "Is this what you like to do?" he asked. She nodded, uncertain.

He put two hands under her and lifted her up effortlessly, as if she were a small child. He licked between her thighs. "You liked this last night," he said, and she realized he'd been watching with the men who took the pictures. "Is this what you like to do?"

She pressed herself against his tongue, and let him see that she liked his touch. He didn't react, and he put her down. He turned her over on the couch, with one easy motion, putting her on her knees, facing away from him. He moved up behind her, pressed his groin against her. He lightly slapped her ass. She didn't react. "Is this what you like?"

She didn't move. She did nothing at all.

Reidus walked away from the couch, leaving her there. She rolled over and sank down against the pillows, watching him. He went to the breakfront with the silver dishes. He opened the glass doors gently and slowly, and took out some silver dishes.

"Silver is soft," he said. He bent several of the dishes in his hands, twisting the metal until each curved object had new edges, sharp and bright, even in the low light of the room. "Is this what you like?"

He brought the pile of metal over to the couch, as if asking her to select the ones she liked. When she didn't react, he spilled some of the misshapen silver over her body. She covered herself with her hands, but the sharp edges of the metal cut her, and little drops of blood appeared on her cheek, at her hip, on her shoulder.

He bent over her, picked up one of the silver dishes, and turned the edge of it toward her, using it to slowly cut a line, thin, but firm and straight, from the base of her neck to the top of her groin. It was the kind of cut that even if tended would leave a scar. She put every bit of strength she had into pushing him away. With all her effort, she got nowhere. He didn't even seem to notice. He held her down with his left hand, using his right to guide the silver edge into her skin. It hurt very much, but she found she didn't have to feel it. All her practice in numbing herself to men had developed a talent for numbing herself to everything. She was able to look up directly at Reidus. More than anything else, she had a sense of disconnection, as if she were watching him hurt someone else, not herself.

Reidus paused for a moment, perhaps noticing that she had stopped struggling, interested in the reason. Her expression gave him no answers. He went back to cutting her, creating more lines in the perfect skin, beginning to do deeper damage. He was systematically cutting her open, and she was bleeding heavily. Despite her numbed mind, her body jerked, and the more he cut, the more apart she felt from herself. He stopped for longer intervals now, to look down at her, look at her eyes. He could read nothing, no emotion, no cry for help.

Though she was detached from her pain, she realized she was dying, right here, right now. She hated him and thought she knew how to hurt him before she died.

"I know why you do this," she said, gasping the words out, taking little breaths. He was still now, listening. He was showing no anger, but she knew it was there, all the time, never ebbing.

"I know," she said. "You can't stop doing it. That's what it is. You'll always do this. You're . . . predictable. You're no different than the others, just like all . . ." He put a big hand over her face, shutting her mouth, and she couldn't struggle free enough to say another word. He cut across her throat with one short stroke so she couldn't speak anymore, but was still, for a moment, alive. He turned away from her, dropped the bloodied silver on the carpet and went to the door.

The blood at her neck stirred a bit with her last breath.

"Did all your other men do this?" he asked.

33

I WAS OVER AT Simon's apartment, packing. I'd promised to bring some of his things to his sister. I had the television on as background noise while I tried to decide what to take and what to leave. I heard the name "Laura Thompson" as if shouted out at me from the eleven o'clock news. I turned up the volume. A reporter, standing alongside a highway, was saying, "Apparently she lost control at this curve, then she spun off the road and hit the utility pole. She and her eight-year-old son died instantly."

Reidus hadn't shown up at work in the week since the scene at the mall. Sara had been searching for him unsuccessfully. Now I knew what Reidus had been doing. He'd learned of my deal with Carlton to restore Hatley, and he decided to involve himself. So he'd killed the woman with whom he'd begun things there, Laura Thompson. Next he would kill the man who'd interfered.

I called George Howard at the hospital, but got a recording that said patient phones were off for the night. No use calling the front desk. How can you warn them against Reidus? I drove the rental as hard as I could, but still it took forty minutes to get there.

I hit the hospital building running, taking the stairs up, past a startled nurse, double-checking my direction by the arrows painted on the walls. As I swung open the door to Howard's room, I saw an empty bed and Howard's body, beyond it, folded in the corner. He was alive and awake. He looked at me, but his voice was unsteady, hard to hear. The room had signs of a fight but the signs were odd. The bed was several feet out of position, but the mattress and sheets were neat. A dresser was lying on its side with a lamp neatly upright on one of the drawers. A wastebasket was overturned, the contents intact. I'd raced Reidus to get here, lost, and somehow Howard was still alive.

"Reidus," Howard said.

"I know. But where?"

Howard, apparently in shock, took time answering. "I think he wanted to kill me, throw me out the window. Then he just dropped me. He was happy to see her . . . the woman."

Sara, I thought. She'd gotten here first. The only prize Reidus would choose over Howard. From Howard's window, I glanced down into the parking lot, saw nothing, then hauled Howard back onto the bed. He was still talking. "They were fighting, but without any noise. No noise." I didn't understand what he was saying. The hospital was quiet, but the silence seemed wrong, impossible. If Sara had arrived, and Reidus had gone for her, then somewhere close by there was a war. People would hear it.

I stepped out into the corridor, looking both ways, listening. Nothing. An old woman was pacing up and down with a box walker, its rubber-clad feet making no sound. Down the hall, two nurses were pulling a medication cart. Soft, dull clinks, the click of metal and glass. Nothing. The air-conditioning sliding its white noises into the air. That was all. Maybe it was already over, I thought. But maybe they were still fighting. "No noise," Howard had said. I suddenly pictured it. The two of them, Reidus and Sara, fighting out their hate, she interrupting his intent to kill Howard, but both totally unwilling to involve others, especially the law they both, for different reasons, held in contempt.

Unless she was dead, Reidus still wouldn't want any noise. Where would he go? Where in a hospital would all noise be shielded? I ran up and down the corridor. No sign of Reidus or Sara. No one had seen anything.

Then I ran down to the basement, near the generators, the most isolated parts of the building. Nothing there. At the end of a long hall, next to a large green door, there were signs for the radiation area. I opened the door and went through. Laboratories. No patients, no clutter. There were two X-ray rooms. Heavy doors with the radiation sign with the circle and the cross. The doors were not latched shut. I went into the first room, looked around, under the tables, saw nothing. Then I pushed open the door to the second.

She was lying on a large table under the X-ray machine against the far wall. No sign of Reidus. I walked over. Sara was alive, but unconscious. Her face was very pale. I tried rousing her but got no response. Whatever Reidus had done had left no wounds visible on her face or arms.

I heard the slight whoosh of the thick door before it closed. When I turned Reidus was standing at the entrance, smiling and silent.

"I'm leaving," I said. "With Sara." I looked around the room and saw a wheelchair farther along the wall. I went to get it.

Reidus stepped forward. He spoke softly but blocked my path.

"If you try moving her in this condition, she'll almost surely die. I'm tempted to let you. I haven't figured out if you really care about these people, but if you do, letting you be responsible for her immediate death does have some appeal to me."

"I'm interested in Sara but not in you. She's the reason I'm here."

"You'd really leave, just like that?" Reidus asked genuinely surprised. "You know what I'll do to Hatley. The deal with Carlton is off." He paused as if thinking about his employer. "Carlton," he said with disgust, shaking his head. "Weak. Predictable. Ordinary, after all."

"Once Sara's taken care of, we can talk about Carlton or Hatley, make a new deal," I said. "I have a feeling Carlton will be taking some time off, maybe going somewhere with Meredith."

Reidus froze for a second, then he smiled at me. He couldn't have made it clearer with words. He'd done something to Meredith, something horrible.

"I'm not interested in a new deal," he said. "I don't want to deal at all, I want to fight. But you won't do it. That's why she's here. For incentive." He looked at Sara. "She's tough. She came very close to killing me before I could even get out of that room up there. If I didn't have the big man as a shield . . . I'd say she's just had a run of bad luck."

"What did you do to her?"

"I basically caused her a lot of internal bleeding. It's easy. If you beat someone badly enough and keep them alive it happens automatically. Pull up the blanket and take a look at her left side."

I removed the blanket. On Sara's side, by the waist, was an ugly blue bruise.

Reidus joined me by Sara. "She can be our unconscious spectator," Reidus said, putting a hand on her arm. "They say people can process everything while they're unconscious—see, hear. There's a problem recalling it once you regain consciousness, but they say everything that happens gets stored away."

He reached up to the X-ray machine with one huge arm while he talked.

"These babies are heavy," Reidus said, tapping the machine with his fingers. "About as heavy as cars. But it's no effort at all to move them. They're built with pneumatics and hydraulics. It's like pushing a small car with one finger."

I watched warily as Reidus moved the machine up and down and side to side over Sara's body. Each time he let it go it kept moving just a bit more.

"You have to be able to move it close up to whatever part of the patient's body you're shooting," Reidus said. "As heavy as it is, you have to aim it pretty finely, get the thing situated just right."

He brought the machine down to Sara's stomach and the tube pressed into her flesh. I grabbed the machine, pushing it hard away from her.

Reidus let go, laughing. I moved the machine up, easily.

"Of course, you could hurt someone with this thing if you weren't careful," Reidus said. "You can crush someone. Get it going, let it move, and it goes right through the patient. Models newer than this one have a little rubber ring on the tube to prevent that. As soon as the ring touches anything, the machine freezes."

"I'm taking Sara to a doctor," I said. "Now."

I walked past Reidus. When I reached the wheelchair, I saw near it, on a shelf, a row of black metal boxes. They looked heavy, about the size of briefcases. I grabbed one and threw it hard at Reidus. Then I threw two more. Reidus caught the first one and dodged the next, but the third one hit him cleanly in the gut. He dropped to one knee but was almost up again, though still off balance, by the time I reached him. I cut behind him, swept his feet out and pinned his arms to his back. I tried to break his arm, hoping to buy time to get Sara out.

Reidus made no attempt to get away. I had leverage and position, but Reidus was too strong. He rolled over, pinning me under him, then stood up and lifted me a few feet in the air. He swiveled and sent me crashing back down to the floor, but he held on to my right leg. I tried to roll out of his grip but couldn't. He planted a leg under mine, and, using it as a wedge, slowly bent my lower leg over his own until the bone broke. I must have been yelling in agony for a minute, my vision completely blank, and then I passed out. Next thing I remember, Reidus was leaning over me. I heard him clearly, despite the pain.

"It's a clean break," he said. "Nothing compound about it. It'll heal neat, if you make it out of here."

He picked me up and carried me to the wheelchair. He set me down gently.

"You know, in the orthopedics area they have a machine that breaks bones to reset them. Maybe I'll take you there." He laughed.

He looked down at me, as I grimaced and held my leg with both hands. The area by the break was swelling like a balloon. Reidus looked concerned, and his tone was reassuring. "Don't worry about the swelling. It'll stop. When the bone breaks through the skin, you don't get that. But yours wasn't that bad." Then he laughed again. "You wouldn't have gotten out of here anyway. I rigged the door so it takes about a minute to open now. It's just wound wire. Easy, but you do need about a minute to work in peace. I won't give you that."

"So we're in here all night," I said. I was startled at how difficult it was to get the words out. My throat was dry, as if all the liquids in me had been drained. "For what?"

"Great place," Reidus said, covering the room with the sweep of his arm. "They use radiation to take pictures, they expose cancer patients to radiation for healing. Radiation. It's like prayer. Invisible energy that heals. It also kills. It's all in the timing and the dosage."

I looked at Sara. She seemed to be having trouble breathing. My own pain made it hard for me to follow Reidus. He seemed to notice I was distracted and waited until he had my attention again. Then he continued talking, with enthusiasm.

"The X-ray machine is on. We're getting dosed right now. You and me and Sara. Radiation does get you sick after a while, but no one knows just how long it takes. It's hard to test, you can imagine, especially in human beings. Most of what's known about the stuff is from accidents and bombings, like Hiroshima. We've been in here about ten minutes. If we left right now we'd probably be okay. Another twenty minutes and who knows? I think in about a half hour, at this level, we'd hit a radiation-poisoning threshold. That would shorten our lives. Hard to say by how much. If we stay in here another two hours or so, the radiation poisoning would get lethal and we'd be dead in two weeks."

Sara stirred a bit. Reidus glanced over at her. Every time she moved or made a sound, Reidus seemed to get excited, and he'd begin talking about something else.

"Do you know how to teach a man to defuse a bomb?" Reidus's tone was serious. "You teach him how to make one. Every intelligence service in the world trains their people that way. If you can make something, you can take it apart. Same way with the body. Teaching doctors to knit bones and sew skin together is also the best way to learn how to take the body apart. I never went to medical school. But it's clear enough in the books. The thing is, you do need to experiment a lot."

Sara moaned. Her eyes weren't opened, but she was drawing her feet to the side, trying to roll over.

"A tough woman, as I said. Very strong. She might live with that kind of bruise for hours. Most people would die in about thirty minutes. They'd drown in a mixture of blood and the poisons their kidneys aren't cleaning up."

I moved my wheelchair over to Sara. The bruise appeared to be spreading. Reidus went over to a table in the corner and picked up what looked like a small toolbox, latched and locked. He opened the box by breaking the small latch off with his hand.

"Don't be impressed," Reidus said. "It's made to be opened that way. Easy access in emergencies."

He took out a syringe. The needle was much longer than an ordinary one. It was the size of a kitchen knife.

"They call this a Bristojet kit," Reidus said. "It's used to revive patients when they're having heart attacks. You put the needle right into the heart. First you fill it with this stuff."

He held up a small clear glass bottle with a thin rubber top, filled with an amber liquid. There were several of these bottles.

"It's epinephrine. Pure adrenaline. It brings you up, heart rate, breathing, everything. I've tried it. The rush is incredible. No street drug could compare. Be down from anything and it brings you right up. The head stays clear. It only lasts a couple minutes, but it's strong enough to wake you from any sleep, no matter how deep."

He plunged the tip of the big needle into one of the small bottles. The amber liquid snaked up from the bottle to fill the tube of the syringe. Reidus walked toward Sara holding the needle up like a spear, squeezing the plunger gently to spray droplets into the air, checking its working order.

I rolled my chair between Reidus and Sara. Every time I turned the wheel, I felt a new surge of pain, and I was afraid I might pass out again. Reidus stopped a few feet away, holding the tip of the needle toward me.

"I could bring your friend some relief with this. Give her back some energy. Wake her up. Let her feel things. But it's taking a chance. The needle goes into the heart, it penetrates, it comes out. You can stick the heart like a pincushion, with hardly any damage. The person lives. But strike the big artery, the aorta, and the person dies immediately. I could play her like an instrument, race her engine like a car. It's just mechanics. Do this, she responds. Do that, she responds. I could show you now. That would really bother you, wouldn't it? I could use this on you first, and then on Sara."

Still pointing the needle at me, he slowly turned toward Sara. He was grinning.

I looked over at the locked door. At that moment, Reidus plunged the needle into Sara's chest, pressing down on the syringe. For a second, there was no reaction at all. Then Sara's eyes shot open and her body stiffened. She began shaking, and her hands clenched. She cried out in pain.

PAYBACK

I wheeled toward Reidus, reaching out for the syringe. "You bastard," I yelled. "Stop!"

While I was still moving, Reidus reared back, suddenly, unexpectedly. Sara's arm was around his neck. He tried moving away, but she held tight. I rolled myself to the table and grabbed his arm. I managed to get the syringe away, but Reidus curled his leg up against the wheelchair and kicked it, rolling me back across the room. Sara tightened her grip and pulled Reidus down onto the table next to her.

Reidus turned his head to Sara, only inches away, still locked in her grasp.

"You are a tough lady, aren't you?" Reidus said. He reached a hand up to the X-ray machine and pulled it down toward her.

I had hit the wall hard. I felt barely conscious, but somehow I managed to wheel myself back to the table. Reidus noticed but didn't seem to care. The machine was coming down smoothly, only seconds away from crushing Sara. I stood up on my good leg, propped the knee of the other leg on the table edge, and wrapped my arms around the large black metal casing of the X-ray machine. I pulled the machine toward me and away from Sara, then hung from it, my weight quickening its descent.

Reidus saw it coming, but it had the momentum of a car on an oil slick, pneumatics and hydraulics working smoothly. The tube pushed down into Reidus's chest. In an instant, it opened a pathway of blood and skin, and then it stopped as it broke several of his ribs.

Reidus's head snapped back on the table. He still had an arm around the machine. The other arm was under Sara, who was now devoid of all energy. The epinephrine was wearing off in a hurry. I got myself back into the wheelchair and rolled to the front of the table. I could see that Reidus was badly injured, but the expression on his face hadn't changed. It lacked surprise or fear or anything but calm.

Reidus was trying to speak. The chest injury made it difficult. I leaned over.

"Everybody dies," Reidus said.

Without thinking much about it, I braced myself with one hand on the table, put the other on the machine. I guess my instinct was to push it up and away from Reidus, but I didn't. I just held my hand on the side of the object, lightly, loosely. Reidus freed his other arm and

219

reached up. Pulling hard, he brought the machine the rest of the way down, through his chest. His upper body collapsed and spread out under the weight of the black metal mass.

I let go and dropped back in the chair.

Sara had enough strength to turn her head and stare at Reidus. She grabbed his head and turned it to face her.

"His eyes," she said, finally. "Let's be sure this time." Then she passed out.

34

THEY'D PATCHED HER UP to the point where she was able to do everything but get out of bed. Most of her body was bandaged, but her face hadn't been touched. I was the one visiting, but my jaw and neck were swollen from blows, and I was maneuvering a cast for the support my broken leg wouldn't provide. The leg was wrapped in concrete-stiffened gauze from foot to groin. My toes were free, and I moved them around once in a while, just to remind myself the object was mine. Her face worked fine, and she laughed out loud when she saw me.

"I should just move on over," she said.

"It may not show," I said, "but they must have put you in there for a reason. Maybe there's some damage under those bandages."

"I actually feel pretty good," Sara said. Then she looked away, then turned back with a defiant air. "I'll tell you one thing, though. I wasn't as good as him."

I smiled. "I'd say that's a compliment—not being as good as Reidus. The way a Reidus usually gets stopped is by running into someone just like him. People who like to hurt and don't hesitate about it—they cancel each other out. Let's hope we never run into anyone as good as Reidus. He's not someone you'd want to be compared to."

She didn't respond.

I managed to get seated with my legs spread out on the floor.

"He killed Meredith two nights ago," I told her. "They found his fingerprints all over her house. He killed her with a piece of silver that he'd bent with his fingers. Almost as if he purposely left an imprint of his entire hand on the murder weapon."

"You think he wanted to get caught?"

"No, not exactly," I said. "Maybe he did, maybe he wanted to contend with police, that's something I could see. But more likely he didn't think about it at all. He knew it wouldn't matter, one way or the other."

"He was right about that," she said.

I studied her face. She seemed truly happy that Reidus was dead. And relaxed. I didn't pursue it.

"The person who seems most upset about Meredith's death is Foley, the *Tribune* police reporter," I said. "He's the one who gave me the details. He's not taking it well at all. I guess she meant a lot to him. Sad. I think he'll quit and take an early retirement."

"What about Carlton?" she said. "Did you deal with him yet?"

I told her about the arrangement with Carlton, and about Hatley. She was skeptical. "I don't think he'll stick to it. In a few months he'll just start up some other scam."

"Maybe so," I said. "But he'll leave Hatley alone because he really doesn't care about Hatley. It's just a question of relative costs. Guys like him are businesslike. No matter how emotional he can get, when he takes the time to think it out his real concern is money. Anything for money."

I managed to get up and limp to the nurses' station down the hall. I'd asked them to hold onto the box with the ebony horses. I brought it into the room. I took one of the statues out and handed it to Sara. "I believe this belongs to you," I said.

She smiled. Then she handled the item for a good long time before looking back up at me. The smile was gone.

"The hunting and the shooting weren't what I cared about. Just killing Reidus. Am I a killer?"

"I don't know. Are you?"

"No," she finally said. "I'm not."

The sea was endless from the beach, a window on the edge of the world, so that when the big waves came, they were visible from their very beginnings as small, wind-flicked risers miles off. Lying on the smooth, colored sand of the beach, eyes aimed right, one could see each swell and dance of the waves on the lap of the wind, making slow and steady progress like the world's largest creatures, making their inevitable way to the land. In the endless run of calm days on Bequia, we had rested in the shade of coconut palms like dogs at a fire, day after day, calming in the slow, flat sight of the crystal blue and green waters of the reef. The colors were one perfectly matched line between the end of the sea and the beginning of the sky, and looking straight up to heaven was one of the privileges of being there. At night the sea turned a very dark blue, and the sky in its God-guided shifts turned black. Then the stars came out, turning into a wide bank of heavenly fire. And there was nothing to do but look up.

I'd picked Bequia, a dot of an island way down in the Caribbean, closer to Venezuela than to Florida. The island had absolutely nothing. Nothing but hills and tropical foliage and friendly people and what had to be one of the world's prettiest sheltered harbors. The only way to get there was by boat, and not by cruise ship or even by twin-hulled ferry, but by a local schooner. We stayed at a small hotel built around a 250-year-old coconut plantation set in a valley and facing a bay. It was comfortable and quiet. Hammocks, shaded spots under palms, little paths into the headlands. No gambling, no nightlife, no entertainment, unless you happened to be there one of the few times in a year when someone spotted a whale, and the local men went out in pint-sized dinghies carrying their hand harpoons and hoping for the big catch.

We were sitting on one of the small headland cliffs overlooking the water. It was too far into dusk to see much, but all around were the rhythmic sounds of the island birds, the coqui.

"What ever happened to those two cops in Wakefield, the guys who attacked you?" Sara asked.

"That was pretty funny," I told her. "I walked into a bar one night and approached them from behind. When the tall one, Hayes, saw me coming, he almost fell off his chair. He thought I'd come back to finish the fight. I told him to relax, which was easy, considering how much he'd been drinking. When I laid out all the evidence I had on their little shakedown operation, they looked at each other with what appeared to be a certain display of pride. Then they laughed. I laughed too. They paid for my beer.

"A couple weeks later, I got a letter from the court in Chester County saying the charges against me had been dropped. Case closed."

She smiled, and leaned over, resting her head on my lap. "What about the reporter who worked with Simon?" she asked. "Did he go back to the newspaper?"

"Baines? Yeah, he did. I called him and tried to explain the whole situation, but I don't think he believed me. He said he'd decided to go back to work anyway, even if Carlton's people went public with the pictures of him and the woman. He said he told his wife about the affair. She was pretty upset, but they're staying together."

"You didn't think they had enough to blackmail the guy in the first place, did you?"

"It's an odd thing about blackmail," I said. "It's not always what you have that matters. It's what the other guy thinks, or fears. In this case, they may have done Baines a favor. Helped to straighten out his life. Knowing Carlton, he'd probably take credit for that, if he ever found out."

A strong breeze came up from the west and we took the short way back to the rooms, almost beating the rain. When she was sleeping, I went back out, and walked the length of the plantation.

The storm had gone as quickly as it had come, and I sat again on the headland cliffside. When the night clouds rolled off, the stars came back and I looked up. We'd heard the weather in Philadelphia was rough, cold, an early winter. No problem. This time I'd taken a big chunk for a fee. I had plenty of time.